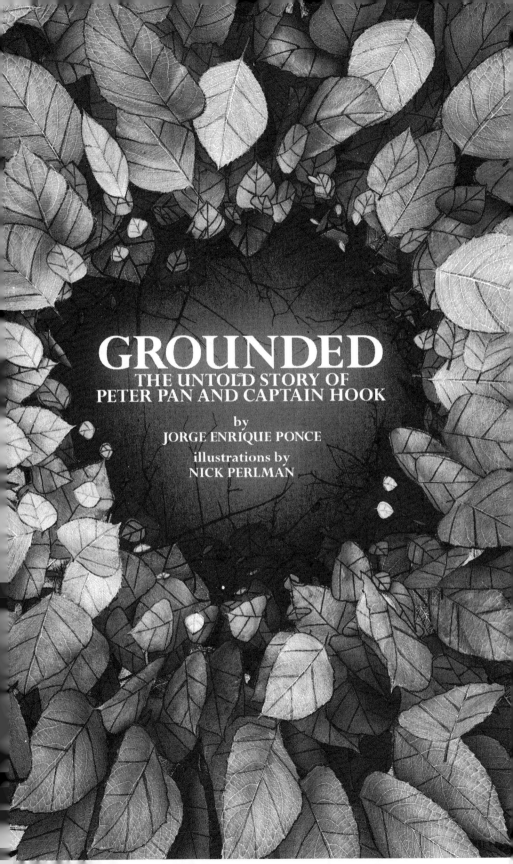

GROUNDED
THE UNTOLD STORY OF
PETER PAN AND CAPTAIN HOOK

by
JORGE ENRIQUE PONCE

illustrations by
NICK PERLMAN

G O O

Published in the United States by Goo Factory, LLC, in Los Angeles, in 2014. First Edition.

Goo Factory ISBN: 978-0-9912974-2-9

Cover by Chris ONeill
Illustrations by Nick Perlman

www.goofactory.tv

Printed in the United States of America

For Kyle,
Don't be afraid to grow up.
It's only a trap if you forget how to fly...

GROUNDED
THE UNTOLD STORY OF
PETER PAN AND CAPTAIN HOOK

Inspired by J.M. Barrie's novels
"Peter & Wendy" and "Peter Pan in Kensington Gardens".

NCE UPON A TIME...

PART ONE.

Sometimes you wake up.
Sometimes the fall kills you.
And sometimes, when you fall, you fly.

— NEIL GAIMAN

I.

A BOY NAMED JAMES

S HE FELL INTO the grimacing jaws of the crocodile, Captain Jas. Hook recalled the wonderful time when he could soar through the skies; the wonderful juncture when he defied gravity. The smell of the clouds. The luminous stars. But the memory slipped away, as the flickering pages of his mind took him back to one distant night. One when innocence still lingered inside his shadowed heart. Back to that one special night before the turn of the century in Bloomsbury, London, when his life was transformed. He smiled as the memory held fresh in his mind, the essence of that evening clearer than the present. So fresh he could see the unclouded skies, the tiled rooftops, and the smoky chimneys enveloped by a new moon's kiss. So fresh, he could smell the crisp breeze filling the air with the aroma of spring. As he recalled from that night, colorful fireworks had been erupting in the distance, blending momentarily into the star-crusted blanket above. The North Star was shinning brightly. The second star to the right shone just as bright, a turquoise glow.

Neverland.

Yes. He remembered. His memory sharp as ever. As he had once promised a friend, he would never forget...

The crackling lights trickled down, crowning Kensington Gardens with a halo of enchantment. Laughter spread up and down the cobblestone streets and past the gas lamps as boys and girls of all ages made way merrily with their parents.

An inviting faint glow flowed warmly out of the second floor window of a Victorian home. The inside exuded an oppressive dullness compared to the vibrant fireworks arresting the sky. The hallway's massive cuckoo clock ticked its way into oblivion, marking the beat, each *tic* devoid of life—a reminder of the fleeting rapidity and effervescence of being.

Eyes locked on a dusty arithmetic book, James Hope's fragile fingers turned a page, revealing more convoluted equations. The blue sparkle in his eyes wavered, fighting back the restlessness of a thirteen year old, trying not to look outside. He knew what he'd find, but he also knew it was not for him. In a moment of weakness, his vacillating eyes left the page and got lost wandering through the glass.

Peering past the ghostly image of his reflection, he caught sight of a happy family inside the home across the street. A young boy was flung in the air by his loving father, his face smiling so hard it seemed to hurt. The boy's mother clapped her hands, chasing both of them with unending elation. Picture perfect. James's lips quivered. He wanted that. His bones ached for it. But that life was not meant for him. The universe was parading an ungraspable joke in front of his eyes.

"Did the words fall off the page?"

James didn't have to look. He knew the voice. Caught, his eyes instinctively returned to the page, scanning frantically left and right, attempting to pick a word out from the pool of drabness. The voice belonged to his father, Lord Jas. Hope—he had shortened his name aiming for finesse and sophistication; *James* was a name suited for children; *Jas.* was the name of a man. A tall and elegant man, both

4

an erudite and socialite in the highest of Britain's circles, he was an exemplary figure to everyone but James. To James, he was an iceberg. An unmovable rock. A structure fabricated from intricate rules and removed from any emotion.

"No, sir," James replied, eyes glued onto dead paper.

"Come down off your cloud, son," he added, "keep your feet firm on the ground". It was his own personal motto for non-idealistic realism. He was a practical man with no time for fantasies or delusions. *Time is of too much value to be wasted with your head up in the clouds.*

James, of course, did not feel this way. His face distorted in disagreement, as if he had just tasted something sour. His father caught on, his own eyes looking past James, out into the streets of London, which brimmed with life. After some careful consideration, he retrieved a small shiny object that fit perfectly in his hand: a gold pocket watch. Pouting his thin lips, he stared at the moving dials as if they were an abstract painting. James's father loved that gem dearly. He would open it every night, cleaning and oiling its inner mechanics. "It will tick until the day I die", he would say.

Like an epic underwater creature fit for a sailor's nightmare, the cuckoo clock struck deeply, filling every gap of silence with an oppressive density.

"You deserve a little break," he added after what seemed an eternity. "When the ticker hits nine, come find me."

He handed James the gold watch, bringing a half-smile to his face. If you are to be rewarded, you'll have to work for it first, his father would say. Even though the idea of 'reward' brought a hint of joy to James's heart, it felt too far away a reality to embrace fully. The reward had become an unattainable idea, a myth long forgotten; melancholic and bittersweet. And as such, an idea that would never be a reality.

"It's yours now," he said, referring to the shiny ticking device. "This way, you'll always know the exact time. The educated with proper jobs always know the exact time, all the time, every time."

Great, James thought, more ticking invading his head.

"The only job those boys will have in their futures," his father added sternly, nodding at the window, "will be mopping decks on pirate ships." This was his father's attempt to dissuade him. He loathed the 'sailing scum', as he often called them. James, however, felt differently. The idea appealed to him, instantly tickling his adventure bone. But he knew better than to speak his mind regarding such matters.

"Can I see mother?"

A frown altered his father's forehead as if James had spoken in a primitive language. Mr. Hope pointed to the gold watch in James's hand, *when the ticker hits nine*, before slipping back into the room across from James.

For a brief second, his forever wandering eyes caught sight of the woman inside the bedroom. The woman lying on the bed. The woman he so strongly wanted to see, but was kept away from. The door snapped shut as fast as it had opened.

Once again, he was alone in the lonely hallway. The cuckoo clock ticking away.

A deep sigh left James's hopeless body.

If only... he wondered as he looked up at the starry sky. If only, what? he thought.

The streets had cleared leaving behind a faint mist that diffused the surrounding gas lamps. Silence had become so loud no one would've believed the streets had witnessed a celebration a few hours earlier. The children were now at home, tucked in bed, possibly having a story read to them, if not two.

It was well past nine o'clock, and Mr. Hope was nowhere in sight.

James had not moved an inch. The sound of the cuckoo clock, however, had managed to grow deeper, rumbling the formations of the house with somber aridity.

The bedroom door across the hall creaked open, wide enough to allow the middle-aged doctor out, followed by Mr. Hope, who closed it firmly once he was out. As the doctor went into details regarding a medical condition, James's ears perked up from behind the book. Remembering they were not alone, Mr. Hope lowered his voice and led the doctor down the stairs, far from James's audible reach. His eyes followed them until their elongated shadows disappeared. Then it was back to silence, except for the cuckoo clock hammering rhythmically, not once missing a beat. He fidgeted with the book, anxiety creeping in. No matter how hard he tried to zero in on the words, the shapes had ceased to make sense; his concentration had completely abandoned him. His eyes had no energy left for studying; their immediate focus was latched onto the bedroom door across from him.

It was haunting him.

Calling him.

Overtaken by frustration, he slammed the book shut and left it on the chair behind him.

Half-heartedly, he pushed the heavy door open, allowing enough room for him to squeeze in. A body lied in bed, breathing deeply. A woman, her face covered in sweat, drained by exhaustion.

Nerve wracked, James approached the bed. "Mum?"

No response. Silence.

Hesitant at first, he extended his hand and touched his mother's shoulder. She reacted, stirring slowly, her eyes heavy with a fever. A faint smile appeared on her face at the sight of James.

After sharing a moment of uninterrupted silence, James moved his hands, swiftly changing shapes by maneuvering his fingers. He was performing skilled sign language.

What is going on?

With great effort, his exhausted mother raised one hand to reply: **Nothing to worry, darling. Just a little fever.** She then added: **Will you stay, my darling?**

With brooding eyes, James replied: **Yes. I will never leave you. Never ever. I'll stay by your side. I promise.** He placed his head on her lap. He held this position for a beat or two, enjoying her delicate touch, her fingers brushing against his onyx hair.

"What are you doing here?" his father's voice spliced through the silence with unforgiving edge.

Startled, James faced him. "I wanted to see her—"

"Go to bed, James." It wasn't a request. It was an order.

The mother's pleading eyes reached her husband's, wishing James would stay, but she didn't object.

Yet James couldn't hold his silence in the house of whispers. "Why?" he muttered, his little heart slowly breaking.

Attempting to avoid a scene in front of his sick wife, Mr. Hope dragged James out of the room.

Alone in the hallway, Mr. Hope grabbed James firmly by the shoulders. "Do not test my temper, James."

"Why won't you let me see her?" he asked, holding back tears. He desperately wanted to understand, but couldn't. "You promised!" he exploded.

"Can't you see your mother is ill?" his father scorned.

"I want to be with her!"

"Stop acting like a child, James."

"I am a child!" he barked back. "Let me be one!"

Mr. Hope released James's shoulders. The boy was obviously distraught.

"Well then..." he began, after a languid pause, "I'm sorry to tell you, but only adults are allowed inside. It's not a place suitable for children. Go to your room and pack your bag. We will be departing to 'The King's College of Our Lady of Eton' at dawn." He paused again. Then added, "Perhaps when you grow up and become more like me, you'll see things differently."

Feeling betrayed, James trembled with rage. "Maybe I don't want to be like you!"

"Lower your voice, James."

But there was no stopping him. Something inside him had been awoken, bottled up for too long. "Maybe I don't want to grow up!" Aiming to sting, he added, "I'd rather be the son of a pirate!"

When without a warning, a slap whacked him across the face. James had successfully pushed all the right buttons, poking on his illustrious father's ego, sending him right over the edge.

James's burning gaze locked on Mr. Hope. Hot tears glazed his young eyes. But he refused to cry; out of pride—unwilling to give his father the satisfaction. Hardening his fragile heart, he repressed every emotion.

With controlled movements, James lifted his chin proudly and walked past his father, disappearing down the hallway. Barely audible, his bedroom door clicked shut.

Silence.

The slumbering golden pendulum swung endlessly, uninterrupted.

Tickey-tockey.

Tickey-tockey.

II.
A BOY NAMED PETER

HE SOMBER, VICTORIAN RESIDENCE seeped into James's bedroom, crushing down any attempt on his end to rouse the child inside him. Kicking a toy train out of his way, he marched towards the window, stopping halfway. His gaze was caught by the overbearing shelving, encyclopedias and scholar texts, all judging him from above with their noses raised—snotty judges sniffing on their own farts. Textbooks suffocated shelves, sandwiching storybooks at a crushing level. Factual reality would always triumph over short-lived fantasies, for everyone knew, fantasies came to an end once childlike innocence was lost.

He stared at the books' worn-out spines. How he loved those stories. Tales of far off places, magical creatures and sword fights. How could one resist? Yet no matter how hard James held onto this fantasy realm, the reality of his world kept hammering down on him like a stampede of wild elephants. And in that particular instance, it was hurdling down full force.

Following a fit of rage, he shoved all the books off the racks. Boring editions and storybooks both met the same fate around his feet. As he ripped through pages of anatomy, flora, and fauna, a sudden clanking outside got his attention, sparing Greek mythology from the massacre.

Through his bedroom window, which he had looked out of a hundred of times, James spotted an unusual sight. A garbage can had toppled down, landing on its side. It had been knocked over with a small broomstick, maneuvered like the sharpest of swords by a young boy about his age. Maybe a tad younger. Green overalls covered his white shirt. His clothes might not have been as nice and iron-pressed as James's, and his shaggy ashy auburn hair might not have been as combed and clean-cut as James's, but he was still a regular boy, just like him. A cat leaped onto a second trashcan. Reacting promptly, the boy raised his guard, engaging fully with the new enemy.

"Ha-ha! Surrender now, you leathern-jerkin, puke-stocking, flesh-monger heathen!" he threatened the feline.

Perhaps not that *regular* of a boy...

The cat purred.

Then it licked its paw.

Purrrr...

He poked the second garbage can, startling the cat, causing the container to stumble down the cobblestones, trash spiraling everywhere.

The boy looked around, lowering his guard for the first time. Taking a moment, he scoped his surroundings, ensuring no one had witnessed this sudden mishap. More so, because it was an embarrassment towards his swordsmanship skills. The mess was none of his concern. He shrugged and was about to resume his merry-way when, as if reacting to a sixth sense, he looked up. James's bedroom window was caught in the crossfire. James didn't flinch. He didn't pretend. Why should he? The boy should have been the one looking away after causing such a mess. But the boy did not falter. They looked at each other for what seemed like ages; a clog in the hourglass of time. Like a mutual agreement bereft of verbal confirmation, they had started a competition. A staring contest, if you may. James had all night; he didn't have anywhere else to be. He could stand by that window for hours if that was what needed to be done to show the boy.

The boy, on the other hand, seemed to be on a schedule—that or he was naturally restless; most likely a combination of both. He tilted his head sideways, initiating a conversation with the slightest of gestures.

This caught James by surprise. Why doesn't he walk away? he wondered. Unsure of what to do, he got fidgety. Should *he* look away?

Breaking the delay, the boy with the broomstick sword waved.

Almost instinctively, James waved back.

That's when things got serious.

The boy... he motioned James to come outside. An invitation, reassured by the friendly smile that had just appeared on his face.

James smiled back, continuing with the mirror exercise. However, his smile quickly fizzled once he remembered his current situation. He was surely grounded. Chances were he wouldn't be leaving his bedroom anytime soon... Until he had to leave for Eton come morning, of course.

But the boy wasn't giving up that easily. Furthering the invitation, he dug out a broken broomstick from a neighboring trashcan. He offered it, reaching out in James's general direction. The invitation could not have been clearer. Garbage cans can't be the most exciting of adversaries, James thought; the boy was lonely. Until then, James had borne his solitude stoically enough—losing himself in textbooks—without realizing how alone he was himself. Every swordfight needs a challenger.

Overtaken by childish joy, he ran to the back of his room, past the encyclopedia slaughter, and dug out a toy sword of his own. Back by the window, he victoriously raised it above his head.

The boy outside responded with a poised *en garde* maneuver. It was James's move. The decisive move. Taking a deep breath, he opened his window, allowing the nighttime crisp to flurry in.

"What are you doing?" James asked. In all fairness, he couldn't come up with anything smarter to say.

"Training to become the best swordsman in the world!" the boy blurted out, swinging his broom-sword around.

Tilting his head sideways, James observed the young boy, finding his bravado and vigor both confusing and amusing. The boy's freedom sparked a tinge of jealousy in James. He looked down at his own spotless Eton uniform, forced to wear by his father even when out of class. Why couldn't he be free like him?

"When I grow up, I'll be the fastest, strongest, and mightiest swordsman there has ever been. I'll always have perfect form. You'll see!" the boy added proudly—almost too proudly. He leapt onto the overturned, unstable, slippery trashcan, almost losing his balance. Waving his arms around, he was able to save face. A bit too late, however, as James was already holding back laughter.

"You knocked over my garbage can."

"It wasn't me," the boy said, his face too serious—not a trace of playfulness.

"I'm James, James Hope. What's your name?"

"Ahoy, James!" the boy billowed from atop the trashcan, broom-sword pointed towards the sky. "I'm Peter."

The boy's name was Peter.

"How old are you, James?"

"Thirteen. You?"

"Twelve and a half."

And a half? James thought. What an unusual thing to say.

"Do you go to school, Peter?"

"Maybe," he responded playfully, a devilish smile creeping up on his face.

"I go to Eton," James said.

The boy named Peter grimaced. "I hear boys who go there are rotten haughty twats."

"Most are, unfortunately."

"Are you a rotten haughty twat, James?"

"Oh, no. Not in the slightest," he replied. Then added, "I'm a haughty pirate!" Fetching a pirate hat from under his bed, James

13

made a menacing face while swinging his toy sword. Yet the fun was short-lived. The playful spirit quickly waned from his blue eyes as footsteps—slow, paced, cumbersome; his fathers'—echoed down the hallway. Overtaken by fear, James froze. The footsteps approached and stopped by his bedroom door. James held his breath. A second or two later, the footsteps resumed, gradually fading into complete silence. James let out a sigh of relief. He's gone, he thought.

"James, the pirate, ruler of all seas," Peter, down below, summoned his attention. "Want to come out and play?"

"I can't," said James half-heartedly, removing the pirate hat, reality crashing down.

Peter frowned. "Why on Earth not?"

"Father won't let me. We're leaving at dawn. Back to Eton, that is."

"Oh, for heaven's sake!" he bellowed, swatting at the air, as if an invisible fly had just become a nuisance.

"Did your parents let you out?"

Peter shrugged, cocky. "They let me do whatever I want."

"That sounds nice."

"Neither parents, nor Eton, would ever stop a real pirate," Peter added, challengingly. "Unfortunately, I cannot stay and chit-chat, I have adventures to attend. Nice meeting you, James!" And just like that, Peter turned on his heels and strutted down the cobblestone road.

After a brief pause that seemed to last a lifetime inside James's head, "Wait!" slipped out of his lips. His curiosity had been enticed. That was clear.

Peter halted, directing his attention back to the window. He crossed his arms, waiting by the gate laced with ironwork—waiting for what? He wasn't really sure.

Although nothing happened at first, James had already decided. He had decided not to be a prisoner, not to be tied to the ground. Earlier that night, he had been promised a reward; a reward he had earned—a reward that was rightfully his. And he was going to take it.

14

Extremely hesitant, James slipped his sword under his belt, before carefully climbing out the window. He mounted the windowsill, looking down.

The color instantly drained out of Peter's face. "What are you doing?"

Taking advantage of a sudden rush of—lunacy?—bravery, James leapt onto the white fence latched against the wall, hanging onto the thick ivy webbing. Losing his footing, he kicked the air, holding on with only his hands.

Peter latched onto the iron gate below, his wide eyes following, never leaving James.

After repeatedly trying to hook his foot onto the ivy, James had successfully stabilized himself. It was only a few steps down before he could jump onto the front lawn and land safely. And that's exactly what he did.

Regaining his composure, he brushed off a few leaves sticking out of his jacket and wavy hair. He pushed the gate open and he was out in the street, where Peter awaited.

An old soul at heart—who'd had formality and orderliness drilled into his head for years—, James offered him a firm handshake. "Pleased to meet you, Peter."

Peter stared back. For the first time since his arrival, he could really look at him. Up and down. The Eton jacket—the *bum-freezer*—a cropped version of the required tailcoat known as the 'Eton Suit', and the stiff white collar which looked like white rigid feathers sticking out of a bird's neck. So proper for a crazy fool who'd just now climbed down his bedroom window, Peter thought. "Ahoy! Ahoy, sailor!" he hollered, snapping back into his game. "Pleasure is all mine!"

As Peter shook back, James couldn't help but notice how he was a bit taller than the boy with the broom-sword. It wasn't that he was petit, but James was unusually tall when compared to the boys his age. Besides, Peter did say he was half a year younger; that is six months. A sprouting boy can grow quite the amount in six months. At that point in time, neither of them could have imagined Peter would not be sprouting anymore.

"I thought you were going to flap your arms and fly out the window." Peter narrowed his golden-brown eyes, wrinkling the few freckles that dusted his small nose.

"That's foolishness!" said James, educating the younger—and now shorter—boy. "Pirates don't fly, Peter. Everybody knows that."

With that, the trash-can-killer and the window-climber were off, down the cobblestone road, between the gas lamps, making way through the deserted streets towards the sound of music.

At that precise moment, an unusual friendship was born.

III.
TAVERNS, CLOUDS & PIRATES

OUPLES STUMBLED OUT OF every parlor, joint, and teeming tavern in the square, dancing clumsily, stepping on their own feet—ale generously spilling—as they howled and sung into the night. A man with a stump for a leg played the accordion elastically, marking the beat. Another man tripped into a fountain, causing a third to point and laugh boisterously. The harmonious cacophony of life seemed so much more disjointed and chaotic to James when scrutinized up close.

Inside one of these roaring establishments, the men slammed their pints onto the wooden tables, booming with thunderous laughter, as the big-bosomed women cackled at the spectacle unfolding before them. Their eyes followed the boys' feet atop the wooden table. Back and forth, the toy sword clanking with the broom-sword, a match of epic proportions. The Roman Coliseum had been brought to their pub, and the two feisty gladiators—no matter how small—were giving it all they had.

"You can't defeat me, you bloody mongrel!" screeched Peter, his broom-sword cutting the air with grace.

"My sword will end your evil reign, you pussing maggot!" James sneered back, maneuvering himself out of a locked attack.

Even though Peter was used to such attention, this was all quite new to James. Not once had he seen the inside of a tavern, let alone had a sword fight on a table. His father would never have approved, neither of his behavior nor the type of personnel currently crowding the house of ale. Actually 'never approved' would have been an understatement. He would've referred to them as 'regular commoners' without batting an eye—without giving them the time of day. James didn't understand such disdain. Their clothes might have been different, their jobs might have been more burdensome, but how did that make them any different? Sheltered as he had been, James had a natural quality for seeing the best in people, and at that exact moment, these 'regular commoners' were cheering for him. How bad could they be?

"Go back to yer mothers, lads! Before you scrape yer knees!" bellowed an ironsmith the size of a house.

"Go back to yer mother, lad! Before you scrape yer knees!" Peter imitated him, with impressive precision. His vocal chords were as flexible as rubber.

The room was immediately dazzled. The ironsmith was not.

"That was brilliant," James said impressed.

"Why, thank you," Peter said with a bow before resuming the fight. "We are motherless runaways, old man!" he yelled back at the ironsmith, never losing sight of James's maneuvering attacks. "We are pirates in search of adventure, running away forever!"

"Ha! Mark my words, scug! Running away forever is a fool's game. You won't be running for long!" the ironsmith insisted, fuming at the mockery.

"Scug? I beg to differ, you low-born, bounder bastard!!"

Rising to his feet, the ogre-man bellowed: "I'll make you squeal like a lil' piggy, you filthy mouth rascal! Go, get thee gone to the devil and be buggered!"

But the boys had already made way across the tavern, out of his reach. They were too involved with their game to care, carried away by the excitement of role-play. Swinging at each other skillfully, they showed off their swordsmanship, always attempting perfect form. Perhaps due to his size, James had the upper hand and lunged away, pushing Peter to the edge of the table, close to securing his victory. When finding a slight delay in James's attack, Peter ducked past him, knocked him off his feet, and disarmed him. Victoriously, Peter pointed his broom-sword at the defeated boy's chest. "Do you surrender, sinister man?"

"You may have defeated me," replied James, menacingly, "but my minions will haunt your darkest dreams for all eternity!"

"And I shall slay them just as heroically! Until then—" Peter paused, raising his broom-sword, ready for the final stab. When his expression changed.

"Show me what you've got!" James hollered.

At that moment, something clicked inside Peter's head.

He held out his hand, offering it to James. Half of the tavern *booed* at such a display of weakness. They wanted their bloody ending.

Accepting the offer, James grabbed onto Peter's hand, but just as he was being pulled up, his chest was met with the bottom of Peter's foot. With a slight nudge, James found himself falling off the table and landing on the ale-smothered floor.

The bar-fight aficionados gasped, astonished at the deceit and foul play.

Looking up, James wiped the sticky ale from the side of his cheek. When an unexpected grin swept away the harshness on his face. "Bad form!!" he stammered.

This caused Peter to fall backwards in a fit of uncontrollable giggling. The crowd erupted with thunderous cackle, chortle and chuckle; rejoicing, relieved at what could've otherwise been a rather ugly picture filled with wailing children, tears, and snot.

As the night wound down, the streets of London began to slip into a serene stillness. A drunken pair zigzagged up the street, holding onto one another as they howled at the moonless sky.

Backs resting on a rooftop, milk pitchers in hand, Peter and

James had lost themselves in the star suffused sky. James pointed at the firmament. A white puffy dragon, tail coiling, white fire breathing out of its mouth, had materialized before them. Peter gulped down his milk pitcher, leaving a prominent milk mustache behind.

"You grab it by the tail, climb on its back, and slash!" James said, reenacting the heroic act with his toy sword. "You cut the dragon's head off!"

"Slash!!" Peter repeated, snorting and chortling as milk sprayed out his nose. "How ripping! You make it sound so easy."

"It is. It can be. Unless it breathes fire on you..."

Peter took a large bite off a loaf of bread while the white dragon shifted with the wind. It had become an amorphous, misshapen blob. Quick on his feet, Peter spotted another one. "Look!" he yelled out, pointing at the sky. "A ship!"

"A pirate ship! Filled with treasures and adventures!"

"You tell good stories, James," muttered Peter, mouth stuffed with bread, the words barely making their way out. "I like stories. And clouds. I love clouds."

Like a long forgotten memory trickling back with fermented bitterness, James's feet were pulled back down to the solid ground. "Come down off your cloud, feet firm on the ground..." the words slipped out, almost by accident—a withdrawn whisper.

"What was that?"

Overtaken by another thought, James said out loud, "What you said, about us being runaways," he started, "did you mean it? As in forever?"

Peter shrugged. He took another large bite. "Maybe not tonight," he mumbled. "Maybe not tomorrow night, and maybe not forever..."

"Aren't you afraid?"

"James, James, James. Don't you know? I'm not afraid of anything. There's no time for boring things like *fear*," stated Peter—a gleam in his eye—trying to impress his new friend. "Just imagine, the action! No one telling you what to do, where to go, no *don't do*

20

this, no *don't do that*, no *don't set the kitty cat on fire...*"

"It does sound like a dreamland," said James, melancholy growing inside him. Fighting back the rigid thoughts forced down on him by his father and his dogmatic Eton reality—as he was to depart come morning—, James became unaware of his surroundings. He did not see Peter, who, perplexed, sat up, rubbing his eyes, squinting, making sure what he was observing was not just a light residue from the fireworks.

"What's that?" he asked, nudging James.

Finally looking up, James caught sight of Peter's source of interest. A faint glow bled through Kensington Garden's treetops in the distance. It pulsated sporadically.

"The gardens..." James replied, somberly.

Peter locked his wide eyes on him, as if saying: *I smell a story! Tell me more!*

"You really don't know?"

Peter shook his head, eyes agape.

James's mood swung back into dreamland, his feet slowly pushing away from the ground; he always loved a good story.

"All the magical creatures come out late at night," he began, "that's why they close the gardens. It's the lockout. To keep them in."

All at once, Peter was irrevocably enchanted. A spell had been cast over his senses. His innate curiosity had not only sparked, it had set off an entire wildfire. When a thought hit him. His smile reversed. "Or to keep us out..." he added, sudden fear creeping onto his skin.

Seizing the spurt of adventure inside him, James leapt off the roof with an eager: "let's go see!" He figured he might as well enjoy his one night of freedom before returning to his tedious reality.

Caught by surprise, Peter sat motionless for a second. Then he pocketed his bread, pushed himself off, and climbed down. For some reason, he no longer shared James's excitement. His curiosity had fizzled out. His façade of bravery was slowly crumbling, being replaced by a tinge of fear. And like his previous spark of curiosity, this much darker flame had begun spreading, and was now taking over.

IV.
THE LIGHTS AT
KENSINGTON GARDENS

AMES ADMIRED THE IMPOSING gates with growing courage. Once caught up, Peter wrapped his tiny hands onto the sturdy metal bars and pulled on them just slightly, as if to confirm a doubt. A sense of relief seemed to take over.

"That would have been sooooo exciting, James!" he said, almost too dramatically, as he pulled onto the gates, throwing his body back like a maniac, feigning misery: "But oh, bullocks! The gates are locked!"

"We climb!" James exclaimed.

Peter could hear his relief balloon deflating. His skin went porcelain white as he observed James climb up the gate with ease.

Halfway up, James stopped, noticing he wasn't being followed. "What's wrong?"

No response. Peter stared at the gate expressionless.

After dropping down on both feet, James looked up. He noticed Peter's hesitation. The younger boy's gaze lost on the ground.

"It's our adventure, Peter. Just like you said, maybe not forever, but tonight... we're free."

Peter knew James was right, although he would have hated to admit it. Releasing a small sigh, he added, "And then we go home?"

What was Peter afraid of? James wondered. Where had his courage gone to?

"And then we go home. I promise. Pirate promise."

"There's no such thing as a 'pirate promise', James!" Peter hollered, flashing his playful and devious smirk. "Everybody knows that."

"How about a 'James Promise'?"

With an emphatic smile, Peter offered him the end of his broom-sword as an invitation to seal the agreement. James responded by tapping the broomstick with his own toy sword. Then he climbed up the gate.

"Here, take my hand," he said, stretching out his arm invitingly. Before they knew it, they found themselves on the other side of the gate, inside the magical Kensington Gardens.

Eerie fog slithered through the darkness between trees and bushes, like claws reaching out longingly from the grave. Both boys came to a halt upon seeing the glowing light deep in the heart of the park. They both gulped, their mouths dry with dreaded anticipation. There was something exhilarating about the mystery, James thought. Peter, however, didn't seem to feel this way. He loved adventure, but the moment unknown darkness and uncertainty swept in, a wave of fear consumed him.

Out of breath, they ran down the bridge, stopping halfway. Leaning over the railing, James pointed, his finger extended— "There!"—at the sight of the small island in the middle of the Serpentine Lake; the source of the pulsating lights. They pushed through the thick foliage for what seemed an eternity. When they finally arrived at the shore, the dark cold water rippled at their feet loomingly, seducing them into the endless vacuum. The somber lake was the only obstacle stopping them from reaching the glowing lights; from reaching the magical island.

Shivers crawled up and down Peter's spine. He hated water. *Really* hated it. For starters, he couldn't swim.

"Oh well," he announced, faking disappointment. "Time to go back now."

James looked around, his daring spirit slowly fading, as Peter eagerly made his way back into the maze of twigs and foliage. Yet James was granted a glimmer of hope.

As the slithering fog receded, a small wooden boat appeared in James's peripheral.

"Wait!!" he shouted.

Peter stopped in his tracks, immediately regretting it. He should have kept walking. By the time he'd made way back to the shore, James was already running down the shoreline to fetch the crummy boat. The young boy's hands were clammy; cold sweat covered his skin. He breathed deeply. I'll be safe in the boat, I'll be safe in the boat, he repeated; a failed attempt to calm his nerves.

The broken oar splashed the oily water, almost too loud a splash, as James rowed the dingy thing. It barely fit both of them, their knees closely pressed under their chins. Peter squirmed every time the dark liquid splattered onto the boat; slimy hands reaching out for him, eager to pull him into the depths of the inky emptiness. Focusing on the task at hand, James rowed blindly, finding rising gloom wherever he'd look. Neither one said a word.

Once they saw the ominous island break through the thick wall of fog, James stopped rowing, entranced by the gruesome sight. Peter dug his nails into the wood. There was no way James would be going back now, Peter thought, not once he'd stepped on that island.

Black birds croaked at their arrival. The island was surrounded by wooden spikes, protruding off shore threateningly, like a deformed, giant urchin. Some of these stakes had become the forever homes of dead birds and torn kites. A communal graveyard designed to crumble even the bravest spirit. Peter didn't stand a chance.

The worthless dinghy buried itself onto a clear strip of dirt under the sinister prongs. James stood in awe of the haunting island.

"James..." Peter uttered, half a whisper, half a plea.

"Peter..."

"Can we go back, now?" he asked, quite aware it was already too late. They had come too far to go back; his safe, familiar world had already been left behind.

Winged creatures *coo*-ed and *croak*-ed as James and Peter made way through the dense forest that was Serpentine Island; an interwoven organism of vegetation and the creatures who called it home. Peter walked inches behind James, constantly looking back in fear.

After an indistinct amount of time, the darkness began to retreat, like the withdrawing tide. The pulsating light radiated from behind a tall thorny bush. They had arrived.

"We can't go through that," Peter blurted out.

To James's dismay, he was actually right. There was no way they could go through the prickled wall of vines. It was a boundless shark mouth infested with thousands of jutting teeth. But where there's a will...

James's gaze went up and around. It followed the branches of a tree that leaned over the horned obstacle. Peter saw what James saw, and let out a resigned sigh. James was to climb the tree. Peter did not want to come off as a coward, so he didn't protest. After having survived the eerie lake and the darkness, the tree looked harmless in comparison.

As James made his way up the uneven tree trunk, Peter tried to do the same, but slid back down instead. "Help me up!" he whispered, stretching up his arms.

Holding onto a branch, James pulled him up, trying to be as silent as possible. Once on the wooden limb, they crawled towards the vines that had been blocking their view. Suddenly, they stopped.

The light now illuminated their pale faces, eyes widening with awe, mouths agape with bewilderment. Had anyone told them what they would be witnessing moments earlier, they would not have

25

believed it. They would've called it 'rotten foolishness'.

"Odd bobs, hammer and tongs," James whispered amazed. "Are those—?"

"Fairies," said Peter, equally astonished.

Fluttering a safe distance below them, in a small clearing deep inside a pit protected by horned vines, gnarly winged creatures, as tall as a pint of ale, swarmed like vicious hornets over a mound of decaying fruit, meat and vegetables. Their earthy tones were the perfect camouflage had anyone caught sight of them from a distance. They could've easily been confused with bats or giant dragonflies; they were underground creatures and cave dwellers by nature. Some had dried leaves growing out of their backs in the shape of wings. The number of flapping appendages varied with each creature; some had two, some had six. The same principle applied to their limbs; some had two legs, some had a set of eight, like a spider. They continuously flew in and out of the various pockets in the pit; a fairy hive of sorts. A pair savagely fought over a pork leg, while another eagerly waited for the right chance to snatch it.

Dazzled by this sight, the boys' fear quickly disappeared, replaced with saturated excitement. How could they be afraid of such enchanting and seemingly harmless creatures?

A small fire burned at the center. On a tiny pedestal made out of found objects—shoes, buttons and twigs—, lounged a larger, fatter, more menacing fairy. The queen of the topsy-turvy hive. Queen Mab, James thought—the queen of all fairies. A sappy yellow goop oozed out of her crooked mouth.

A smaller, daintier fairy sneaked past the others—distracted by their own prize—, and grabbed a small chunk of meat. She was a female and much younger than the rest, as her wings were not as disheveled. She wore a skeleton leaf clumsily tied around her frail body. The boys would later call this magical creature Tinker Bell. But it's still too early to go into names and titles.

A bulkier fairy hissed at her, claiming the snack as his property. The petite fairy squeamishly flurried away and hid behind a rock.

Frustrated, she banged on an old kettle with a tiny rock, unleashing her pocket-sized fury.

"What is she doing?" James whispered.

"Tinkering?"

Having witnessed the unjust and purely shameful interaction, Peter's sense of justice kicked in. Of course he was by no means going to jump into the pit of fairies, but he was willing to turn the tide. A short boy himself, Peter despised when bullies picked on others smaller in size.

Retrieving the bread from inside his pocket, he snapped a small piece and tossed it to the tiny fairy. James realized this a second too late, and was unable to stop it. To both their surprise—and the fairy's—the piece of bread smacked her head, knocking her off the rock.

Annoyed, the fairy sat back up, searching for the perpetrator frantically, whipping her head back and forth. A second piece of bread cut through the air but this time her instincts ignited on time. She dodged it and caught it mid-air, sniffing it suspiciously, like a squirrel sniffing out an acorn. Finally giving in, she tore off a crumb and took a couple of tiny, tiny nibbles. She liked it. Really liked it. She nibbled at it more and more, chewing faster and faster, rashly looking around, studying her environment, hunting for the source.

A third piece cut across the air in her direction. This time, she sped to it catching it mid-flight. Her wings perpetually whisking, she looked up into the trees, searching for more raining bread. However, her tiny eyes came across something else. Peter and James did not move an inch, finding themselves in quite an unexpected predicament.

"Perhaps she didn't see us," Peter whispered. But he was terribly wrong.

It took the fairy a couple of seconds to grasp what she was witnessing. Then her face wrenched in realization. Aghast beyond her senses, the bread boulder slipped out of her hands.

A few feet below, the bulky fairy fed on his reclaimed piece of meat, until the crumb bounced off his head and hit the ground.

Foaming at the mouth, he snarled, looking up at the petrified fairy. But the fairy's fear wasn't his doing. She was unaware of him; she was looking at something else. Following her stunned gaze, the bulky fairy's snarl went slack. The boys. Intruders. Releasing a piercing war shriek, he ripped a threatening thorn from an adjourning vine and propelled off the ground.

Reacting to the fairy amber alert, the other fairies created a menacing swarm around the fiery pit. Growing in size, the infestation of fluttering and shrieking creatures rose like an all-wrecking tornado, armed with sticks and stones, fangs and claws, rising above the horned vines surrounding them.

Losing her bearings in the fluttering turmoil, the young fairy got knocked out of the way, landing hard, and knocking herself unconscious.

Completely frenzied, Peter and James climbed down the tree with reckless speed. Halfway down, James jumped off, landing safely with a loud *thud*. In an attempt to do the same, Peter leapt, but lost his grip, and came crashing down onto his ankle. He shrieked in pain.

Without thinking it twice, James helped him up, wrapping Peter's arm around his neck. "Lean on me!"

The raging winged-creatures broke through the horned barricade and flew over, raining pebbles and needle-sharp sticks onto the boys. Peter limped, getting nowhere fast. The storm swarmed around them, entrapping the boys in a savage winged whirlpool. Having no place to run, James retrieved his toy sword and waved it around aimlessly. It was almost impossible to look up, as the fairies kept jabbing at the boys' faces, aiming for their eyes.

A few slow fairies fell victim to the sword's blind swatting, but too few to make a difference. Scratches and cuts began to appear on the boys' skin. Hands and clothes, they all fell victim to the barbarous horde's slicing onslaught. Hope was rapidly fading away.

Behind a rock, not too far from the brutality, a pair of leafy wings began to awaken. The fragile fairy swiftly hovered over the rock, shaking her head in confusion. Her beady eyes caught sight of the uneaten piece of bread on the ground. It took her about three to four seconds to fully understand what was going on around her. Horrified, she propelled herself up, leaving a trail of dust behind.

While resisting the winged havoc, James spotted something on the ground. A small cove protruded from the tree next to them, almost within arm's reach. Lifting Peter from under his arm, James dragged him hurriedly towards their only hope for safety. Once inside, he hastily blocked the small entry with an old log.

Spiked vines—which had tangled themselves into and under the old tree—had suffocated its roots, draining it of all resources; leaching it dry, transforming it into an empty casket. The boys curled up into a ball, keeping their every limb away from the needles surrounding them. It was futile. Their hair raveled itself around the horned vines. They had nowhere to go.

Peter looked up, holding back tears. "James, I'm scared."

Regret.

That's all James could feel when looking into Peter's hopeless eyes.

Regret.

Why had he insisted on breaking into the gardens? Why did he have to walk through the darkness, across the gloom, without a sense of direction? He'd witnessed so many red flags, so many obstacles had blocked his way, yet he chose to push through, stubbornly. If he was going to return to Eton the next morning, he had to have a taste of freedom. At least for once, he had to be free— free like Peter; he needed it. But at what cost? His life wasn't the only one on the line; Peter's life was also at stake. He should never have gone into the gardens, he thought. He should never have gone into the tavern. He should never have climbed out his window.

Regret.

All these thoughts clouded the young boy's mind, as anger boiled inside him, aimed at no one but himself.

What James could not see at that moment, was that this place was exactly where he was supposed to be. For adventure was calling their name. And adventure was merely starting.

V.
FAIRY DUST

HERE WAS NO TIME for relief. The fairies stabbed and hissed through the rotting barricade—cutting and pushing—their vicious will growing, surging. It wasn't the fairies that had been locked out. It was the boys who had been locked in. They had accidentally trapped themselves. They had become easy prey with nowhere to run—nowhere to hide.

A small one, the size of a marble, bit its way through the edge of the old log. It darted towards James and scratched his face with a thorn bigger than itself, drawing blood. Reacting, Peter smacked the violent creature with his hand. The might of his blow hurled it across the air, impaling it into the thorns. Motion left its puny body instantaneously.

But the others were not too far behind. They cut through, attempting to squeeze themselves in, a handful at once. This, however, slowed them down.

"They're breaking in!" Peter shrieked.

When a little 'tug' got James's attention. The fragile fairy, from earlier, repeatedly tugged at his shirt. Both boys squirmed, cornering themselves against the decaying log. They expected her to attack. But she didn't.

Wasting no more time, she pushed herself off the ground and flew over the boys, making way through whatever little room there was.

"Stay back!" James yelled, waving his hands around. But she was quick. She maneuvered past swatting hands and thorns. As her fluttering got faster, a sparkling moth-like dust materialized from her wings. She produced the most unusual sound. A metallic squeaking. Like the clinking of a tiny bell.

Not expecting this, Peter looked up, drunk with confusion. "What is this? What is it doing?"

The log behind them was coming unhinged. A larger fairy pushed half her body in, slicing James's ear with a deep *hiss*.

Ow! He recoiled, trapped between the glowing dust and the ruthless fairies.

Peter sneezed uncontrollably. The golden dust had enveloped every inch of the cove, making it almost impossible to see.

"Make her stop!" Peter shouted, choking, sneezing and coughing, all at the same time.

It was then that James stopped panicking.

He forgot all about the deadly fairies.

He forgot all about the thorns.

His attention was fixed on one thing only.

"Peter..." he muttered, his face white as snow.

Amidst sneezes, Peter followed James's gaze. He was looking up; at his own hair. James's hair was floating; swaying in the air like underwater algae.

As Peter looked down, he noticed James's shirt had also begun to rise.

Looking at his own shirt, Peter realized the same was happening to him. A storm of emotions swept through. Confusion. Panic. Terror.

When a fairy squeezed in.

Followed by another.

And another.

And another.

Surrounding the tree outside, a thick cloud of batting wings *hissed* and *buzzed* in unison.

Unbeknownst to them, something was brewing inside...

When the fragile log blew outwards, shattering into a hundred pieces as a massive force shot out of the cove like a canon ball, pushing past every fairy, and into the night sky. Dazed, the enraged fairies followed.

The whopping bundle of light was made up of two small bodies, holding onto each other for dear life—a glowing winged creature led their way. The fairies buzzed, chasing after them, but they were no match; they quickly fell behind.

Flying past the clouds, James half opened his eyes and looked down. London's blinking lights grew smaller and smaller. Before he knew it, streaks of gray covered the city. And then he could see the ocean. And then he couldn't see a thing. His eyes rolled to the back of his head and he fainted, his arms wrapped around Peter tightly.

Propelled by momentum, the two boys unconsciously kept shooting forward, magically secured by the fairy's lead.

Anyone looking up at the sky that night could've gone on and on about what a fascinating sight it was; an unusual streak of light broke through the stratosphere towards the turquoise celestial body neighboring the North Star. Unfortunately, not too many took the time to look out their windows onto the starry night. They were all too busy. Busy with their lives far from the sky, safe on the ground.

VI.
NEVERLAND

OW THE BOYS SURVIVED the journey is to this day a complete mystery. Furthermore, they had no recollection of it. They had both lost consciousness soon after breaking out of the cove, and did not awaken until sometime after arrival. The landing was a separate issue on its own.

When he woke up, James realized he had landed on a field of giant mushrooms. His groggy eyes opened with difficulty, as he blocked the sun's blinding rays with his hands. Tall grass caressed the sides of his face gently. Once he sat up on the sizable spotty mushroom under him, James was able to get a sense of his bearings.

He was surrounded by thick forestation—that much he could tell—with trees as wide as houses and as tall as the eye could see. It was daytime. Had he slept through the night? Was this some unfamiliar section of Kensington Gardens he'd been kept away from? No, this forest was far denser and more tropical. It was covered with foliage he had only ever seen in biology books. The colossal mushrooms, for example: they were low in height but wide on the cap; dark and gangly, they were all covered with small spores. The one directly under him was terribly bruised—the result of breaking his fall. His toy sword was nowhere in sight. A *tic* got his attention. From inside his pocket he retrieved his father's watch. The needles had stopped moving. They retracted on the spot. The ticking sound, however, continued. He pocketed it and took a deep breath. The sweet nectars of spring infused his nostrils. He was alone.

"Hullo?!" he shouted. "Peter?"

Silence.

Fear trickled down his spine. Did Peter survive the fall? Where did they fall from, exactly? How did they get here? Questions poured over James's mind with so much power that the spot between his brows began to hurt. Overwhelmed, he dropped back onto the bruised mushroom and wished he could simply close his eyes and reawaken inside his bed. But that, of course, didn't work.

When the slightest of groans caught his attention; his body jolted up. He looked around, straining his eyes, trying to pinpoint the sound.

"Peter?"

The groan grew louder. It was coming from behind.

"Peter!"

James pushed past smaller—yet, still knee-high—mushroom caps. Soon, he stumbled upon Peter, lying over a bed of spores. He rubbed both eyes, fighting off confusion.

"Mum?" he asked with a sleepy whimper.

"Are you alright?" James checked for wounds.

Peter's face lit up at the sight of him, suddenly awake. "James, I had the strangest dream—" but his words trailed off the moment he noticed his surroundings: the trees; the mushrooms; the scratches on James's face. He stood up, taking in his new reality; eyes wide open, fearing that if he blinked, it would all evaporate.

When a luminous smile appeared across his face. "We were flying, James!" he screamed, ecstatic. "Flying! It wasn't a dream! It wasn't a dream!! ...Right?" he asked, pausing, as a hint of doubt deflated his joy.

Flying. James had forgotten about that. How could he forget? "I don't know," he finally managed to say. "How's your ankle?"

Peter looked down; moved his foot around. "It feels fine."

Had it magically healed? James wondered. Looking around, "Where are we?"

"Are we dead?" Peter blurted out; his speech pattern had become a handful of staccatos, not once stopping to catch his breath. "Pinch me," he said offering his arm. "Pinch me, James. Pinch me!"

"If we are dead—" James added, ignoring Peter's ludicrous request— "is this... heaven?" His wide glassy eyes wandered, dazed. A gentle breeze rustled down from the treetops, pushing orange leaves off the ground, spinning them around in dance and play. They brushed his hair with inviting warmth.

Peter was too distracted pinching himself to notice the beautiful patterns of nature.

"What about the fairy?" James asked, suddenly remembering. "Where's the fairy?"

They looked around. No fairy in sight. Peter looked under his shoe.

"Did we step on her?"

"Her?"

Peter shrugged. "Looked like a her."

An opening between two soaring trees lured Peter in. The deep afternoon rays warmly kissed his cheeks as he stepped into the pool of light.

Lost in the memories that led him there, James covered his face with his hands, his fingers brushing against the several cuts blanketing his skin. It wasn't a dream, he thought.

"Peter..."

But Peter was gone. Following his trail, James made way between the trees, calling his name.

Blinded by the light, James squinted his eyes, hurting from the blazing sun. Once his vision had adjusted, he was able to *see...*

Peter stood at the edge of a cliff a few feet away.

James wearily made way to his side, the extensive island

revealing itself before him. An enchanting sight. Mystified, he allowed the colossal light beam to cloak him completely.

In the distance, a compact ridge comprised of small peaking mountains had trapped a cluster of technicolor clouds, wearing them proudly like a puffy, heavenly crown. At its feet, the dense green forest housed a symphony of croaking and chirping, orchestrated with exorbitant life. Grandiose water falls dropped from sharp cliffs—weeping rocks—, sparkling like a shattered mirror and pouring into the vast twinkling ocean surrounding them; a dark emerald hue. Up in the sky, the source of the blinding orange light: a sunset new to their yearning eyes; a sunset with two suns. As the first majestic golden disc tinted the sky and ocean with lilac undertones, a second orange disc, of smaller size, lingered behind it, still too early to set. Regally poised behind the two suns, three moons, all different sizes and various shades of gray, had slowly begun to appear, fading into the streaking skies like a memory. A bewitching sight.

James failed to swallow the lump in his throat. "Where are we?"

Peter answered with silence. Unlike James, he wasn't frightened. He was no longer an anxious wreck clouded with doubt. No, something miraculous had happened inside Peter. The elaborate beauty of the island had captivated him fully, sweeping him off his feet; it felt as if he were floating off the ground. A smile of abnormal proportions had locked itself from ear to ear.

Bordering on tears, "Dreamland..." escaped his lips. His gaze was lost deep in the burning sun.

It was love at first sight.

VII.

THE NATIVES

TTEMPTING TO UNRAVEL THEIR
unexplainable circumstance, both boys made way
through a field of tall grass, which brushed halfway
up their chest. Trees had been left far behind. The
second sun had begun to set.

"And then the fairy appeared," James recalled, "and we could
fly."

"No reasonable explanation," Peter added.

"No reasonable explanation..." James pushed two fingers
against his temple, straining, hoping to make sense of the nonsense.

"Then perhaps," Peter said, his eyes growing wide, "perhaps
we still can."

"I think we would know."

"Would we?"

The tall grass had come to an end. A vast landscape of
solidified lava laid before them. Sharp rocks of all shapes and sizes
jutted out from the ground as steam crawled from nooks in the
volcanic fissures; a magma graveyard.

In the distance, a single tree protruded from the ground.

Round objects hung from its otherwise bare branches. A feeling of unease crept up on James. Peter was too distracted climbing up a large rock to notice. Once at the top, he looked down at his worried friend.

"Am I supposed to flap my arms?" Peter asked.

"I don't remember there being any flapping..." James replied.

Peter jumped.

Dropped.

Getting up, he brushed the dirt off his hands. The fall was not hard enough to cause any injuries; this put James's mind at ease.

Resilient, Peter climbed onto the rock again. "Maybe I need to build momentum."

This time, he flapped his arms.

"Maybe..." James added, scanning the area. Something didn't feel right.

Peter dropped. Frustrated, he let out a *hmph!* and climbed once again.

"I think we need to find that fairy," said James, not that Peter was really listening.

Driven by his sense of curiosity, James wandered across the volcanic plane towards the lonely tree, past the steam geysers, past the thick layer of smog. Peter was too caught up in his own pursuit of flight to notice.

Upon arrival, the veil of fog gave way. James squinted, finally able to detect more than just a silhouette. What he saw, however, he did not expect—not that he was expecting anything in particular. Stagnated by fear, his muscles stiffened. His feet, his hands—they stopped responding to any mental command; even his voice had gone cold. Hanging from the coiled branches, tightly wound with dried-up vines, were six... ten... twelve shrunken human heads; leathery, haunting, each and every one of them with wiry black hair. One even had a full set of frail looking teeth fixed into a tiny smile. James could not share its smile. That haunting smile. Numerous small skulls had been incrusted into the dead tree's ashen trunk. James couldn't avert his eyes as the hollowed sockets stared back in

silence. It was a gruesome sight.

"Um... Peter..." the words finally came in the shape of a whimper.

Peter jumped.

Dropped.

Repeated.

"What is it?" he asked out of breath. "I think I'm getting close. I can feel..."

He dropped.

"...my body..."

Again.

"...getting..."

And again.

"...lighter..."

And again. Hitting the ground harder and harder.

"PETER!!" The stress of James's current fears materialized through his voice.

"WHAT??" he shrieked back, annoyed at being interrupted.

Seeing that James was not moving, nor responding, Peter

groaned and stomped across the clearing towards him.

"What is it, James? I was *this* close—" but his words quickly trailed off once he reached the lonely tree. Speechless, Peter's mouth hung ajar.

An unusual and ominous silence flooded the terrain. Every bird and living creature had simply muted. Both boys shared a queasy look, but there was not enough time to follow with an exchange of words. Before either could blink, extremely sharp blades made of volcanic rock materialized around both of their necks.

Neither moved an inch.

Both held their breath.

Home seemed so far away at that moment.

A discord of primitive drums rumbled across the wasteland. Moonlight three times as powerful as what they knew back in London, illuminated the island, draping everything with an ethereal glow. Had the circumstances been different, this could have been a night of magical wonders. But that was not the case.

Rumble.

Shackle.

Rumble.

Shackle.

At the center of a wide clearing surrounded by trees, a burning crater tinted its surroundings crimson red. The Gates of Hell, James thought. Large baskets, woven from vines and fibrous vegetation, hung off the tree trunks like termite nests in the distance. Cloaked by partial darkness, shadows crawled in and out of them like spiders.

Near the all-consuming caldera, a slab of black rock had been erected. James and Peter squirmed by it, attempting to free themselves from the ropes restraining them. Their bodies tied back to back, their hands and feet bound. They had nowhere to go.

"I want to go home, James, I want to go home!" Peter pleaded.

"Let us go!" James demanded, but it was no use. Who would listen to a child?

The drumming pounded the core of their very bones. The

kidnappers—the men playing the drums—were a terrifying sight; their skin was gray and crackled, ashy-white like dry clay. Fangs, sharpened wood, and bones, all protruded from their grisly flesh; each one of them was a unique display of physical distortion. Some walked in the nude, others wore shreds and patches of animal skins on their ghoulish bodies. They were the island's natives.

A single figure parted through the beating drums. Wielding a staff decorated with a human skull, every inch of his body was covered with ornamental bones, piercing the skin on his chest, face, arms, and back. He had to be their leader, James thought. Distinctive red markings streaked across his paleness like a tiger. Blood?

The drums grew silent the moment he arrived at the rock by the crater. Although his mouth opened and sounds followed, James could not make out a single word; it didn't sound like any language he was familiar with. More like guttural gibberish. One of the natives understood the command. Leaving his place by the drums, he lifted both boys off the ground with a single hand. No matter how violently they swung or kicked, the massive native—built like a mountain—did not flinch.

"We didn't do anything!" Peter wailed, hopeless.

The native dropped them atop the black rock with incredible ease. The boys' blood boiled in terror, as the blazing fire flickered a mere drop away.

The chief looked down at them, his face as blank as a canvas. With clumsy brutality, he grabbed onto James's hair, pulling it in his fist; the boy let out a sharp cry. But the pain became a secondary concern once the remorseless man raised a sharp, curved hatchet, wielding it high above his head. He was going to strike. James and Peter wailed in horror, tears streaming down their flushed cheeks. Wrapping his hand tighter around James's hair, the leader pulled the boy's head up, exposing his young neck. This is it, James thought; the grand finale. The man would aim for his neck and his blood would gush generously onto the black rock, trickling down into the burning pit. That was how James envisioned his life would end. He would never see his mother again. He would never see his father again. He would never find out how he got to the island, or if he indeed ever did fly. All these concerns congested his brain.

At this, a booming voice made the wheels of death stop in their tracks. A weight had lifted. The Grim Reaper's burdening presence had unexpectedly vanished.

The chief lowered his weapon with as much ease as he had lifted it; his gaze directed towards the crowd behind him. He was not pleased.

The boys readjusted. Being closer to the edge, James was able to spot the intruder. It was a girl; both beautiful and extremely disheveled—not a day over sixteen. She stood imposingly, parting the ghastly crowd. Animal skin covered her body. With nonchalant serenity, she carried half a dozen dead rabbits over her shoulder.

She made way towards the chief, dropping the dead rabbits at his feet. Not once did she look at the boys. Guttural sounds escaped her lips with firmness, as she faced the leader with powerful vigor. The fire's glow flickered on her face. Were they arguing? James thought.

Flustered, the chief flung the hatchet into the ground and pointed at the boys, yelling incongruences. He snatched the rabbits and walked away.

What were the rabbits for? Were they a part of some kind of market barter? James wondered.

The natives went back to their daily routine without question. Nobody seemed to mind this unexpected exchange. They returned to skinning animals, feeding their young ones, and sharpening their weapons... Funny as it were, they didn't appear to be threatening once they were minding their own business... when sharp objects were not being held up to the boys' necks.

The girl retrieved a knife—more sharp objects—and with one quick move, sliced through the rope binding the boys. Both flinched. For all they knew, the natives could merely have been switching executioners.

Something about the dark pits of her eyes disarmed James

completely. A strange pressure squeezed his chest. All at once, nausea and joy consumed his body. It was unlike anything he had ever experienced before. It was a sense of belonging he had lost since arriving to the island. He somehow felt at ease; and all because of her eyes. Oh, those eyes, James thought.

Fearless as a tiger...

Hypnotic as a lily...

She motioned the boys to follow her. Every movement she made was precise; her pacing, fast; her will, tenacious. The boys hastily leapt off the rock and followed, worried that once she was gone, the chief would resume that day's head shrinking activities.

With her, James felt safe.

VIII.
MERMAIDS

IGER LILY—AS JAMES would call her from that day on—cut through the somber rainforest with fierce resolve, neither looking back nor saying a word. The boys followed, failing to keep up with her quick but steady pace. They shivered, fear chilling them from the inside, and the night's frost biting them from the outside. Unsure of their immediate future, they followed the girl into uncertainty. After all, she had saved their lives. Why? James had no idea.

The darkness was absolute. They could barely see their hands when brought up to their faces. Their fate was as grim as their surroundings. A wolf-like creature howled in the distance.

"Do you think our parents will be looking for us?" Peter stuttered, amidst shivers.

"I'm sure they are worried sick. But we'll be back in no time, I know it."

To this came the expected pause, foreboding the expected question.

"But how do we go back, James?"

Silence was his only response. His eyes remained fixed on the back of Tiger Lily's head, not once losing sight of it, not even to blink.

"Where are you taking us?" Peter asked.

She didn't respond, nor acknowledged the question, for that matter.

"I don't think she can understand you, Peter."

A jerky scuffle behind a bush made the entire party come to a stop. Tiger Lily's knife was, without delay, unsheathed. Her eyes wide open in alert. Minding each step, she positioned herself between the boys and the rustling bush, ready to defend. The scuffling intensified. Something was making its way through. Getting closer. Closer to them.

Peter and James found solace behind her, almost too afraid to look up and face sudden death for the second time in one night. Her hand tightened on the knife, ready for whatever would spring out into the aphotic night.

Rustle. Rustle. Rustle.

When it finally pushed through the shrubbery, a small warthog snorted and scuffled, desperately trying to eat through a piece of fruit. Noticing their presence, it fearfully scampered back into the wilderness.

The boys released a half-hearted sigh. Half-hearted because although they were afraid of the warthog, they were quite glad it was more afraid of them—or at least more afraid of Tiger Lily. She sheathed her knife and resumed her step.

The mysterious howling had significantly escalated. As they grew closer to it, it started to sound less and less like a wolf. It was too melodic. The howls resembled wailing with musical undertones; a melancholic tune. Both incredibly sad and heart-wrenchingly beautiful.

Upon walking past the trees and into the moonlight, they reached a murky, swampy lagoon that fed into the ocean. A massive, jagged boulder, taller than Peter, taller than James, protruded from the center of the smeary waters, like a devil's horn, bearing a warning. The water wasn't entirely dark. Sporadic bursts of light pulsated from underneath the surface.

"The water," Peter said amazed. "It's glowing."

Captivated by this magical gift of nature, the boys halted; their complete attention captured by the lagoon. The wailing augmented, as did the glow.

Seduced by a sensuous spell, they both gravitated towards the swamp, walking into it without hesitation. Unnoticed by them, the jutting rock began to move. It seemed to be alive. That was not possible. The rock wasn't moving; something on top of it was. Its slimy surface mirrored the moonlight—slithering down the rock, uncoiling, arms moving, slipping into the waxy waters. A ragged fin flipped in the air before submerging completely.

The sirenic wailing increased its vibrato as both boys submerged into the water, first up to their waist, then up to their necks. Their pupils fully dilated. Their eyes wide open. In a matter of seconds, the viscous liquid had engulfed the entirety of their heads.

The moment they disappeared, Tiger Lily's hands plunged into the water, pulling their heads out. Their bodies followed.

Dark water poured out with every cough. Peter collapsed on the pebbled shore, dry heaving. James hurled violently, emptying his bowels of all its contents.

Clapping her hands together, Tiger Lily snapped them back into attention. She placed her index fingers inside her ears, in demonstration. She nodded, egging them on. They obeyed, mimicking her.

Grabbing a couple of rocks a bit larger than her fist, she tossed them into the lagoon. The wailing stopped almost immediately, replaced with a shrilling shriek and the splashing of water.

Unaffected, Tiger Lily resumed her walk. The boys on the other hand, couldn't hide their panic.

Peter stared into the inky waters, horrified. "We were in the lagoon... weren't we?" he turned to James, losing himself. "James, we were in the lagoon! We were buggered over! We almost drowned!"

47

James narrowed his eyes, searching, but finding nothing in the—now still—night. "Were those...?"

"We could've drowned! We could've drowned!!" Peter shouted like a lunatic.

"...mermaids?" James was too caught up inside his own head to be carried away by yet another possibility of death. He hadn't had enough time to properly digest his encounter with the natives, or the fairies before that.

"I want to go home, James," Peter pleaded. "I want to go home." A fear new to James clouded Peter's eyes.

James nodded, without really knowing what that nod meant. Were they going back home? There was only one way to find out, James thought, as their anxious eyes followed Tiger Lily up the rocky mountain.

IX.
MOTHERLESS

FTER CLIMBING UP A petrous slope, the boys followed Tiger Lily into a cove, hidden against the side of a cliff. Colorful flowers covered the entire interior of this vast cavity. Its mouth was narrow, but its ceilings were vaulted. It wasn't a tunnel, but a wide pocket with a single entrance. At the center of the uneven ceiling, a natural skylight framed the moonlight, creating perfect beams of light. Golden particles of dust danced around in these upright shafts of luminescence. The boys looked around, wondered. Curious, Peter poked one of the flowers. It recoiled instantly into a bud. He stepped away, uneasy, and kept clear of every wall.

From inside a leathery pouch, Tiger Lily removed a rudimentary instrument carved out of several bones, similar to a flute. It was cream-colored, quite small, and fit easily in her hand. She blew on it, producing a hollow nasal sound, like that of a goose.

"What is she doing?" Peter whispered.

Wishing the sound were more on tune, both boys covered their ears.

When a faint light began to bleed from inside one of the budding flowers, producing a phosphorescent coruscation. What followed was yet another captivating wonder of the island. As if marking the beat, glimmers of light began to appear one by one, inside various flowers, creating rainbow streaks across the rocky surface. In a matter of seconds, the entire cove was pulsating with hundreds of shimmering sparkles of light. The night sky had somehow descended and blanketed itself onto the cove. Peter and James looked up in amazement, briefly forgetting all about their encounters with death and the abysmal distance separating them from home.

Then the lights began to move. They pushed through the delicate petals and hovered nimbly, pulsating constantly. Flying particles disappeared and then reappeared, moving across the darkness. Now illuminated, the boys noticed an unusual collection of items hidden among the blossoms; old clocks, bent up pots, mismatching shoes—odds and ends, arbitrary trinkets that somehow had made their way into this desolate cave to die.

As the lights descended, one flickered right before James's eyes. It was a firefly. His eyes lit up with excitement. James had never seen a firefly before. And by the looks of it, neither had Peter, who spun around dazed by the magical event unfolding before him. It had been less than a day, and the island had already led them into an uproar of emotions. Like a rose, they had been enchanted by its beauty one moment, and terrified by its thorns the next.

One of the blinking lights was brighter than the others, and unlike the fireflies, it didn't pulsate, but remained glowing, streaking the air with gold.

James squinted, picking up on an unexpected familiarity. As the light got closer, he was able to see its contour. Its wings. Her head. The metallic squeaking noise similar to that of a tiny bell.

"The fairy!" James cried with uttermost joy.

"It wasn't a dream," Peter jumped frantically. "It was all real!"

Recognizing the boys, the fairy circled around them, fluttering her wings and covering them in golden dust. Peter sneezed.

In no time the boys began to levitate, their feet leisurely kissing the ground goodbye.

"How do we do it?" Peter asked, spinning around, giggling frantically.

"Is it like swimming?" James wondered.

"Oh, I hope not!" Peter replied. "I can't swim, I really can't."

They clumsily attempted to control their flight. The fairy flew over and under them so fast, that her radiance weaved a chrysalis of light around them. Tiger Lily smiled, or so James thought. It could have been a smile. It could also have been a trick of light and shadow.

"I think I've got it!" announced Peter as he spun endlessly in a flying somersault. He pushed forward with his feet, entering the light beam under the moonlit skylight. James followed with some effort.

"Please, take us home," Peter asked the fairy.

Self-propelled, she shot out through the skylight and into the starry night. Peter trailed behind.

Before departing, James turned and gave Tiger Lily one last look. You must realize, at that given moment, he thought he would never see her again. It's true they couldn't fully understand each other, but she had saved their lives. Twice. James smiled and gave her a slight nod, *thank you*. She smiled back. This time, there was no mistaking it.

The breeze brushed against James's skin with a combination of invigorating warmth and crisp coolness. His hair tousled and flowed freely. He could change directions at his whim, no longer tied to the forces that grounded him. It was an indescribable feeling. For the first time in years, James felt like he could breathe—*really* breathe. He took in the moment. The sky was clear of fear. Last time he found himself flying, he had fainted within a few seconds of departure, forming no real memory of it. This—flying—, he thought, was the true definition of freedom.

Peter howled and croaked with intoxicating vivacity. Not only could he mimic voices, he could replicate animal calls as well. He did sequential somersaults and figure eights across the starlit skies. James joined him, their laughter intensifying as they rattled the stars. They flew up high, framing their silhouettes in the brightest of moons, and then dipped back down.

The fairy glowed sporadically, leading the way.

James descended, speeding over treetops while grazing the leaves with extended arms. They flew past the ice caps on the highest of peaks, and blended with the hypnotic magnetism of the island's Aurora Borealis.

Finally, the three figures flew into the night, growing smaller and smaller, until they had disappeared entirely.

The boys landed outside Kensington Gardens, by the gate. It had to have been long after midnight as the streets were dead silent and the gas lamps burnt dim.

The fairy flew into the gardens after her task was done, hopping from one flower to the next. Without a second to spare, Peter bolted home, running across the cobblestones. When, suddenly, he stopped. James wasn't running with him. In fact, not only had he not walked away from the gardens, he was climbing back over the gate.

"Don't you want to go home?" Peter asked.

"I'm getting mother flowers. She loves lilies."

"Let's go on more adventures tomorrow."

"We can fly around the park," James assured him. Yet he knew this would not be so. Eton awaited first thing in the morning. He couldn't bear disillusioning his new friend. James dreaded good-byes. He would just disappear, he thought. Making it painless.

With excited anticipation, Peter gave him a firm nod, before resuming his run back home.

Clacking footsteps echoed rapidly past rows of middle-class Victorian houses. Peter ran through the streets relentlessly, eager for home, missing his mother's voice, missing the warmth of his bed—all of this, was to be his again; the nightmare was finally over.

He slowed down upon arrival and took a moment to admire the place he knew as home. It wasn't much. It was old and rather small, but it was his. He walked up to the door and was about to knock, but stopped. All the lights were out. Everyone was surely asleep. Thinking it over, he decided to surprise his mother, by having her find him tucked in bed come morning. It was the perfect plan, he thought; *she'll be so overjoyed!* Looking around, Peter made sure he was alone before he pushed himself off the ground and slowly rose to the second story window—his bedroom window.

Peter was ecstatic. Such was this happiness, he felt in tune with the world.

When he reached the window, he paused. This was it, the moment he had been waiting for. But something was amiss. His smile vanished. Solid metal bars were blocking his way. He wrapped his small hands around them. *What's this?* They were cold. He didn't remember there being any bars. He wondered *why?*

Approaching, he pressed his face against the glass. Inside he saw a white crib. Not his bed. Not his toys. Confused, Peter pushed himself away from the window and looked around. Could this be the wrong house? he asked himself. As if to erase a doubt, he flew to the house next-door and looked inside one of its windows. But it wasn't his. Digging his hands into his hair, he shook his head heatedly. *This can't be right.* Hoping it was all a big misunderstanding, he returned to the first house, to his bedroom window, and pressed his face between the cold bars once more—his breath clouding the glass. There it was, unmoved.

The white crib.

A new child.

His replacement.

A tremor crawled up his skin, piercing it like needles. He felt as if the ground had been suddenly yanked from under him. When angry tears stung his eyes. His jaw clenched in fury as he pulled on the bars repeatedly, but they didn't budge. Finally, a strangled cry rasped out of his throat. They'd betrayed him. They'd abandoned him.

His bed was long gone.

His toys were long gone.

His parents... were long gone.

Suddenly consumed, Peter weightlessly drifted away, like a loose leaf, lost without a home or destination.

He couldn't understand.

He was only a boy.

How could they leave him all alone in a world that's so cold?

X.
THE PROMISE

HILE DRIFTING AIMLESSLY THROUGH the London skies, a thought crossed Peter's mind. Although his body was drained out of energy, *this* thought, he had to attend. Hovering past rooftops, he recognized the gate laced with ironwork. Curious, he gravitated towards the second story window—James's window. A faint light lured him in. What Peter saw next rattled his wounded heart.

The bedroom window had been left wide open, strangely inviting for such a cold autumn night. Peering inside, Peter saw what looked like a boy's bedroom. Books on shelves, toys neatly arranged. Just like James had left it. Yet there was more. Sunk in a chair, sleeping from exhaustion, was a man. A tall, lanky man in a wrinkled, elegant, suit, with several days of unkempt scruff. James's father. An open storybook lay on his lap. James's bed was perfectly made, immaculately kept for the day of his return.

Why wasn't James's window barred? Peter thought; Did James's parents love him more? Did mine love me less?

The obvious situation took Peter by surprise: he'd been

abandoned. Forgotten.

And James hadn't.

His fragile worn-out heart refused to face it. He was afraid. He was too afraid. He simply couldn't face it alone.

He needed a friend.

He needed James.

Lilies slipped out of James's hand the moment he heard the news, landing on the plush evening grass.

"Are you sure?" James asked, a slight tremor in his voice.

Peter nodded. Firm. Assertive.

"It's not possible. How long were we gone? Maybe a day? Two?"

"Maybe longer."

"This is a mistake. I need to talk to them," James raced across the gardens.

"They don't want us anymore, James!" Peter yelled. "They don't want us."

"She's my mum, Peter," James cried out. "My mum... she would never..."

"They forgot about us."

Refusing to believe this, James climbed onto the gate. "I have to see her!"

"No!" Peter pulled him down—sitting on his chest, pinning him at the shoulders with his knees.

"Get off me!" James struggled, kicking. "I have to see her! I have to talk to her!!!"

"No, you don't!" Peter insisted, holding him down.

"GET OFF!!!" James shrieked as an uncontrollable sob escaped his lips.

"Fine!" Peter got up, his brows furrowing—his face burning red. "You don't believe me. Do whatever you want, James." Without waiting for an answer, Peter walked away—away from the gate—back into the gardens; into the shadows.

Dumbfounded, James wiped the snot trickling down his lips. "Where are you going?"

Peter did not respond; he kept walking.

Concerned, James sprung up and followed. "Where are you going—?"

"You think I'm a liar, James!" Peter turned, facing him, furious. "A liar!!" Peter grew more agitated with every word, pacing back and forth in a shapeless circle.

Puzzled, James didn't know how to react.

"Why would I lie to you, James? Why?? I'm your—*friend*." Peter allowed those last words to sink in.

Looking down, James sniffed. "I'm sorry... I didn't mean to—didn't mean to hurt you, Peter."

"Well you did! My mother abandoned me too, James! You're not the only one who got tossed away!"

James came to a standstill, and looked up—his eyes bloodshot from crying. "I'm not—I—" he whimpered, unable to finish his sentence. Then, he took a deep breath. "I—I believe you. I believe you, Peter." He shook his head, dry heaving—the reality of his situation came crashing down. "Why would they do that to us?" Tears burned down his cheeks

Peter shrugged. "Perhaps they never loved us as much as they said they did. Perhaps they lied."

"But why?"

Why? asked the wounded child.

"I don't know, James. Grown ups... they're simply... rotten. That's it. All grown-ups are rotten. Rotten to the core."

James's gaze was lost in the space between his feet.

"I didn't want you to see," said Peter. "It was a revolting sight. I did it for you, James."

Something shifted inside James. An unblemished crystalized innocence had suddenly found itself tarred black.

James wiped away the tears. "I don't want to be homeless."

"We don't have to be."

"An orphanage?"

"I'd rather sleep among the dust bins. We—" Peter paused— "we can go back..."

The thought had crossed James's mind, but for him, the island was tainted. It had robbed him of his home, of his parents. Although this was not entirely true, these were the rationales concocted by a young boy when faced with adversity.

"What about the mermaids?" asked James. "And the natives?"

"We'll be ready for them this time."

"And leave everything?"

"There's nothing left for us to leave, James. It will be our big adventure, like we said. This is our calling. This is it. It's our chance! We'll fly the skies forever and ever!"

"Forever is an awfully long time…"

There was an eerie optimism burning in Peter's eyes. James saw it, but he couldn't put his finger on it. Why wasn't Peter crying? James wondered. He seemed perfectly put together for a boy who'd just been abandoned. Calculating even. Something had hardened inside Peter, repressing a memory, burying away the pain. But James was too paralyzed by shock to see it. Peter had decided it was all for the best, as mothers weren't that great to begin with.

"How do we survive?" James asked.

"We hunt."

"Hunt? We can't hunt, Peter!"

"Yesterday we couldn't fly either," he snapped back.

James sunk on the grass—his back against a tree—and buried his face between his hands. "How could they do that?"

"We can do this, James. But I can't do it alone. I need you to come with me."

James was too weak to rebut and Peter was too eager to give up. Hopeless, James looked up, meeting Peter's eyes.

"We make a promise," Peter began, pacing around in a circle. "A pact, never to become them, never to forget, never to grow up." Then facing James, he added, "Promise, James. Promise me you'll never grow up. Promise me you'll never forget."

Silence shrouded over them.

"I promise," James finally said.

"No," Peter stammered, his face grave, somber. "*Really* promise."

Getting up, James took a deep breath. "I promise. A 'James Promise'." He raised his right hand ceremoniously. "I, James Hope, will never grow up. I will never forget."

At that, Peter smiled. "We'll make it our new home, James, you'll see. A land where we never grow up!"

"Never-grow-up Land?" repeated James with a frown.

"Never—" Peter paused; a single eyebrow arched playfully— "Land. Neverland! Where you never grow up."

The name gave their unexpected misfortune a sudden appeal. The island sung to their shattered hearts, calling them home like jungle drums in the distance.

Peter stretched out his hand, offering it to James. "It's time, my friend. Will you join me?"

Hesitant, James looked around, expecting a sign, something to tie him back down to the ground, back to London, back to home. But no sign came. Perhaps that was his sign—his sign to leave.

Shaking Peter's hand, "We'll never grow up."

After finding the fairy among shrubbery where they had left her— they needed her golden dust and sense of direction—, the boys parted through the clouds in pressing silence. Neither one of them spoke a word. With Peter and the fairy at the lead, James took a second to look back down at the sleeping city.

At his home.

At his life.

At his mother.

One last look...

He took a deep breath and with no further adieu, he flew out of sight, straight into the white clouds, and into the night.

XI.
BACK IN NEVERLAND

REGNANT CLOUDS CLOAKED THE island. The two boys and the fairy pierced through the air and broke into the dense cluster. They found themselves trapped inside a turmoil of layers. Absorbed in their gelatinous darkness, the boys tried flying through for what seemed an eternity.

Finally, the clouds spat them out, tossing them into a current of walloping winds, pushing them back and forth, constantly knocking them off their balance. They couldn't tell up from down. Torrential rain covered the island as far as the eye could see. The fairy was instantly swept out of sight.

"Peter, hold my hand!" shouted James, barely audible over the roaring storm.

Peter struggled. He tried to move closer, but got swayed back and forth like a piece of lint. "I can't!"

"Try getting closer to the trees!"

Fighting against the sweeping gusts, James reached out for Peter's hand, but failed to grab it.

When suddenly a violent gush propelled him against Peter, locking them into a knot of arms and legs, cannon balling directly into the treetops. They torpedoed through the dense canopies; branches snapping and cracking, helping break their fall—and luckily for them, none of their bones. They plummeted past the last few layers of branches and hit the jungle floor hard. No giant mushrooms this time around. They moaned and groaned in pain. Soaked to the bone, they looked for a place to hide. But the jungle was pitch black, branches blocking whatever moonlight made it through the impenetrable wall of clouds; bolts of lightning sporadically illuminated the jungle floor.

"Come over here!" yelled Peter from somewhere.

James followed, doing his best to trace Peter's voice. He found him hidden under a large willow, partially protected from the downpour. James crawled under it.

Shuffling noises rustled in the darkness as unseen creatures made way among the foliage. Terrified, both boys pressed their backs against the sheltering tree. James's hand felt through the dirt, wrapping itself around a sharp rock. He held it tightly.

Lightning.

Darkness.

Lightning.

Darkness.

Without a single blink, the boys looked around, their nerves on edge. With every shred of flashing light, they expected a creature to appear from within the night and make them its dinner.

Was this to become James's new home? This reminded him of something his mother had shared with him when he first started at Eton. He refused to leave her side. Look at the moon for solace during times of tumult, she had told him, for the moon is the same wherever you may go, and I'll be looking up just the same and my heart will be there with you, and you will feel at home. Yet no matter how hard James tried, he couldn't see past the luscious treetops— past the loaded clouds. And even if he did, he knew neither one of Neverland's three moons would connect him to his mother.

Home, he thought. That night he expected to cry. But no tears came.

"Are you sure this was a good idea?" he asked, shivering.

"There's no going back now, James. There's no going back."

James could only see but an outline of Peter's face. That's when he noticed; something had changed inside Peter—something had been lost after their return to London. What is he hiding? James thought as he looked into Peter's hard-bitten face.

Light.

Dark.

Light.

Dark.

XII.
BROTHERS

FLOCK OF LONG-feathered birds with plumage as orange as fire crossed the morning skies. Crisp white clouds parted in the distance. In survival mode, Peter swung a sturdy stick around, clearing the path before him. Just like the first time, their ability to fly had inexplicably worn off. They assumed it to be normal.

Trees unfolded around Peter; their low elongating branches spread like tentacles, weaving in and out of one another. Both soil and trunks alike were delicately coated with green moss and blue spores. The island had more than one face, they soon discovered; dense jungles, gloomy forests, volcanic fields.

As the days went by, James tried to think less and less about his mother. But the image of a barred window gnawed at his heart with every breath. He appeared from between the trees behind Peter and followed closely, carrying dragon-fruit-like goods, the size of tangerines. Like many things in Neverland, they had no name.

"I found these," James announced, fruit-goop spread all over his face.

"Did you try them?"

"Yes, they are sweeter than the other ones."

"How could you tell they were not poisonous?"

James spun in his tracks. "Poisonous??"

Moments later, they reached a clearing; the magma graveyard. This time around, they easily spotted the lonely tree and its shrunken heads from a distance. They did not take another step.

Overlooking the island, Peter mapped their surroundings on the dirt. The cliff provided them with a perfect view of the entire landscape. Using a pointed rock, James attacked a coconut-like fruit—sweat dripping off his forehead—but his efforts were pointless; the shell was impenetrable.

"We can go around the clearing, through here..." Peter pointed at the dirt, then at the landscape. A valley extended past it, following a river into the ocean. "I can see the ocean. It's not too far."

"What's over there?" asked James, pointing in the opposite direction. The mountain range crowned with clouds blocked their view.

"I think that's where the girl took us. The cave," Peter said reminiscing. "The mermaids... we should find something sharp."

James tossed him his jagged tool, now entirely blunt. Peter examined it before disposing of it.

"No. *Really* sharp. Or else they'll eat us alive."

"*They'll?*"

"We don't know what else is out there, James. We need protection."

Spotting a stick on the dirt, Peter picked it up, studied it, and snapped it in half. He lifted the serrated edge up to his face, smiling proudly at this discovery.

The rest of the afternoon was spent scouting for acute rocks and sticks. Anything that looked blunt or feeble was immediately discarded. They used dried vines to attach the ragged slabs onto branches. Other rocks were kept as hand blades. The boys were now armed, but even they knew it was but a mere false sense of security. Fencing lessons and playful make-believe would not cut it. When faced with immediate danger, they would have been torpid. In this kind of scenario, one could only learn through actual practice; and practice was only enhanced through raw experience—meaning surviving.

They arrived at the waterfall by early afternoon. Peter skipped on the boulders surrounding the lake—as large and white as prehistoric eggs. He was able to get a clearer view of the wildlife it harbored; rainbowed fish the size of his arm swam carelessly close to the surface.

Waist-deep inside the basin, Peter and James launched their spears into the water, missing repeatedly. Frustrated, Peter chased the fish, splashing and tripping under the surface. His head reappeared, gasping for air, his arms swatting around in a failed attempt to swim.

That night they ate more of the dragon-fruit-like-plant. Neither of them said a word.

As the days went by, James began carving small incisions onto the interior of a fallen and hollowed tree. They had found shelter inside. It wasn't the safest of places, but it provided them with a dry roof over their heads. The fresh new carving was the last one in a set of crisscrossed lines. James had been tallying their days spent in Neverland to keep track of time. Except this proved to be quite difficult. After the first few nights, they quickly discovered Neverland had more than a day inside a day. This can be quite easy to understand once the dynamics are explained. Soon after the main sun—they agreed it was the main one, as it was the largest one—had set, and the smaller sun had followed, the boys noticed something peculiar; once night had fallen, several hours later—or so they calculated—, the smaller sun would rise by itself, creating a not-so-bright, half day. During that time, the larger sun was nowhere to be seen. After the small disc would set, nighttime would continue uninterrupted. Eventually, the main sun would rise again, followed by the smaller one shortly after. This would have caused great confusion to anyone used to the standard sunrise and sunset schedules—as were the boys at first. They had no way of measuring time. His father's watch was of no use. It ticked, but the hands were frozen. For all they knew, the island did not share the same twenty-four hour cycles a regular day did. For boys who feared growing up, they were quite consumed by the task of recording time. Especially James. It was hard to tell if he was indeed counting up a collection of days since his arrival, or if he was counting down, waiting for their departure date, as inmates do in prison.

"They would help us hunt. And build a shelter," Peter explained.

After ruminating in silence for a period of days, Peter had finally shared his thoughts with James. Apparently, he had been working out the logistics—which James thought had not been worked out at all. Peter wanted to bring other boys to Neverland. In fact, he was determined to. James knew that once Peter got something in his head, it was a done deal.

"So we just tap on their windows and ask, 'hullo there, lad, we don't know you, but would you like to leave your mummy and daddy and join us on an adventure?'" James asked, mockingly. "'We have mermaids, but don't go near them, they might try to eat you; we have natives, but don't go near them, they might also try to eat you...'"

Sensing James's grounding nature, Peter interrupted: "Maybe we shouldn't tell them about the natives. Or the mermaids. They don't have to come if they don't want to. They have a choice. But think about it, James, so many boys out there, just like you and me, who have nowhere to go. Where should they live? On the streets? And become beggars?" Peter wisely pulled on James's heart strings, playing them like a skilled violinist. "We'd be saving them, and they'd do as we say—"

"They'd do as *we* say?" James interrupted, brows knitted.

Peter shrugged.

"Like their parents?"

"No..." Peter caught himself, and started backpedaling. "No, not like parents. But like—" he looked for the right words, "—like older brothers! Older brothers with more experience."

"Peter, we have no experience."

"But we will!" he said assertively. "We'll tell them which fruits are sweeter, where not to go, how to avoid the mermaids' spell... they'll become—" he said with a twinkling gleam in his eye— "our brothers. Our little brothers."

Whether he wanted to admit it or not, James liked the idea. Who knew, perhaps if Peter had grown up, he would've been a superb salesman. "I've always wanted a brother."

"I'm your brother, James. We," Peter paused. Then added, "brothers and parentless. We have to stick together. We have no one but each other. And *they*..." said Peter, pointing at the sky, "those boys need us. We have to rescue them. Rescue them from being abandoned."

This struck a chord in James. The word 'abandoned' had left a forever-bitter taste in his mouth.

"They'll starve on the streets," James finally said.

"Tucked in an alley like a pet you forgot to feed!"

"They'll become thieves. And orphanages are pure torture."

"They are worse." Peter's answer caught James by surprise. Had he ever been in one?

"You're depressing me." James had never personally seen the inside of an orphanage, but had only heard horrid stories. "What about girls?" he inquired, a lump of air suddenly stuck in his throat.

"No girls. Girls are too... complicated. Besides that would be just like having a mother." Peter stated, puffing his chest. "We don't need any girls around."

James decided not to push further. "And we won't force anyone," he added. "If they want to go back, they are allowed to go back. No hard feelings."

"No hard feelings. But why would they? When they could have

all of this?" Peter motioned at the entirety of the island, spinning in a circle, arms wide open.

Their uncharted playground.

XIII.
THE LOST BOYS

ETER APPROACHED THE MOUTH of the cave with caution. It was still bright out; the mermaids were nowhere to be seen. Just like he remembered, the interior was decorated with beautiful and exotic flowers, their sweet intoxicating smell lingering in the air. The random trinkets remained stuck onto the walls, among the greenery. He strode past hundreds of rows of blossoms, following a barely audible banging. Coming to a halt before one, he motioned James over while pressing his index finger on his lips; *shhh.*

Upon arriving to the mysterious bloom, James peered into the large petals, standing next to Peter. This flower was unusually large; its petals spread wider than the boys' heads. Hiding inside was their fairy friend, keeping herself occupied by banging a small— out of shape—pot with a tiny rock. The flower was large enough to house her and her selective collection of pots and clocks. They both realized she was the one heaping all these mismatching items. She was the tiniest hoarder they had ever come across.

"Hey, there Tink," James smiled.

"*Tink?*"

"She's always tinkering."

Startled, the overjoyed fairy shot right out of her flower dropping clanking items all over the cave. Her squeaky voice reverberated across the rocky walls.

"And she sounds just like—" Peter started.

"—a tiny bell," James added.

"Tinker—"

"—Bell," finished James with a Cheshire grin. "Tinker Bell!"

And just like they had named the nameless island, and James had christened Tiger Lily with a name, the boys found themselves naming things without reservation, like pioneers in a new world. Drunk with excitement at their sudden discovery, the boys screamed her name as Tinker Bell fluttered over them. A cloud of golden dust bathed them entirely, and in a matter of seconds, the boys began to fly.

They made it to London by late evening. Most boys had been kissed goodnight and were tucked in bed, minutes away from drifting into dreamland. Both Peter's and James's flying skills had greatly improved. They were in control of the air around them at all times; graceful and fluid.

Peering through a bedroom window, a loving mother read her daughter a bedtime story. Peter frowned and stuck his tongue out in disgust.

Onto the next one.

A father kissed his son goodnight before dimming the lights.

Peter huffed and puffed.

Onto the next window.

This time, they found a picture perfect sight—to Peter's standards, that is.

A rotund boy about thirteen—with cheeks so flushed he looked like he'd been standing next to a fire—, stormed into the bedroom slamming the door behind him. Fat tears varnished his face as he leapt onto his bed in a striped nightgown that made him look like a bell. Digging under his bed, he retrieved a plate overflowing with pastries, tarts, and slices of cake.

Tears flowed gratuitously as he stuffed handfuls of sweets into his tiny mouth; his cheeks growing larger with every bite, stretching to their limits, about to explode. Every sob was a failed attempt to breathe amidst the sweet mush.

Two soft knocks by the window interrupted his stuffing, crying, and heaving fest. He peered around his bed, startled. Nothing. Shrugging it off, he scooped another handful of goopy confiture and ingested it. Two more knocks. Louder this time.

Getting up, he looked around the room, annoyed at being interrupted mid-nosh. Curious, he approached the window. What could he find out his window this late at night? Probably nothing, he thought. Except he was wrong. He found Peter.

The flying boy's friendly wave caused the rotund boy to lose his step, tripping backwards, stumbling over his toys, and choking on the lumps of dough caught in his throat. Hyperventilating, he got up with surprising agility and ran back to the window. He pushed it open, sticking his head out. His eyes had not deceived him. He rubbed them with both hands, expecting to wake up. That's when James appeared.

Two flying boys.

Two.

Both appeared to be around his age.

"Why are you crying?" Peter asked.

The boy didn't quite hear him, or simply had more important matters to address. "How are you doing that?!" he shrieked in a whisper, pointing his stumpy finger at them. "How are you... flying?" His eyes widened, huge as billiard balls at the mention of the word.

"I'm Peter, this is James."

"Uhu, uhu, right. How are you flying?" the boy pressed on, frantic. "Teach me!!"

"What's your name?" asked James.

"Nibs," he replied briskly. "HOW DO YOU FLY?!" his face

71

boiled red with anxiety—and a sugar high.

"Well, you see, Nibs," James said, educating him, "we can fly, because we have no mothers."

"Oh," young Nibs deflated.

"Want to learn how to fly, Nibs?" asked Peter, twirling in the air.

"Yes!!" Nibs cried, chocolate spread all over his face. "But... no mother?"

"It's the only requirement, otherwise the magic doesn't work," Peter lied.

"You can always stay here," James reassured.

Not liking this, Peter intervened. "But do you *really* want to stay? Who made you cry, Nibs?"

"My parents..."

"Why?"

"They wouldn't let me eat cake," Nibs accused, outraged.

"Exactly!" Peter howled. "And isn't that so extremely unfair?"

"It's appalling!"

"Rotten!" Peter added, getting the boy even more worked up. "Is this how you want to be treated for the rest of your life? In a prison where you're not allowed to eat cake?"

Nibs shook his head.

James watched, skeptical. There was something about Peter that made him feel uneasy. Yet, part of him also felt it was unfair the boy didn't get to have cake. It reminded him of his own father, when he didn't allow him to see his sick mother, or to go out and play. Which made him wonder. Should he go home? Peek through his window? Face his fears? A sharp pain crept on his chest. No. *No*, James insisted. He missed his mother. But he couldn't allow himself to miss her. He couldn't miss someone that had abandoned him. Someone that had forgotten all about him.

"We are boys! We should be able to have cake whenever we please!" said Peter, encouraging Nibs's tantrum. "Leave these buggers behind!!"

"YES!!!" he replied, hanging on Peter's every word. Then, he hesitated. "But... who'll tell me stories?" He looked at them for several long beats.

"James will. He's pretty good," said Peter, as if to secure the deal.

James smiled warmly.

"Do you know the story of Pan and Apollo?" Nibs asked.

Matter of fact, James knew that story like the back of his hand. It was one of his favorites and, even though he refused to admit it, he had not heard it in quite some time. Pan, the Greek god of shepherds and nature, was a fantastic musician, widely known for his invention of the Greek pan flute. An instrument that emitted a sound so sweet, that he grew blinded by his pride and challenged Apollo, the sun-god, to a musical duel. For those not familiar with Pan, he was a woodland creature with the legs of a goat, devilish in nature. He was known for his mischievousness, always getting in trouble. Hoping to punish Pan for his vanity, Apollo agreed to the contest. Pan's music was so wild and coaxing, it tickled all the other faun's furry little ears. But once Apollo held his golden lyre, a music so perfect it hadn't been heard by mortal or god before, captivated everyone's ears; Apollo was immediately proclaimed winner, and Pan was left to relish in his own jealousy and contempt.

"Oh, how I love the story of Pan and Apollo," Nibs squealed as he held up a storybook displaying a beautiful illustration of the god. Peter fancied the leaves draping over Pan's body and the scalawag quality of his nature. Tearing the page off the book, Nibs folded the image and stuffed it inside his pocket.

"But where will I sleep?" he then asked, worried.

"Neverland!" Peter's eyes sparkled like shooting starts whenever the name escaped his lips.

"Never-*what?*"

"A magical place where you never... ever... grow up," James added.

Nibs considered this. He looked around his bedroom. What was left there for him?

"Is there cake in this Never-place?"

"Sweeter desserts than your tongue has tasted," Peter replied before James could answer. "We even have pies!"

"What kind of pies??"

"Apple pie, cherry pie, pear pie... and mountains of tarts!"

Why was Peter lying? James wondered.

Nibs released a shrilling hoot and then smiled. "I want to do it. Now, how do I fly? Do I just—" he muttered as he climbed onto the windowsill— "jump?"

"NO!" both boys yelled, arms stretched out.

"You need some... fairy dust," Peter said with a grin.

"Fairy dust?" Nibs grimaced, a true non-believer.

James called out for the fairy, who swiftly appeared upon hearing her name. With elegant moves, she circled Nibs, sprinkling him with sparkling dust before he had time to react.

"What's this? Is this sugar?" he asked, licking his hand.

When his feet gently pushed off the ground. His body rose like a small hot air balloon. "Oh, my goodness!" he squawked in realization. "Oh! Oh! I'm flying!!"

The three boys crossed the London sky, Nibs clumsily swirling behind, as they made way to a new window. The 'brother recruitment' went on until the early hours of dawn. After several hours, not three, but eight silhouettes bobbled through the moonless night, all led by a blaze of light.

As they grew smaller and smaller, Kensington Gardens glowed below them. A long fairy with six legs hovered over the treetops, keeping guard. Her straining eyes caught sight of eight puny dots drifting in the distance. They were all led by a shimmering star; Tinker Bell. Overtaken by a sense of urgency, the long fairy buzzed back into the foliage, back to its nest, back to alert the others.

XIV.
TIME

WEEK–OR SO they estimated–had gone by since their latest departure from London. The acclimatization process had gone by smoothly. The boys' eagerness to please their 'Older Brothers' was stronger than any kind of loyalty.

Hanging from a tree, was Tootles. He was the oldest of the lost boys–only younger than James–and the same age as Peter; however, this wasn't an issue when it came to establishing the pecking order. Tootles was also taller than Peter and possibly the most mature out of the boys. You would always find him hard at work, doing all the annoying tasks the other boys would rather avoid. No matter how dangerous, no matter how grueling, Tootles would do the job with no hesitation. He was also the most serious and quiet, always hiding behind his sharp, round spectacles. He was a stone-faced intellectual. It was almost impossible to get a laugh out of him.

With meticulous care, he picked the dragon-fruit-like produce off the highest branches and tossed them down. On the receiving end–at the bottom of the tree–, were the twins. For reasons unknown, they refused to reveal their individual names and always spoke in unison. James pointed out that perhaps they enjoyed being considered a joint individual, glued together; like a boy with two heads, four arms, and four legs. So they were known as 'the twins'. Whether it was a twins' thing or not, it was hard to say, but they quadrupled the other boys in energy. They were like frenzied gerbils, always in motion, always caught up in their own brotherly conversations, which the other boys did not partake in. Erratic and clumsy, the twins reached up, eager to catch the same fruit, bumping heads and dropping on the ground.

A few feet away was Curly, sharpening a branch with chilling precision. During his first week in Neverland, he'd created a game called 'lick the toad'. The other boys had found it amusing for a while, but lost interest once finding the right toad became a grueling task. One thing must be understood about Curly; he was the shortest of the boys, but he was also the most notorious. One couldn't let his full, red, kinky hair, and sprinkled freckles deceive them. He was a wicked boy by nature. He loved hunting. Not because it was exciting to hide behind bushes, but because he enjoyed inflicting pain. Dead animals were his joy and he loved skinning them the most. Which is why his weapons had to be the sharpest, the strongest, the deadliest. This made his friendship with the other boys a bit combustive on a daily basis. Peter enjoyed his company, and thought he was a fantastic hunter and cook—mainly because none of the other boys (except maybe Tootles) wanted to be near a bleeding carcass. However, his attitude proved problematic at times. He teased Nibs for being overweight, which in turn compelled Nibs to devour everything in sight. *Why doesn't he like me,* Nibs would ask while stuffing his face with fruity mush.

With delicate ease, Curly gutted a frog, skewered it with a stick, and placed it by the fire. His childlike curiosity got the best of him as he sniffed the frog's steaming entrails.

The remaining two boys sat around Peter, as he drew a floor plan on the dirt. He was designing a cottage they could call home. An incident involving Nibs getting stuck inside a hollow tree trunk had destroyed their last shelter. One would think the plump boy

would be a little less plump after a week (or so) in the wilderness, but he'd instead gotten heftier. Perhaps because he was constantly eating—every minute of every one-and-a-half days—, as he was at that very moment while watching Peter draw in the dirt.

"I'm famished! Where are all the pies, Peter?"

"What pies?"

"The apple pies... cherry pies..." Nibs replied.

"Did you hear that? He wants some bloody pies!" Curly mocked him. "Would you like some tea with your pie, your royal highness?"

"There are no pies here, Nibs," said Peter.

"But you said—"

"What did I say, Nibs?"

And that was the end of it. Nibs then proceeded to eat a handful of dirt. It was rich in minerals and nutrients, he would insist.

And then, there was Slightly; the eighth lost boy. Even though he sat directly next to Peter, his imaginative mind wandered somewhere else, distracted, captivated by a butterfly. He had a heart of gold, but not a day went by without the boys wondering how he had managed to stay alive. Slightly was incredibly naïve. His overt positivity made him easy prey for tricks and puns.

These were the boys. All except one.

James was nowhere in sight.

In a state of extreme awareness, James made way stealthily through the dense jungle, his spear sharp as glass, lingering above his head. His face was strategically masked with dirt and his clothes were shrouded with leaves. *Camouflage.*

A cracking branch halted his movement. His ears perked up. He crawled through the underbrush, ready for his prey. But his eyes met a better prize.

Climbing up the rocky slope, Tiger Lily made way across the jagged path towards the cave. Tinker Bell's clutter cave.

James smiled.

Sneaking past the flora and rummage inside the cave, James surveyed the area, hoping to go by unnoticed so he could surprise the girl—but he couldn't find her. James frowned, perplexed at the sudden turn of events. He knew he had seen her walk in. Where had she gone?

Suddenly, the air was knocked out of his lungs, as a force fell from above, nailing him to the ground. He wheezed as a blade hugged his neck. He blinked repeatedly with anxious terror.

Tiger Lily's dark eyes burned with bloodcurdling determination. Then something in them softened. She took a moment, then leaned closer to his face. She sniffed him. Two sniffs. Softening her expression, she stepped off of him and helped him up.

This caught James by surprise. She could have killed him. She had acted as if she didn't remember him. How could she not?

"Do you remember me?" James asked, mouthing the words carefully.

The girl tilted her head, unsure of the noises coming out of his mouth.

"*Parlez vous francais?*" James tried again, having taken a few French classes at Eton.

Nothing. She responded with the same puzzled reaction.

Letting out a deep sigh, James's hopes of communication grew dim. Just as he was coming to terms with the idea of a friendship without conversation, an idea sparked inside the corridors of his mind. Sign language. He maneuvered his hands with slow, controlled movements. But Tiger Lily was unable to understand him. Yet there was a familiarity in the motions that caught her attention. She had seen something similar before. At first she had difficulty figuring out where, but in a matter of seconds the memory fell into place. Caught in the moment, she briskly grabbed him by the hand and dragged him out of the cave with zero explanation.

The main sun was setting outside. Nightfall would be coming soon.

Tiger Lily made way across the native's camp with James close behind; hesitant, the memory of that terrifying night still lingering.

As the last rays of sun bled through the horizon, smoke rose out of a single tent separated from the rest of the camp. The girl frantically pushed James inside, taking a seat by the faint fire pit.

A fragile woman with wrinkles deep as canyons sat by the fire, smoking a long wooden pipe. Her little eyes were sunken deeply into the crevices of her skull—a gleam sparkling off the black dot that was her iris. Her skin was as leathery as the tent—a dried-apple quality—worn out by age and the scorching sun. Her long, dirt-caked nails adjusted the fire with a poker.

Tiger Lily communicated with her in their native tongue. Smoke flowed out of the side of her thin mouth, as she shifted her gaze towards James with a warm and approachable smile. Tiger Lily signaled with her hands towards James—her own version of sign language. He understood.

James moved his fingers, communicating with the old woman.

My name is James Hope.

May the spirits guide you, James Hope, she replied, taking her time.

James paused for a moment, unsure of what to ask.

What is this island? he finally signaled.

All the points unite. Timelessness flows out of the unity. Timelessness holds the secret to its magic.

This confused James. **What do you mean 'timelessness'?**

The woman's beady eyes spotted the golden watch in James's pocket—his father's watch. He'd been carrying it everywhere, always keeping it in sight. Not as a sentimental gesture towards his father, the iceberg, but as his only remaining link to home.

The woman extended her withered hand gently, asking for the object. Understanding, James relinquished it. With her bony finger, she tapped at the watch's face. Like before, the watch ticked, but the hands emanating from the center of the dial were still.

Suns set. Suns rise. The dance repeats. Yet the river of time does not move. It doesn't exist. The roundabout spins, dances, but we do not move. We dissolve, as does memory.

This got James's attention. **Memory dissolves?**

We live for the moment. Memories hold you back; their weight crushes your spirit. The island helps your spirit; it helps you forget. Faces slowly dissolve. You too will soon forget. We have been on this island since the dawn of man. Once the island makes itself your home, you'll never be fit to belong anywhere else.

A growing discomfort had started spreading in James's gut.

The mermaids' wails haunted the night. The old woman looked up, appreciating the sound. It was simultaneously beautiful and broken.

They were once creatures of heavenly beauty. But they fed on the darkness for too long. The darkness... it blinds you. Their hunger for death consumed them. They lost their shadows. If you ever leave this island, you'll understand. For the one who arrives, will never be equal to the one who departs. Change. That's what this island is about. Yet if the island takes ahold of your shadow... there's no letting go...

James's face distorted with worry. **How do you stop it?**

The woman smiled. **How do you stop a frozen river?**

James's heart sank. Anguish welled up in his chest and threatened to register on his face.

Unarmed, James cut through the dark jungle with extreme urgency. His breathing short and erratic. The encounter with the native woman had disturbed him deeply. The conversation kept replaying inside his head, causing the hairs on the back of his neck to rise. *Memory dissolves.* James did not want to forget. He couldn't forget. He might have left home, but he did not want to let go of that memory.

Once he arrived, he found himself facing a rudimentary cottage made out of branches, rocks, and leaves. Nothing a storm couldn't easily wipe. But James couldn't move. He felt paralyzed.

Muffled conversations could be overheard coming from inside. Laughter. Then silence. Nibs spotted James through a tiny crack.

They playfully shushed one another inside. Then they giggled.

"What's the password?" Nibs asked, feigning a deep, threatening voice.

But James couldn't reply. He stared at the hut, expressionless.

"Maybe he didn't hear you," Slightly said.

"He's right outside, you bloody idiot! Of course he heard him," scowled Curly.

Nibs cleared his throat before proceeding, this time deeper and louder than before. "What's the passwooooooorddddddddd?" his words elongated.

"Maybe he doesn't know," said Tootles.

"Wait—We have a password...?" asked Slightly, confused.

"Bloody idiot!!"

Finally, Peter stepped out. Concerned, he looked at James. Nibs followed, tossing dragon-fruit skins out. Not acknowledging their presence, James kept staring at the ground, rooted to the spot.

"Nibs, go back inside," Peter ordered.

He obeyed, closing the giant-leaf-door behind him.

"You look ill."

James looked up, fear in his eyes. "We can't stay here."

"Didn't you see our hut?" Pride sparkled in Peter's eyes. "Tootles found great wood we'll use to reinforce it tomorrow—"

But James interrupted. "We have to leave."

Peter winced, not appreciating James's firmness and tone. "Why?" he asked, irritated.

"This island... it's going to make us forget."

Sensing his friend was more troubled than he lead on, Peter's annoyance quickly dissipated. "Right..." his brows knitted nimbly. "Forget what?"

"About everything!" James stammered, growing agitated. "Forget where we came from, forget about London, forget our parents..."

Peter scoffed. "Is this some kind of game?"

"*Game?*" James found himself shaking, losing his wits. "This is no *game*, Peter. This is serious."

"That's just bullocks, James. Islands don't make people forget things. Everybody knows that."

"It does! This island does. It's magic. And its magic—it erases time. Or stops it. Time doesn't exist here."

Peter stared at James blankly. Frustrated, James let out an exasperated groan, his face flushing red.

"I think you were out way too long in the sun, Captain," sneered Peter. Was that condescension in his voice? James was pale. Sweaty. He looked ill. "You should get some sleep. And I mean that."

Defeated, James wrapped his head between his hands. Perhaps he was overreacting. Perhaps Peter was right. How could an island make people *forget*? That was impossible. Then again, so was flying. And so were mermaids. Doubt lingered. Had Tiger Lily momentarily forgotten about him?

"But what if... what if we do forget?" James finally asked.

"We went into the gardens, didn't we? We climbed that tree, got attacked by a swarm of rotten fairies, I hurt my ankle and then you carried me to safety. Saving my life. Protecting me. See?" he placed his hand on James's shoulder. "I did not forget. And I will never forget. How could I ever forget that? You're my brother, James. You have to trust me." Peter's words were finally getting through.

He had to be right... right?

"Now come inside," he continued. "I want to show you something. We have a small fire set up. Oh, and that's not it. We also—are you ready? We also have a chimney."

That evening the boys shared stories, laughed, and ate, but their voices filtered through James's mind without leaving a trace. The joys of the present suddenly found themselves lost amongst his burgeoning fear of forgetting his past.

Withdrawn.

Dejected.

They didn't understand.

Or perhaps they simply did not care to.

XV.
THE DARK LAGOON

HE SKY RIPPED AT its seams, roaring and thundering into shards of luminescence. Trees swayed furiously. Some were cleaved clean, extracted, leaving behind nothing but a lacerated gash. Drops the size of grapes cut through the air with stinging speed.

The boys' hut was no match for nature's wrath. The structure rattled about to cave in. Chaos seeped into it.

Tootles rubbed two sticks together, trying desperately to start a fire. Curly held a leaf over Tootle's head; keeping him and the sticks dry.

"What's taking so bloody long?" Curly snapped.

"It's not working! It's too damp!"

"Maybe you just don't know what you're bloody doing!"

"Shut your mouth, Curly! Or I'll shut it for you!" Tootles threatened, pointing the stick at Curly's face.

Tension levels kept rising as the twins ran around holding onto the walls, trying to stop the cottage from collapsing. However, the storm wasn't the only cause of their worries. Peter was ill. Very ill. He had fallen under the weather without a warning. Slightly had found him unconscious by the waterfall. Heat and exhaustion could have been the catalysts, but something else in his body was spreading like venom, taking over his senses, destroying his strength. He hadn't awoken since then—two days ago, in Neverland time—, sleeping without water or meal.

"How is he?" James walked in, soaked, carrying lumber.

Slightly placed a wet rag on Peter's feverish face. The circles around his eyes were deep and dark. He trembled sporadically, completely benumbed.

"He's getting warmer and warmer," Slightly reported.

Nibs was nervous-eating. "That's good right? Right...? Warm is good, right??"

Taking over, James dropped on his knees. "No, it's bad, very bad."

The shivering increased. "Mum..." Peter's weak voice whimpered.

"Peter? Peter, can you hear me?" But James got no response, as his friend was drifting in and out of consciousness at rapid intervals.

Suddenly, a small, but promising flame, burnt gently on the dried leaves. Tootles howled victoriously.

"We need to get him out of here," James said.

"Nonsense! He's safe here!" rebutted Nibs.

In under a second, the roof of the hut was wiped clean exposing the boys. They were drenched by pummeling raindrops. Nature has a way of positioning herself atop the food chain, frequently reminding bottom feeders of her omnipotence during those times of human haughtiness. Tootle's flame never stood a chance.

The boys shrieked and panicked. They ran around in circles, bumping into each other, as the torrential downpour stuck to them like a second skin.

"HEY!" James snapped them into attention. There was no time to waste. "Tootles, grab his feet." He did. "Nibs, grab me a few large leaves."

"In the dark?"

"Did I stutter?"

Nibs squirmed.

"Twins, grab him from the sides. Curly, get under him."

Between the five of them, they were able to raise Peter off the ground. Nibs returned promptly carrying a set of giant leaves. With the help of Slightly, they used them as umbrellas to cover Peter, keeping him dry—or at least attempted to keep him dry.

"Where are we taking him?" Curly asked.

"To safety."

The boys marched into the jungle, one behind the other, lifting Peter on their shoulders. The walk to safety could easily have been confused with a funeral procession.

They marched through a boulder-lined clearing, suddenly exposed to the unpredictable winds. Slightly lost his leaf umbrella and was forced to join Curly in the ranks holding Peter up. The thunder and downpour had no intention of decreasing. On the upside, lightning was the only glow illuminating their way.

With no trees to protect them from the merciless gale, a turbulent gust knocked James and the twins, causing them to lose their footing. Out of balance, they almost dropped Peter.

"Get up! Up!!" James screamed, hoisting Peter's head back onto his shoulder.

They fought against the windstorm, minding every step on the uneven surface.

If there's anything mermaids crave more than human flesh, it is a sublime monsoon. The fresh water mixed into their murky swamp as they bathed in its heavy droplets and wailed to the thunder beats—a celebration of their animalistic qualities.

As the somber procession approached their lagoon, the water began to coruscate from within, the enigmatic wails fusing into harmonious incantations.

"Cover your ears!" James barked.

The boys instantly readjusted. Some of them stuffed premade leaf-mush-balls into their ears, while others—like the twins and Curly—used their forefingers to block the sound while balancing

Peter on their shoulders. Slightly sang himself gibberish, hoping to drown the creatures' cries.

They arrived to the native's campsite safely. The boys looked around, dreading the worst. They had been told repeatedly never to approach the natives or their campgrounds. Now, they were walking on their turf. Curly squeezed the handle of his blade in one hand. Slightly couldn't bear to keep his eyes open. Yet there wasn't a single body in sight; the natives had all sought shelter from the storm. A faint strip of smoke materialized from the elder woman's tent.

Shivering, they all crouched inside the tent and around Peter. The wise woman chanted while blowing smoke at the inert boy. Buried under a mound of animal skin, Tiger Lily awoke, stirred by the commotion. She noticed the boys squatting around Peter, and the growing concern on James's face. She knew something was wrong. Dangerously wrong.

As the wise woman's chant came to an end, she placed her puny hand on Peter's head, gently caressing it. Looking up, she shook her head with deep sadness.

James's watch ticked away in his pocket.

Tic-toc, tic-toc.

Whether time froze in Neverland or not, James could feel the clock of life ticking away, fading into silence. Every tic was a precious moment of Peter's future, slipping away. However, despair wasted no time in feeding the boys' fear.

"What do we do now?" Nibs frantically chewed on a dragon-fruit.

"James, there has to be something we can do," Tootles attempted to reason.

"We can't let him bloody die!!" Curly was fuming.

Lost in thought, James withdrew from the ruckus. The boys were right. He couldn't let Peter die. He felt responsible for his life. At the end of the day, it was Peter who saved him from complete abandonment in London. But then again, it was James's fault they were abandoned in the first place. He blamed himself for their current situation, as he was the one who'd insisted on breaking into the gardens on that dreadful night.

Yet none of them seemed to notice Tiger Lily sitting in silence, her mind churning, ruminating in a corner. That was until she decided to take action. With unexpected strength, she swung Peter onto her back and darted out of the tent.

"Where is she taking him?" the twins shrieked in unison.

Tiger Lily wasted no time making way across the clearing, fast and steady. The boys spilled out of the tent chasing after her, calling out, yelling at her to stop, pleading obscenities as the gorged raindrops struck them like bullets.

Had everything worked out according to Tiger Lily's calculations, they should have been out of harm's way upon arriving to the flowered cave in the mountain, by the mermaids' lagoon. However, these things rarely work out as planned.

As she made way past the uneven surface of the rocky slope, a faint buzz broke through the clouds, cutting through the rain; getting louder with every passing second. Exhausted, Tiger Lily looked up at the black sky. A swarm of angry fairies tore through the firmament, headed in her direction. Small and sharp, spears and arrows pierced her skin. As she yelped in pain—losing her balance—Peter escaped her grip, tumbling down the mountain. She wrapped her fingers around his limp hand while he was still at arm's reach.

The boys broke through the dense jungle, stopping at the sight of the violent attack. Tinker Bell aside, they had never seen a fairy before, let alone a vicious fairy. James recognized the winged creatures instantly. They had left Kensington Gardens and sought them out. Fairies may be tiny creatures, but they hold onto a grudge for years; err them and they will never forget.

Tiger Lily shrieked, arrows like needles stinging her flesh. This snapped the boys out of their daze. Reaching out for anything that could inflict damage, the boys set off into the war zone with branches, rocks, and an ear-splitting war cry. Tootles swung a stick back and forth furiously, knocking the fairies off their winged balance. The twins spun on the spot, hurling rocks the size of their fists at the flying creatures, getting a lucky hit every few throws.

A fairy spear punctured Tiger Lily's arm, drawing blood. She recoiled in pain, once again letting go of Peter. Tumbling down the slope, he splashed into the murky waters of the mermaids' nest. His seemingly lifeless body sunk with ease, as pockets of air bubbled to the surface.

Like a spider sensing the vibrations across its web, the slimy creatures uncoiled and slithered off the rock at the center of the lagoon, slipping into the waxy waters, sniffing out their prey. Lit from within, the swamp pulsated with a brilliant glow, announcing the start of the hunt.

Tiger Lily's face went slack with fright. Filled with manic rage, she seized her small ax and twirled it across the air, slicing arms, legs, and fairy wings with spine-chilling precision. Yet the fairy's numbers didn't seem to decrease. They circled the boys, surrounding them completely. Their attacks grew closer and closer, cutting through flesh like a thousand razor blades. The boys' self-confidence wavered. Unable to see through the thick rain, they fought back, perilously.

Breaking through the fluttering wall, James snatched a handful of rocks and hauled them at the water surrounding Peter. The mermaids were unaffected. Crossing the shore with five long leaps, James bounded into the lagoon, diving in Peter's direction.

The moment he reemerged—simultaneously pushing Peter's head out—, he knew they were cornered. The mermaids blocked their way back to the shore, as they sluggishly closed in around them. With nowhere else to go, James dragged Peter towards the black boulder jutting out of the swampy water.

Having cleared through some of the menacing fairies, Tiger Lily was able to get an unobstructed view of the swamps, spotting James on the slimy rock. He inched Peter onto the moss-covered shore. The mermaids were a mere two feet away. Pulling on Peter's unresponsive arm, James dragged his limp body up the steep terrain. That's when the first mermaid crawled out of the water and onto the rock.

Desperate, Tiger Lily pressed her bone flute to her lips and blew on it. Louder and louder. The dissonant tune struggled to be heard. Thunder roared, challenging its might. The twins stared at her astonished—they had never seen the instrument before.

Tootles and Curly swatted at the last set of fairies, finally overturning their numbers.

James drew his jagged spear and pushed Peter behind him. If the mermaids were going to prey on Peter, they were going to have to go through James first. That was the first time he saw one of the creatures up-close. She was like nothing he could have imagined; like nothing he'd ever read in his storybooks. Her skin was sickly-pale-green, oozing with live moss, as water flora sprouted from under her scales. Fingers were partially webbed and had shapeless, sharp claws protruding from the very ends. As she clutched onto the rock, James saw her hairless scalp, bone-ridges deep as valleys, and its gruesome tentacles extending down the back. Malformed protrusions bulged on both sides of her head. She hissed at him, revealing rows of needle-sharp teeth. And where her eyes should have been, perse, bulbous protuberances with narrow slits took their places. These creatures were blind. Blind as bats.

James jabbed his spear into the air hoping the mermaid would retreat. Sensing his maneuver, she recoiled, but did not withdraw. Livid, she clawed at him but missed. Seeing an opening, James kicked her off balance, knocking her off the rock.

But this encounter had only been a distraction. A second mermaid had already snuck past James, unhinging her jaws over Peter—mucous and saliva dribbled on his face.

James didn't have time to think. His every muscle tensed at the sight of the creature. Once again he was facing death, and once again he was determined to defy it. He had failed his mother, surely losing her to the bittersweet eternal sleep. He was not going to fail Peter.

With surpassing fury, the spear rose high and came down heavily, clasped tightly between his fingers. Cerulean blood trickled between his hands as the creature shrilled and squirmed. He knew

one blow would not be sufficient. One blow didn't guarantee that it wouldn't return. One blow simply wasn't enough.

The weapon was yanked out of her—liquid sapphire blood oozing—before brutally impaling her once again. The creature shrieked cries James had never heard before. Consumed by a sense of loss, he drew the spear out and stabbed her again and again, with relentless savagery. Emotions, previously repressed, exploded without restraint. Tears streamed down his scorn-stricken face as an act of self-defense had turned into an act of violence by his rampant outburst. After the third stab, the creature stopped wailing. The creature had stopped moving. However, James couldn't stop stabbing her. He had to erase her beyond death. He wasn't killing. He was destroying. And so, the boy who would have never hurt a fly, had killed.

After a loop of ceaseless jabs, James finally stopped. The mermaid's corpse had been limp for some time now. Energy had fled James's body, leaving him in a deep state of inertia. Numb, his shoulders caved in. His head slugged down, defeated.

He could hear Tiger Lily's flute. It sounded far, far away—out of his reach, out of his world. Where was it coming from? James couldn't see it. Couldn't feel it. He felt as if he were sinking; falling deep into an endless well; dropping fast, but getting nowhere faster. The falling motion ceased to feel like falling. It had become a feeling of idleness, as if he'd been caught in the middle, suspended midair. It didn't feel like flying. It felt like a hollow, empty deadness.

Like a dark lagoon.

The boys called out his name, their voices breaking, cracking, hurting. But James was unresponsive.

Tiger Lily's relentless musical efforts had finally worked; a trail of sparkling dust shot out of the cave, circling her eagerly before fluttering towards the lonely rock.

Tinker's squeaking snapped James out of his stupor. He yanked the spear out of the legless carcass and climbed down to the bottom of the rock, where three mermaids had emerged. He was able to keep them at bay by slicing the air and hurling rocks. But he knew this wouldn't work for much longer.

Tinker's glimmering dust cloud covered Peter entirely. The sky seemed to have lit up around her; it truly was a sight to be seen. Never had Tinker produced such vast quantities of dust, which in turn was physically exhausting her. Yet Peter remained limp. She fluttered her wings even faster, draining herself, her glow gradually waning, flickering.

Outsmarting James's tactics, the mermaids spread around the rock, climbing up different sides. The boulder was too wide for him to stop them simultaneously. He was able to distract the first two, but the third slithered past his guard, clawing to the top, reaching for Peter.

Tinker saw James struggling, as a second mermaid began closing in on the dormant boy. Gathering every ounce of energy left in her tiny body, Tinker fluttered her wings faster, releasing a final burst of dust.

At this, Peter's body separated from the ground. He levitated, the air beneath him pushing him upwards, keeping him afloat like a feather. The boys cheered victoriously from the shore.

The weakening fairy kept fluttering as her light grew dim. Peter's body had risen significantly, hovering over the rock. Seeing this as his only exit, James crawled up, and jumped, grabbing onto Peter's limp arm.

Led by a debilitated Tinker, Peter and James flew out of danger, making way to the mouth of the cave.

Tiger Lily climbed past the uneven slope, followed by the boys who sang 'hurrah! hurrah!' behind her.

Amidst their celebratory chant, they failed to notice when Tinker Bell collapsed mid-flight, spiraling away, carried by the turbulent winds.

Inside the cave, James and the boys gently pushed Peter back in tune with gravity, placing him on a bed made out of petals and leaves.

"What happened to Tinker Bell?" Slightly was the first to observe.

A sense of anguish took over Tiger Lily as she approached the mouth of the cave. The storm wasn't giving in anytime soon. She couldn't see her light. She couldn't feel her presence. She blew on her bone instrument a couple of times. Nothing. Distressed, she wandered back into the cave. Had she known that Tinker Bell was safely tucked inside a nook under a rock, Tiger Lily would've had an easier time letting go of one of her worries that night. She crushed a few flowers inside a bowl and fed them to Peter. Yet he remained unresponsive. Following an ancient ritual, she breathed life onto his lips. Then, she adjusted a small drum on her lap and broke into a healing chant. Soothed by the steady nature of her drumming and her undulating voice, the boys were easily lulled to sleep. They all clutched onto their found weapons, finding comfort in them like teddy bears.

James kept guard by the opening—eyes agape. His insomnia was fueled by the fire sweltering inside his chest; haunting images of him maneuvering the spear flashed before his eyes. Sleeping would mean dreaming. Dreaming would mean reliving that moment in an unending torturous hell. He refused to go to sleep. He couldn't. Those evening's events, he knew, he'd never forget.

Tiger Lily's voice flowed into the night. The storm would eventually clear, as the boys' wounds would eventually heal. All would happen come morning, but morning was ways to come.

XVI.

PAN

HAT MORNING, THE SUN filtered through the clouds, tinting the sky coral. It illuminated the mouth of the cave, caressing James's shoulder warmly. Despite his resistance, he fell into dreamless sleep not long before dawn, overwhelmed with exhaustion.

The golden disc rose, parting between the storm's leftover clouds. Light gradually chased darkness away, permeating every crevice, every crack. The newborn ray of radiance beamed through the spotlight—gently pouring through its shaft with luscious glow—bathing Peter entirely in a golden pool of warmth. The muscles on his face twitched. Then, as his body began to stir, he floated upward off the ground.

Being the closest to him, Tiger Lily awoke—a light sleeper by nature. As Peter continued to rise, Tiger Lily shifted, studying this abnormality up-close. This was rather unusual, she thought.

The floating boy...

Suspended in a sunbeam...

The burning heat on James's face woke him. He turned his head groggily, averting his face from the blazing sun. He squinted

his eyes open, checking on the boys, hoping to ease back into sleep, but he didn't. His eyes remained open. Wide open.

Still not fully conscious, Peter had managed to levitate four feet above the ground; stretching his arms and legs, he let out a long, deep yawn. Finally, he opened his eyes.

"Good morning, boys!" The vibrancy in his voice, the rosy flush in his cheeks; James had never seen him so alive. He was seemingly unaffected by the previous night, and the illness that had taken over his body for days.

The boys stirred, rubbing their fatigued eyes.

"Boy, don't you all look like lily-livered, scrofulous poxy!" howled Peter, noticing their long faces, scratches and bruises. "What's for breakfast?" he asked patting his belly. "I'm famished!"

James and Tiger Lily exchanged questioning looks. Not only was his extreme recovery unexpected, but by Neverland's laws, he shouldn't have been flying. If James was certain of anything in Neverland, it was that the fairy's golden dust wore off after a night's sleep. Or so he thought.

Tiger Lily frowned. Something was wrong. *Tinker Bell.*

She quietly left the cave, her flute pressed onto her lips. Once outside, she blew on it gently.

Nothing.

She blew on it again.

This time, a faint squeaking bell caught her attention. It was coming from under the rubble a few feet below. Pushing a few small rocks aside, she found the feeble fairy, wings twitching, powerless. Wrapping her hands around the fragile creature, she lifted Tinker Bell and disappeared into the woods.

Slightly was the last to rise. "Is he awake yet—?" his words trailed off at the sight of Peter.

"Bloody dickens!" Curly blurted out.

"What's the matter?" Peter asked, unaware he was flying. "Cat caught your tongue?"

Silence settled in.

"Peter, you're flying," James said, breaking the dead air.

He was about to rebut, when his gaze landed between his feet. To his surprise, there was no ground directly below them. The gravel covered surface was three to four feet away.

"Well, I'll be damned..." muttered Peter amazed.

Stricken by curiosity, the boys walked around Peter, grabbing onto his feet, examining him—he had become an eccentric anomaly right before their eyes. It was almost as if he had risen from the dead.

"He must've gotten a large amount of fairy dust," Tootles noted.

"When will it wear off?" Nibs asked.

Peter shrugged.

Expecting an answer, Nibs turned to James, who tilted his head with doubt. "I'm not quite sure... there was a lot of fairy dust. More than I've ever seen."

Seeing Peter like this made James incredibly anxious. He wasn't by any means grieved about his friend's recovery; he was extremely glad. It was the magic behind the recovery, which made him worry.

"Is he still ill?" Slightly voiced his confusion.

"*Ill?*" Peter sneered. "I feel fantastic!" He swept across the cave, spinning and turning with perfect grace. Then, "We need a new home, boys!"

"Why can't we stay here?" Nibs asked, munching on the flowers.

"I fancy it here," said Slightly.

"No, it's too dangerous," Peter replied. "The mermaids' lagoon is but a drop away..." he taunted them. "And we don't want to be mermaid food now, do we?"

The twins shook their heads in unison.

"We'll build a stronger, bigger and deeper fortress!"

"Deeper?" James asked in a whisper.

"And where will we build it, Peter?" Tootles asked, adjusting his glasses.

"Underground. Where no one can find it."

The boys cheered with excitement, intoxicated with Peter's vivacious spirit. James, however, couldn't get past Peter's resurgence. It made no sense. He'd been practically dead a few hours prior.

"Peter, what about last night?" James asked coyly, almost too afraid—except he didn't know why.

"What about last night, my dearest friend?" he answered, with a mischievous glint in his eye.

James hesitated. "Are you sure you are all right?"

"James... I've never felt better!" Caught in the moment, he danced mid-air, kicking his feet and playing on an imaginary flute. His whistles echoed inside the cave, his blind elation reverberated on every surface. Nibs squinted. The picture unfolding before his eyes—it looked awfully familiar. He'd seen it before... In a storybook somewhere... The leaves, dangling loosely around Peter's body... The vines adorning his head... The animal skin hanging from his waist... The music, contagiously casting a spell... Feeling as if he'd been struck by lightning, he retrieved the folded illustration from inside his pocket, staring at it blankly, then back at Peter. Yes, it's true the differences between the two were abysmal—for starters, Peter didn't quite have cloven hooves—, but Peter's explosion of wild electricity reminded him of no one other than:

"Pan!!" he shouted ecstatic. "You're just like Pan!!"

Peter stopped mid-air, processing Nibs words. He liked the sound of it. He was very familiar with Pan's impish nature. Something about that puckish, saucy freedom, he found incredibly appealing. He'd be the shepherd, and the boys would be his herd— their rascal leader for all eternity.

Sizing Nibs up, Peter flew to him, staring deep into the rotund boy's eyes. "*Just like*', Nibs?"

He stared at Peter quizzically; sweat forming along his hairline. When Peter skewed his lips into a smile. "I AM the Pan!!"

And with that, he projected himself out of the cave, through the skylight, howling and crowing with powerful ardor.

The boys hurriedly ran outside to witness the spectacle. Peter swirled around in circles, playing with the clouds, soaring at impressive speeds, to astronomical heights and plummeting into great depths.

All of a sudden, his lust for life had become uncanny.

He felt infinite.

XVII.
JEALOUSY

OWN HERE!" TOOTLES CRAWLED out from under an elephantine tree with roots like giants' claws. Deep in the density of the jungle, they'd spent a day and a half hunting for a new home. "It's perfect," said Peter.

The boys wriggled through mud and blue beetles the size of apples. The pocket under the tree was unexpectedly ample. Excess dirt, rotten fruit, bones, and decomposing animals were all removed. Whether a wild animal had been living there or not was something the boys decided to ignore. *Finders keepers*, was Peter's new motto.

Next, two wooden beams were installed in case of a cave-in—not that they would've really helped; they were purely ornamental. Hammocks made out of boar skin were tightened between the beams and the hanging roots of the tree. Seven hammock-beds total; the twins would share. Quaint shelves cleverly designed by Tootles served as candleholders; what the boys referred to as 'candles' were in fact knots or coils of oiled tumbleweed that burned slowly, giving off a faint glow. They weren't too bright, but allowed the boys to walk around their new home freely without bumping into a beam or colliding with a wall. They even dug out a cozy nook for Tinker Bell, who'd become their loyal companion, following them wherever they'd go.

As the days flew by, the boys grew closer to Tiger Lily. Although they couldn't understand a word she said, they were fascinated by her survival tactics and instincts. Peter was a charismatic leader, and they would've followed his word until the end. However, he had been spending more time up in the clouds than on the ground with them. He was becoming unreachable. Tiger Lily had an untamed energy that attracted the boys, which made them miss her whenever she wasn't around. It wasn't a motherly quality—far from it. Tiger Lily had no maternal instincts. She was a friend, and a great one, but mostly she was a hunter and a spiritual being with ages of wisdom. True, her body was that of a young girl, but she had lived through more dawns and sundowns than the boys could ever conceive. She was a force of nature to be reckoned with, and they wanted her on their side. Thanks to her, they were no longer eating frogs for dinner every night as she taught them the secret tactics of catching wild boars and setting up snares—weak at first, only working one out of ten times, usually catching a small squirrel or a malnourished rabbit. They learned to watch out for lurking crocodiles and flesh-eating beasts. She taught them how to recognize poisonous plants and poisonous fruits, expanding their palate past their dragon-fruit laden diet. They boiled eggs in hot springs. She brewed them potions that had them flying without the aid of fairy dust. Thanks to her, the resources in the island were ready and available for their taking. Most importantly, she knew what had to be done when Peter had fallen ill. If it hadn't been for her, they might've lost their dear friend and leader that night.

A boar fed on a fresh piece of fruit, grunting eagerly, rubbing its snout into the ground. Hidden behind a hedge, Tiger Lily and James, still as the night, fixed their gaze on their prey. With one eye closed, James pulled on the bow and exhaled ever so gently, taking aim at his target.

He released.

The arrow spliced through the air and into the beast, impairing it. They sprung from the bramble and landed onto the squealing animal, slicing its throat, killing it instantly.

Silence.

On a different occasion, Tiger Lily had shown Tootles and James which plants were best suited to medicate illness and injuries. As they were picking mushrooms off the ground, Peter broke through the treetops, making his presence known.

"Tootles, are you ready for our dragon-fruit run?"

"Can Curly go, Peter? We are learning about the botanical qualities of the island," he replied, unintentionally contradicting Peter; his studious interest overpowered his otherwise regular judgment. Peter wasn't pleased; as this wasn't the first time he'd been turned down.

A few days prior, he'd attempted to go fishing with Curly who was too busy learning how to properly skin a rabbit. Peter did not dislike Tiger Lily. But he disliked not being looked up to. He *wanted* their respect. He could fly. She couldn't. Yet they seemed to be losing regard for his magical ability.

Hovering in silence, Peter's eyes were everywhere. He could see the boys' every move, like a hawk tracking its prey. He could see Tiger Lily and James fishing by the river, splashing around the water, developing a friendship, having fun. He could see how James was slowly changing; moving on from his ever-so-proper Eton uniform to a more liberating combination of wolf-skin and leaves. Peter's thoughts dwelled deep in darkness. His face cringed at the thought of being replaced. What was that feeling overtaking his body? That burning sensation growing inside his gut? A severe jab of jealousy. It reminded him of a similar crippling pain he'd felt once before, back on that night when he found himself blocked out by icy bars, left alone in the cold, replaced—abandoned. Peter tried to understand. Had James abandoned him? Is that why he was flying solo? Had he discarded him just like his own parents had? The spreading

toxin soon became anger—his face boiling red—as he relived their betrayal. He felt completely helpless, a victim to an emotion—and Peter dreaded emotions. After all, he was only a boy.

That night, the boys slept deeply in the shelter under the tree. Their daily lives were populated with numerous tasks, most of which involved intense physical exertion and concentration, rendering them useless come nighttime. Two of the hammocks were empty.

Outside, not too far from the entrance to their hideout, Peter sat by a small fire, poking it, aloof. His gaze lost in the dancing flame.

James appeared between the shrubbery, carrying five orange fish over his shoulder. He sat next to Peter, unloading the catch.

"Are they asleep?"

Peter responded with silence.

Without understanding why, James felt a strange sense of grief. He continued. "Are you hungry?"

"Are you a lost boy, James?" Peter asked abruptly, with no preamble.

"A what, now?"

"You heard me. Are you one of us?"

James knitted his eyebrows softly. "Of course I am..."

"Oh, don't get me wrong. I know you are. It's the boys. They were wondering."

James was confused. "Wondering what?"

"They thought, perhaps, you were becoming one of *them*," said Peter, nailing him with his eyes.

James did not need to ask. He knew exactly what Peter was referring to; Tiger Lily.

"You've been spending an awful lot of time with her," he continued. "Can't see why they wouldn't think that."

"She's helping us, Peter."

"Is she really? How can you trust them?" Leaning in, with secrecy— "They tried to kill us."

"And she saved our lives. She saved yours three times!"

"It's them! I'm speaking for them!" Peter replied hoarsely. "I don't think they are ready to have a girl as part of our group."

James was silent. Not for a lack of interest. He didn't like where this was going. Peter's attitude was coming off as possessive. Too possessive.

"I think you should stop seeing her. We can't trust her."

"This isn't about them, is it?"

"What are you trying to say, James?"

He studied Peter for a moment. A deadpan look in his eyes.

"Spit it out!"

"You're jealous, Peter."

"Bugger off."

"Do you really think I'd trade all of this to become one of them?"

"Would you?" Peter was not showing any signs of backing off.

"This is madness!"

"This is a boys only club, James!" Peter sprung to his feet, standing his ground. "We didn't come this far to get a new mother. We don't *need* a mother."

Having heard enough, James got up and walked away, departing from the warm glow of the fire.

"Where are you going?"

"For a walk," he called from within the darkness.

"Are you going to see her?"

But James had already vanished into the wilderness.

"Are you a lost boy or not?!" Peter screamed, clenching his fists.

Silence.

In a frenzied fit, he kicked the firewood rabidly, releasing a cloud of burning ash into the air.

That night, neither of them was able to sleep. James meandered through the dormant island while Peter soared through the opaque moonless sky.

Both aimless.

Both lost.

XVIII.
FADING MEMORIES

TILLNESS BREATHED INTO THE hideout under the tree. Night was at its deepest, and so were the dreams; weaving like wool, tangling themselves, taking ahold of the boys' young minds. Yet when memories are not enough, imagination has a way of filling in the gaps; ever so often turning dreams into nightmares.

Slightly was the first one to awaken. Disoriented, he looked around, panting heavily. He only saw darkness and lost it, verging on sobs. "Mum?? Mum?????"

No response. Trepidation seized his throat. He started to hyperventilate.

"MOTHERRRRR!!!!!" he screamed at the top of his lungs, startling the other boys.

Peter would've heard Slightly's desperate screams from outside, had he not left shortly after James's departure; his raving mind was not at ease.

"What's going on?" Tootles got up and made way to Slightly's hammock.

"Where am I? Where's my mum??"

"She's not here, scug. We left, remember?" said Curly, lighting up one of their candles.

A sudden awareness took over poor Slightly. He rubbed his eyes and inhaled deeply. When a thought struck him. Hard. He squinted, as if trying to recall something. A fleeting memory ran away from him, disappearing down a dark, dark corridor.

"What's wrong?" Nibs asked, growing uneasy.

"I... I can't remember her," he looked up, his desperate gaze searching, panic-stricken. He strained, shutting his eyes, trying hard... but the memory wouldn't come. "I can't remember what my mum looks like!!!!!"

Fear percolated in the chamber. The boys traveled deep into their thoughts, searching for that memory, making sure it was still safeguarded in that precious palace of the mind. But they found nothing.

"I can't either," said Tootles, trembling at the realization.

"Me neither," Curly was the second one to admit the ill fate.

"Why can't we remember??" the twins shrieked.

"I can't remember anything!" cried Nibs, setting off a full-blown hysteria attack.

"I WANT MY MUUUUUUUM!!!!!!" Slightly broke down, tears pouring out of his eyes.

"Where's Peter? James?" Tootles called out their names, but the two were nowhere to be found. He felt helpless. Cries bounced off the dirt walls like a dissonant orchestra. Tootles didn't know what to do. The boys all cried and cried. For the first time since his arrival, Tootles felt completely and irrevocably lost. And upon removing his spectacles, he quietly wept.

Fitting to their name, the lost boys were truly lost.

For once.

XIX.
THE LIE

FTER WAKING THE NEXT morning, the boys went through their daily routine, yet skinning rabbits and cutting timber had suddenly become banal. Their energy levels were low. Their movements were weak. The previous night had shattered part of their fragile spirits and they were now wearing their mourning in silence.

Keeping to himself, James cooked, withdrawn, lost inside his own mind. No one had said a word all morning.

The treetops rustled above them as Peter descended. He stared at James, who didn't return the acknowledgement.

"Cold winds are coming from the North. We need to gather more animal skin."

One look. That's all it took for him to notice the boys' energy. They all seemed... defeated.

"What is it?" he finally asked.

The boys shared a disheartened glance.

"Well?"

Nothing. He got nothing.

"Suit yourselves, then."

"Peter," Tootles spoke up. "Maybe we don't have to."

He scoffed. "Of course we do! Unless you want to freeze to death!"

"No... I mean—" the words refused to come—"What I meant was..."

"What is it, Tootles?" Peter barked. "Say it."

Slightly pushed from behind him. "We want to go home, Peter."

Peter fell quiet.

James froze.

Neither one had expected this.

When Peter's demeanor changed entirely. Surprisingly uplifted, he smiled, ignoring Slightly's request.

"It won't be *that* bad! As long as we prepare ourselves and get enough animal skin—"

"Peter, we want to go home," Curly interrupted. "We really do."

"Slightly had a nightmare," Nibs said.

"I can't remember my mum, Peter! Her face... it was gone! I could only see a shadow! A frightening shadow, Peter!" Slightly was frantic.

Peter's smile inverted. Fuming, he faced James. "Did you put them up to this?"

"I did not do anything," James replied without turning.

"We really can't remember, Peter. Can you?" Tootles intervened, trying to sway him. "Can you remember her face?"

Peter took a second. His face strained. He focused on extracting the memory... then his face went blank trying to put the many scattered shards of his memory's mirror back together. But he managed to hide it. He took one good look at the frail, scared boys.

"Can you, Peter?" Nibs asked coyly.

A luminous smile reappeared on Peter's face. "Of course I can."

The boys exchanged a look.

"I remember her as if it were yesterday. And I remember all *your* mothers quite clearly. When they all managed to neglect you... punish you... and forget about you."

"Mother would never!!" Slightly shrieked in a fit of rage. His explosion took everyone by surprise. Even Peter took a few steps back. But this only fueled his determination to gain their reverence, making him come back stronger, making him stand his ground.

"What makes you so special, Slightly? Our mothers forgot about all of us. They found a replacement and moved on. Is that what you want to go back to? A stranger in your bed? A barred window?" Peter pushed his face in, inches away from the crying boy. "To a happy family—happy without you? Tell them James, tell them how your mother forgot about you."

Not wanting to be a part of this, James looked up, keeping his distance. "Peter, stop."

"No! I won't stop! They need to know the truth," Peter was seething. "Tell them what you saw."

Suddenly James's heart dropped. Peter's choice of words had unexpectedly shifted the picture inside his head; as if furniture previously neatly arranged, had suddenly found itself misplaced. It made him *see* things differently.

"Truth is... I never really... saw anything..." The wheels inside his head turned a little faster.

"What are you talking about, James?"

"You did. I never went to see it... myself." Like a tiny seed hiding inside his spine, doubt sprouted throughout him, outstretching its invisible roots with unforgiving force, shattering his fragile heart, pulverizing his confidence into ashen dust.

"And I *did* see it. I saw the barred window, James. And I saw how happy your mother and father were without you. They were dancing!" Peter's words were imbued with bile, sticky with poison. "And your mum, she was smiling... and she even said... she even said 'how happy we are now that he's gone!'"

Time.

Suddenly.

Stopped.

The fog pulled away.

A stone sank in James's stomach. Nervous, images began floating inside his head. Gleaming tears welled up in his deep blue eyes, making them look like tiny crystals. Barely managing to fight them back, he took a deep breath.

"She said that, Peter? You heard... my mother... *say* that?" His voice cracked.

"Did I stutter, James? Or are you deaf?"

James's lips quivered. His hands trembled. *This is not possible.* He shook his head in disbelief. *This can't be–!*

"Do you believe me now?" Peter asked the boys, hands firmly resting on his hip.

XX.
THE RETURN TO LONDON

RAWLING BLINDLY THROUGH THE darkness, James made way across the old native woman's tent, towards a lump wrapped in animal skin. Tiger Lily arose from under the covers, knife in hand, ready to attack. James pushed his finger over his lips. *Shh...*

She lowered her weapon. Remaining silent, James pantomimed a flute, blowing into the air. Understanding, Tiger Lily retrieved her instrument and handed it to him, but she didn't let him leave. Grabbing onto his hand, she pulled him back, uncovering Tinker Bell, sleeping inside a small pouch on a bed of petals.

Handing him the pouch, Tiger Lily released his hand and watched him leave.

That same night James soared through the starry night at full speed, leaving Neverland behind. Bloomsbury revealed itself under the undulating white layers. Gas lamps illuminated his way, like a beacon in the ocean mist.

Time had become a shapeless concept, an abstraction. James

didn't know how long he'd been flying. He hadn't been paying attention to his surroundings. He was too caught up in his thoughts, tangled into a knot he furiously attempted to unravel.

Reducing his speed to a gentle levitation, he approached his old bedroom window.

Then he stopped fully.

The window was wide open. No metal bars blocked his way.

The curtains danced with the breeze, invitingly, calling him.

Building up the courage, James approached.

His bedroom was shrouded in darkness. A surreal sensation took over his being, like an unexpected pulse of vitality in his torpid body. The inside of his mind was torn. The welcoming smell of home embraced him—the musky pages of his books, the burning oil—yet he wasn't fully at ease with the familiarity of the room; *his* room. He wasn't part of it anymore. It had belonged to him in another lifetime. The boy who read fairytales and dreaded arithmetic textbooks was long gone. Who had he become?

A frail moan turned his gaze from the shelves to the bed. A body breathed, rising and lowering under the covers.

James gasped and cupped his mouth.

Approaching the bed, he hovered horizontally, lying on the air, particles swirling below him. His mother slept soundly.

She was alive.

Moisture pooled in the frail boy's eyes.

He outstretched his arm, shaking, tempted to touch her hair. But he stopped at the very last second. He couldn't. Something held him back. He yearned for her embrace so terribly, yet he couldn't wake her. He was afraid. She looked so frail. Consumed with sickness. A pitiful bag of bones. Her condition hadn't improved, only worsened; because of him—because he had broken his promise and left her behind. A brittle little promise—broken. He'd said he would never leave her, and he did. *It's my fault. My fault my mother is dying.* Weakened by a ruptured promise, by a broken heart. How could he? What would he tell her? Ask for forgiveness? How could she not resent him? Resent him for abandoning *her;* resent him for

betraying her. How could she forgive him? The idea terrified James, paralyzing his thoughts and flesh. Yes, he could explain, but it would be of no use. He couldn't bring himself up to face her. What he lacked in courage he made up for in fear. How could he stay after all he had done? He couldn't simply go back to normality. Pick up where he had left off. Pretend. No, James thought. He simply couldn't stitch back the pieces. He didn't know how. Unfortunately for James, that ship had sailed.

Holding back tears, James pushed himself away into the somber ceiling, the rage inside him growing, feeding. This was his home, yet it was no longer *his*.

Sensing his presence, his mother woke up, startled, looking around.

But he was no longer there.

Heaving through the sky like a streaking beacon, James released a pained, guttural cry that echoed past buildings, past clouds, past the twinkling stars.

XXI.
BANISHED

HE OVEREXCITED BOYS CALLED out for Peter from deep inside the forest. He was sharpening a thin blade with a rock by the river; this wasn't one of their primitive weapons, but a real dagger with acute edges. Where Peter had found this item was a mystery on its own. Did he steal it from the natives, find it somewhere in the island, or fetch it from one of his few trips outside of Neverland? There was no way of knowing, as he often flew out during those nights when he couldn't sleep–when sleep would not come.

Curly broke from within the jungle wall.

"What is it? Is everyone all right?" Peter asked, rising to his feet.

Curly nodded, resting his hands on his knees, catching his breath.

"He's back...! The bloody bastard, he's back!" he managed to finally spit out, ecstatic.

Peter's face hardened. He sheathed his blade, making a metallic rasping sound. Taking a deep breath, he pushed himself off the ground.

"You were gone for days!" said Slightly, hungry for stories, as the boys gathered around James.

"We thought the natives had finally shrunken your head!" said Tootles, adjusting his spectacles. "The twins went through every scalp on the island to make sure they weren't yours. They found some really neat ones though..." he proudly showcased a handful of them, holding them in a bunch by their wiry hair. "We even gave them names." He pointed at one with its teeth intact. "This is Franklin."

A deep scar adorned Tootles's face; down his left cheek, below his eye. His left spectacle was cracked. James had only to ask once before he received a very nonchalant explanation. The event had occurred several days prior, or so the boys thought. Nibs snuck up to the fire and devoured most of that day's dinner. In a fit of rage, Curly pinned him to the ground, threatening him with a knife. He would've done some severe damage on the rotund boy had Tootles not intervened. As the twins shrieked in panic and Slightly begged him to stop, Tootles pulled Curly from behind, freeing Nibs. This however, had a serious backlash. Propelled by anger, Curly's weapon sliced through Tootles' face. Apparently this was not the only violent altercation in James's absence. The boys were slowly unraveling, losing control, while hiding behind their vacant smiles.

"Was I really gone for that long?" James asked.

"At least two or twelve days."

"Or seven," said Slightly.

"Or twenty!" added the twins.

This made no sense, James thought. He thought time went by faster in London, yet he felt he'd only been gone overnight. But somehow several days had gone by in Neverland. It seemed the island did not abide by any rule regarding time. *Time*, or what one would consider as 'time', moved at different intervals in Neverland. Days could pass relatively slowly or quickly compared to London time. When in Neverland, there was no way of knowing how their previous world was turning.

How do you stop a frozen river...?

With icy determination, Peter glided over the treetops as Curly ran behind him, at ground level, doing his best to keep up.

Upon arrival, Peter descended, stopping at the sight of James. His hands locked firmly on his waist. Curly followed soon after.

"You look different." Whether the others had noticed or not, Peter was the only one who brought it up. James might have not been physically growing, but something inside him had matured, something inside him had hardened.

"I hear you've been telling the boys how you found this island. How you were born a bird on the island in the Serpentine... and how you were raised by fairies... motherless... is that so?"

"We thought you were dead," he replied ignoring his question.

"I went back to London."

Peter's face didn't flinch. He knew this was coming. "Perhaps you should have stayed there."

Clenching his fists, James used every bit of strength to remain composed. Peter knew; James could tell. But his aloof demeanor revealed nothing. No remorse, no grief. And this infuriated James.

"Why?" he finally asked. "Why, Peter? How could you do that to me? To all of us?"

The boys exchanged a puzzled look.

"Go back, James. No one is stopping you."

"Why did you lie?" James's voice cracked.

Tootles stepped up, noticing there was more to James's departure than they were led to believe. "What is he talking about, Peter?"

"Go ahead, tell them."

"It's obvious you don't want to be here anymore, James. You don't belong. I really think you should leave."

"Tell them!" This time his voice didn't waver; every word instilled with crisp firmness.

Peter turned to address the boys. "James went back to London, in search of his mother and father. Because for him..." and then

117

he proceeded with cautious and meticulous wording, "For him, we weren't enough. He abandoned us, just like our mothers abandoned us."

"What?" James's face dropped.

"We stick together! We need each other. This was *our* adventure, James! Ours!! But so far, you've done as you've pleased, always on your own or with the natives. Never with us."

This struck James. "Peter—" an idea came to mind— "how come none of the boys are allowed to fly?"

"Because they don't need to fly, James. I fly for them. Why waste Tinker's magic?"

"Everyone deserves a chance to fly."

"I am done with having you try to ground me!" Peter shrieked, the veins poking out of his neck, his feet pushing away from the dirt.

The boys found themselves trapped in an emotional labyrinth of confusion, aggression, and despair. They didn't know who to believe, or who to side with. They had never seen them argue before, yet they all sensed this was more than a little tiff.

By that point there was no convincing him; Peter had already decided. "James, you are no longer welcome by the lost boys. As of this moment, you are banished from Neverland."

"You can't do that. You have no authority."

"Who's going to stop me?" Peter rose high above him, clutching firmly onto his blade.

The boys looked at James. He felt their helplessness; their doubt, their fear.

Sensing himself cornered, James turned his back at Peter and paused, as if waiting for something to happen. Something to give. Yet nothing did. Taking one step after the other, James disappeared into the jungle.

Once again, he found himself running.

Running far.

Running away.

Except this time, the memories he tried to force away resisted, always returning to haunt him. Forgetting would have been nice, he thought.

But forgetting was not an option.

XXII.
SMEE & THE JOLLY ROGER

AILORS MINGLED WITH LONDON'S late-night low-life, sleepwalking through the gritty docks and the alehouses surrounding them. A wiry man with an eye-patch stumbled out of one of these forsaken establishments with a jug in his hand, stepping off the boardwalk, and right into the ocean—instantly swallowed by the abyss between two old ships.

Breaking through the heavy fog, James descended, landing in an unlit alley, unnoticed. He felt at peace in the shadows. Darkness held him like a friend, when love would not. Chilled, he wrapped his hands around his bare arms; leaves and patches of fur were no match for the biting winter cold. His breath hung in the air like a lonely cloud that had lost its way.

A lute played nearby, the violent plucking rather off tune. Wooden cases overflowing with fish sat outside, unsupervised on the dock. The salty rotting smell smacked James in the face. A shriveled man pulled a wagon carrying two pigs down the boardwalk—grunting and squealing the entire way.

Unseen, James sneaked up to a small storefront with bread

and fruit on display. Hearing the owner's bellowing voice coming from inside the store, he swiftly wrapped his fingers on a loaf of bread and turned, smiling victoriously.

Unfortunately, he had miscalculated. The towering owner spotted him and grabbed him by the arm, wielding a hatchet above his clean-shaven head.

"Slippery fingers, I see!" he snapped. "You know what we do with thieves around here, hmm?!"

James tugged on his arm, but it was of no use. "Let go!"

"We take their *hands*! That's what we do!" he roared, amused at his own joke. "Slippery fingers no more!"

As James mentally prepared himself for a life of *handlessness*, the thought of throwing himself before the hatchet crossed his mind. Living without his hands seemed almost too unbearable. Besides, what would he live for? With nowhere to go, who would take a handless boy? To end it—he thought—seemed like a more fitting choice.

But as the brutal owner raised his hatchet, a voice interrupted his momentum.

"There you are, *me* lad!"

Both James and the bloodthirsty man turned simultaneously. Trotting in their direction was a short, stout Irishman with a baggy linen shirt, a striped vest two sizes too small, knee-high pantaloons, and oval spectacles. Whereas white scruff covered his face, a receding hairline crowned his head.

"I turned around and y'were gone!" he said frantically addressing James. "I came to tell you, yer money—you forgot yer money!" He stretched out his open hand; a glistening silver coin sat in his palm.

Blank faces were all he got from both James and the owner. Trying to make James play along, he pushed the coin into his face.

"The *money*... you left it behind, aye? For the loaf of bread you said you'd be getting, eh?" The Irishman's eyes widened, expecting a reaction.

The owner turned to James. All four eyes laid on him.

Perhaps he'd be keeping his hand after all. "Oh... yes... it seems I did... leave it behind, that is. Sorry?"

The Irishman grabbed James's hand, removing it from the owner's firm grasp, and placed the coin on his boyish palm. Seeing he was getting no reaction, he motioned towards the owner. "Pay this nice man, now."

James did. The owner lowered his hatchet, still rather confounded.

"We'll be going now," he said, grabbing James by the shoulder. "Thank you, thank you!"

The Irishman waited until they were out of audible reach before turning to James. "Boy, y'want to get yerself killed?? This is no place for a young lad like yerself to be getting into trouble."

Silence.

James's gaze was glued to the boardwalk—hands tightly squeezed on the bread—as they walked past a few anchored ships. It was rare to see any vessel action so late at night. Anyone trading during those ungodly hours of twilight was surely up to no good.

"Well, then?"

"I'm looking for work," James finally said. "At sea."

"Work?" the man let out a belly-filled chuckle and patted him on the back. "Go home, lad. Go back to yer mum."

"I don't have a home. Or a mum."

The man faced him with pity, finding himself lost of words. For the first time, he noticed James's clothes—or lack thereof. "You'll catch a cold, y'know."

"I can hunt," James added. "I can cook. I can do anything. I'm a fast learner and a hard worker."

"Aye... sorry, *me* boy. We already have a cook, and we most certainly don't need any hunters on board, now do we? Perhaps try somewhere else?"

"I have nowhere else to go."

The man sized him up and down.

"What's yer name, boy?"

"Jah—"he stopped. After an abrupt pause; "Jas."

"*Jas.?* Is that short for something?"

James shrugged. *James* was a name for children, his father had said... "Jas. Just Jas."

"No given family name, either?"

"No family to be named after."

The man considered briefly, guarded. Yet through his eyes, past his spectacles, James saw the worried blue of boyishness. Then the man took a long, deep breath. He knew he was going to regret this.

"Call me Smee. Can you work a mop?"

James followed Smee past the hull of a ship and aboard the main deck; a sixteen-gun vessel in a dilapidated state. It sure had seen better days, James thought. A fetid smell defiled his nostrils upon arrival. The rotting fish smelled like jasmines when compared with the new odor. He felt like he was walking through a gelatinous wall of putrescence. But he refused to let this get to him. His spirits had risen, opportunity knocking at his door. Had he known what mysterious cargo hid inside the bowels of the Jolly Roger, he would have reconsidered. But he was too desperate to wonder.

The wretched crew eyed him dubiously as they prepared the ship for departure. Prominent scars, missing teeth, eye patches, missing limbs; truly unpleasant folk—the scum of Europe. He couldn't help but notice the uniformed naval sentinels, sporadically spread around the deck, patrolling, always on guard—like gargoyles on a cathedral. There was no pretending for James. His nerves were shattered.

"Welcome to the Jolly Roger!" Smee smiled a crooked grin.

Jolly indeed, James thought.

"That's the quarterdeck and that's the poop deck," said Smee, waving his thick arm around. "You don't go into the Captain's chambers and you *don't* go below *below* deck, unless yer told so. You mop here and here. You're our very own cabin boy. And for the life of me, don't talk to the rest of the crew; they'll chew your arm and spit your bones out! Ha Ha!" Smee guffawed, wrapping his hands around his belly.

James was pale. Paler than usual.

"Messing with you, boy. But really now, do not talk to them. Here's the mop," he said handing it to him with a bucket. "Make sure to enjoy that loaf of bread you got there. It may be the last loaf you see in a while..."

Shortly after, they departed. The dock's light grew fainter in the distance, eventually disappearing through the mist.

As the night deepened, the Jolly Roger tossed and turned out in the violent, open sea. Towering waves kissed the sky and swept across the deck. James's head hung from the side of the ship. His stomach contracted, expulsing all its contents. Vomit spewed out his mouth as he dry heaved.

Below deck, hammocks aligned side by side like bunk beds rocked gently with the swaying ship. The crew snored loudly. As dawn broke through a small round window by James's hammock, he laid wide-awake, unable to sleep, immersed in thought. He carved a line by the window with a nail, counting the days.

Making sure the coast was clear, he opened a small pouch, allowing Tinker Bell out. He fed her small chunks of meat and potatoes. She nibbled vigorously.

"Do you think he'll forget about us, Tink? We never said our good-byes."

But her only response was to stuff her tiny mouth full.

"I wonder Tink... if you died, would he remember you? Would he remember me?"

Unaware of James's gloom, she fluttered her wings merrily, enjoying her meal.

He picked her up gently and placed her on the windowsill. "Go my friend. Go home. Be free. Not all of us should be tied to the ground. Fly away now..."

Understanding, the fairy swirled around him and flew out the window, straight into the tinted sky.

PART TWO.

Anger is an acid that can do more harm to the vessel in which it is stored than to anything on which it is poured.

— MARK TWAIN

XXIII.
HELL ON EARTH

LIES; THE DEVIL'S FAIRY. They were everywhere; swarming over the ocean; infesting the air; crawling into their nostrils; sticking into their eyes. The summer heat drew them in; the crew's sweat—their sweet nectar—was a feast under the flies' eyes, as if the entire crew was dead but didn't know it yet. In a futile attempt to keep the winged nuisance at bay, a wet mop hit the quarterdeck, wiping off the fish and ale slush. The boney fingers handling the mop belonged to no other than James Hope. For the first time after living in what he considered a pause in time, he had aged. Three years had gone by since his encounter with Smee, since he was irrevocably banished from Neverland, since he had uncovered the truth. Three years aboard a ship of brutal nature had translated into the sun-worn features of his face. His hollowed cheeks made him look more distinguished than malnourished—like chiseled marble. His limbs had elongated, his back had broadened. His china-blue eyes were colder than ever; at no time dim, but bright as the sharpest cut diamond. Staying alive among such a crew was a daily struggle, but his physically imposing presence kept them at bay. He kept his mouth shut and his head low. Most thought he was mute, or simply rotten in the head, which earned him the title of 'loner'. But he watched them; he watched every single one of them through the unruly—fairly long and tangled in places—curls of raven hair draping across his face. And with every sunrise and sunset, he'd mop the decks as he did the day before, mechanically, systematically, dead inside.

Unfortunately for him, the Jolly Roger was not Neverland. There was no forgetting. Not a single day went by when James wouldn't think about Peter and the boys, home and his beloved mother. His antipathy grew with every new moon, slow cooking like a roasting pig on a spindle. For James, the Jolly Roger had become his own personal hell; his punishment for leaving his own frail mother behind; for defying his own father.

Lesser than a pirate ship, the vessel housed drifting souls with no place to call home. They were the unwanted. Scallywags. Trash's filth. And the Jolly Roger was where they had been discarded by the hand of fate. A self-sentenced prison cell detached from the rest of society, wandering the seas.

James had once dreamt about the sea; about its adventures and its sea monsters. But no monster was darker than the will of man.

The crack of the whip whistled across the deck. The Cat-o'-Nine. The sound it produced had such a dreadful familiarity. James mopped harder, attempting to drown the sounds in vain. His spirit may have hardened, but he was still unable to tolerate the brutality commonly displayed aboard. For three years he had pretended not to see, but with each passing day, pretending had become a much too difficult burden to bear.

Fighting every inclination to turn, James threw a quick glance over his shoulder, out the corner of his deep blue eyes. An African woman was being savagely punished. Her hands tied to the mast, bleeding at the wrist. Shackled ankles, covered in dry blood. Her torn tunic exposing her ebony chest and disfigured back, mangled flesh and curling blood—it was no longer human.

The partaking crew was drunk off their wits, passing around a cheap brew, which supposedly replaced ale; a luxury they could not afford. They had found ways of mixing liquids no one should ever mix, producing an intoxicating beverage the flavor of cat-piss.

They laughed vacuously, their glassy eyes barely seeing where the whip was aimed at. One of them threw scraps, potato skins, and bones at her feet.

"Whatsamatter?" he stuttered, biting through the boozer, chewing through his missing teeth. "Not hungry 'nymore?"

The whip snapped on her back; the sound ricocheting inside James's ears, his face flinching at every blow. He squeezed his hands onto the wooden handle. He was past the point of not looking. He was now responsible. Looking away would make him into one of *them*. Merciless. Inflicting pain for fun.

The woman collapsed, her knees caving in. Relentless, the drunken beast whipped yet again. The woman's head hung weakly between her knees, her face kissing the ground.

Dropping the mop, James took two firm steps in her direction, but he didn't get too far. A friendly arm crossed his chest, holding him back. The old, withered man shook his head. James understood the helpless cry in his eyes. But he also understood he couldn't stomach such barbaric torture any longer.

"What's the reason for this commotion?"

The toneless voice shattered all the celebratory uproar. Like a terrified dog with its tail curled between its legs, the drunken sailor wielding the whip took a few steps back, lowering his head sanctimoniously. James knew to look down, his gaze locking between his deteriorating boots.

"She's be–eeing puh–puh–punished, my Lord," the drunk's meek voice breaking, stuttering, shaking.

Escorted by two navy sentries—that stood guard by his cabin day and night—was Captain Claudio Diaz, a Minister of Justice with a distinguished military rank both in Britain, Spain and the oceans between them. His black robe with red stripes had become a beacon for sadism and fiendish tyranny aboard the Jolly Roger.

131

The reasons behind his position aboard the ship were a complete mystery, as his task was one of the most despotic in nature; as so was the essence of the Jolly Roger and the course it had set—*The Middle Passage*. Whether the vessel was sneaking right under royal noses or under strong political pulls—as he was a figure of high-ranking authority himself—was hard to discern. The vessel's sole purpose was to propagate human trafficking—Black Gold; slavery—which had been outlawed by Parliament years prior. This was a clandestine operation between a monstrous triangle: Britain, Spain and Sierra Leon. Some became servants. Some were purchased as husbands or wives. Who was actually acquiring these individuals and how were they kept hidden from society, James did not know. For the sake of order, men and women were packed together below deck, separated from the crew, down where the air was foul and putrid; secured by leg irons, forced to crouch or lay down, like bees packed in a hive, side-by-side, shackled in the darkness. Handfuls perished from disease. Dysentery and fever were the most common. James had been down there once. He would never forget the day he discovered the truth of the Jolly Roger.

The truth.

So pestilent.

So silent.

"What is the crime, if I may ask?" The words slipping out of Claudio's mouth were colder than the gems incrusted in his golden rings.

The paltry sailor dared not look up. "Aye... thievery, my Lord. We found her going through the supply room."

Claudio pursed his lips, smacking the inside of his teeth with this tongue. "A thief. Are you a god-fearing man, sailor?" he addressed the drunkard.

Was this a test? "Ah—ah—aye, my Lord," he stuttered.

Extending his skeletal fingers, Claudio demanded the whip. One of his immaculately dressed guards smacked the butt-end of his bayonet against the ragamuffin's stomach, sending him to his knees. Picking up the whip, the officer handed it over to his Captain.

"And what does our god say about forgiveness, sailor?" he asked, wrapping his fingers around the tainted weapon.

"To fff—ffffoorgive your enemy, my Lord," the slob blubbered, holding onto his abdomen in pain.

Claudio took a step forward. The drunk scurried away, fearful.

"Forgiveness is what separates us from these savages," he said, addressing the crew. "We must learn to forgive." His empty eyes landed on the trembling woman. Blood trickled down her lips. She looked up, terror in her eyes. "However," Claudio continued, "he only forgives... those who repent..."

As the whip tore through the air, the woman buried her face between her arms.

One.

Two.

Three.

Three sadistic blows were all it took to break the crippled woman.

James watched in horror, his eyes stinging at such acts of sociopathic abuse.

But Claudio didn't stop.

"Thievery is a disgusting sin."

SLASH! Harder every time.

"Condemned by death."

SLASSSH!!!

"And the fires of hell."

Before the sixth blow, a voice broke through the quarterdeck. "STOP!"

Time seemed to slow down. The crew parted like the Red Sea, all eyes landing on James.

Smee, grayer and rounder, pushed through the anchored crowd, trying to get to the boy; trying to stop him from making a huge mistake.

"*Stop?*" Claudio repeated, his brow furrowing.

"You're killing her," James said, amidst heavy breathing; his lungs were tightening.

"Who is this?" Claudio asked the guard to his right.

"Smee's boy, my Lord. The cabin boy."

"Ah... the *waif.*"

Claudio approached James. Slowly. Every step placed directly in front of the previous one with meticulous care.

"You need to leave life and death matters to the lord, boy."

"You are not the lord," James rebutted.

The crew members gasped in unison. This was an act of severe insubordination. James could not only get whipped for this, he could be severely tortured and even killed. Yet the icy determination in his eyes did not waver.

"I am the lord's hand on this vessel. And the hand of two prosperous kingdoms."

One step closer.

"I am the hand that yields the whip."

Another step.

"My word is law."

Step.

"Perhaps your law is wrong," James refuted.

Claudio's hand firmly swiped across James's pale face.

Burning with contempt, James's eyes landed back on the frigid Captain.

"Insolent puppy. Be as you wish. I'll spare the beast's life, in order to show... my humanity."

At the snap of his fingers, four crew members seized James by the arms.

"But you'll take her place."

Smee heaved in horror. "No! Please!"

Resistance was futile. James was dragged up to the mast and tied with ease. The poor woman collapsed on the floor beside him, her cream tunic stained red with blood. A blade cut through James's shirt, exposing his back. He didn't fight back. Resilient, his gaze locked somewhere in the distant horizon.

Claudio tightened his grip on the fiery whip.

SLASH!

James's face cringed at the sharp sting of the first blow.

SLASSH!!

He bit firmly into the rope. His refusal to show physical signs of pain infuriated Claudio, intensifying his lashes.

SLASSHH!!!!!!

The hurt woman lifted her head partly, fighting through the pain. A deep-rooted fury boiled inside her eyes.

SLASSSSHHH!!!!

Frantic, Smee pushed through the large crowd that had gathered around the mast. "Out of my way!"

It was one thing to flagellate a slave, but to chastise a crew member with such callous brutality was quite a spectacle. The men roared with each strike.

SLASH!!!!!

The sailors held Smee back, stopping him from interrupting their entertainment.

James's eyelids grew heavier, his eyes rolled back; the pain becoming unbearable.

SLASH!!!!!

His knees caved in.

But before Claudio was able to perform his next blow, the African woman leapt off the ground and tackled him with unexpected adrenaline, ramming him against a set of cargo. The Captain's guards toppled her, attempting to restrain her, but she was able to push her way through. Five seafarers had to join before they were able to fully subdue her.

A rugged sailor helped Claudio up as he dabbed his fingers on his forehead. Blood. A small cut. The woman had desecrated his body. And that was *beyond* forgiveness. With his attention now directed at the slave, Smee saw this as an opportunity to cut James off the mast, freeing him.

"It's all fine. Come with me, it's all fine," he whispered as he lifted James's limp body.

BANG!

The ear splitting shrill immobilized Smee momentarily.

Smoke slithered out of Claudio's pistol. The woman collapsed instantly. The single bullet had perforated her forehead. Not one sailor dared to move.

With the slave removed from the equation, Claudio's gray eyes returned to the mast, finding it bare. He didn't have to search long before spotting Smee crouched over James's unconscious body.

"Tsk, tsk," he said, shaking his head in disapproval.

XXIV.
AT DEATH'S GATE

HAT NIGHT JAMES DREAMT of his mother. She healed his wounds and sung impossible lullabies out of her impossible lips. But her gentle touch—the loving warmth exuding from her beating heart—, was short-lived. A *ticking* suddenly itched James's ears; haunting him, stabbing into his consciousness like a jagged knife.

Where am I? James awoke, startled by his father's watch. His raw whip wounds were infested with flies. Caked dry blood, shirt soaked in sweat; all glued to him like a second skin. Turning to his side, he hoped to alleviate the punishing discomfort of his torn back. As his eyes traveled through the dim light, he found himself in a claustrophobic environment where he couldn't fully sit upright. Surrounding him were lumps of flesh, clouded in shadow. Yet they breathed. They were alive. The sound of clanking chains ignited a revelation in James's mind. He'd seen this place before, but he'd never actually stepped inside; below the deck, in the musky underworld—he felt like Jonah in the belly of the whale. Yet unlike Jonah, he wasn't alone. As his pupils adjusted to the muted light, the African-cargo's gaze met his. James saw no contempt in their eyes, only fear and doubt with an underlying understanding. Faces drained of energy. Many had lost their will to live.

The faint cracking of the whip vibrated above deck. With extreme difficulty, James crawled up to the hatch. Past the partially obstructed view, he caught a glimpse of the action above. Claudio wielded the whip. At the other end of the unforgiving weapon: Smee, screaming in agony.

"Stop!" James pushed on the hatch with desperation, but it didn't budge. "Let me out! Let me out!!!" he yelled at the top of his lungs.

To his surprise the hatch opened. The sole of a boot met his face, knocking him off his balance. All of a sudden, the world around him went black and all sounds went mute.

His eyes flickered open. A streak of red tainted his vision. The dim light from before had completely faded. Nightfall? James wondered; or death? He touched his face, as if to confirm that it was still there. It was. It was also heavily bruised, and there was a throbbing pang in his sensitive nose—likely broken.

A distinctive groan caught his attention. He recognized it immediately. Smee's abused body had been discarded inside the pit, next to his. Shackles on his ankles, wrists, and neck. He was out cold.

"Smee? Wake up... wake up..." James pled in the dark.

The old Irishman's lips parted halfway, words of delusion slipping out. "Black sails... flying... through the sky... dark... dark..." His words ceased—unconscious.

In an act of desperation, James rattled the hatch above him. "Help!! He's dying!"

Nothing. Silence was the only response.

Unwilling to give up, James wrapped the chains restraining his wrists between his hands; creating a hoop, he smashed them against the hatch, creating a raucous, echoing rattle. The human cargo stirred, weary and unimpressed. However, James did not quit. He kept clashing his chains against the rattling hatch, banging harder and harder with no reservation.

Finally the hatch lifted. James covered his face, expecting another vicious kick. But there was no kick. This time, he was pulled out onto the quarterdeck.

James was dropped on his knees upon entering the Captain's cabin. In front of him, a desk made of luscious mahogany with intricate carvings held the centric point in the room. Candle wax dripped unceremoniously. The flames flickered in silence.

Claudio's almighty presence sat behind the desk, too far from the candlelight to register as human.

"Murderer!" James spat out.

Indifferent, Claudio signaled his guards with a wave. The two brutes shoved James's face onto the ground and kicked his torso repeatedly. *White coal.* That's what the garbed ruffians called him.

Curling into a fetal position, James covered his head. But the violent kicks tossed him around with ease. He moaned and groaned; a callous sight to witness. Claudio didn't flinch.

With a second wave of his gem-studded hand, Claudio motioned his men to stop. They picked James up like a rag doll and dropped him on Claudio's desk, face down.

Having all the time in the world at his disposal, Claudio rose from his throne-like chair. His own personal *cat-o'-nine* hung from an iron hook at the side of his desk. He slipped his fingers around it as his men took a step back, leaving the limp boy at Claudio's mercy.

In an attempt to finish what he started, he swung the whip above his head and brought it down, unleashing all his fury. New wounds ripped open over the old ones.

A weakened wail slipped out of James's throat. But he was too weak to move.

SLASH!!!

The torture continued.

The brutality exuding from Claudio's actions made the two

guards grow uneasy. They'd had no problem partaking in the earlier displays of ridicule, but this man was slaughtering the boy; something inside of them veered away from thrill, towards disturbance. Their guts turned into a knot. The smell of flesh contaminated their noses. One of them found himself gagging. The other tried to look away, but it was useless. Their senses were being attacked by the carnage. How many blows had Claudio performed? they wondered; Surely more than thirty—forty? They had lost count. Unable to endure any longer, they slipped out of the cabin. Absorbed by his butchery, Claudio remained impervious to their departure.

However, leaving did not make much of a difference. In the dead of the night, James's wails resonated throughout the entire vessel, invading the crew's dreams. They swept through like the tide, over the deck, and down the hatch into the abyss.

Lost in delirium, Smee's eyes cracked opened, recognizing James's voice. The African cargo looked up in dismay. They were somehow affected by his pain. Although the pale boy was not their equal, his pain was the same as theirs. James had defied Claudio, protecting one of their own—one of the slaves. Helpless, their eyes traveled back into the darkness, shrouding themselves into their desolate silence.

Claudio showed no signs of slowing down. His endurance was impressive. As so was James's.

There he was again, facing death, laid across the desk like a sacrificial lamb—raw and spiritless. His departure from Neverland had changed him—crushed him. He didn't have it in him anymore. He only had himself. And lonely darkness, at such. Yes, he was prepared to die. Defeated, his wails grew weaker. Death seemed like the only way out. The only way... until his helpless gaze caught sight of a *new* option. Life was giving him *another* exit.

SLASH!!!

This time, he didn't wail. Silence. His icy eyes remained open. Focused. Determined.

SLASH!!

140

Silence.

Claudio found this strange; annoying, even. James's wails were music to his ears. Without them... the entire charade was pointless. He vehemently sought a reaction.

"Every man has a breaking point," he said with a scoff. "It seems we have found yours."

Admiring James's destroyed flesh, Claudio yielded the punishment tool high. "And now... it's time to break it."

Before Claudio had time to lay down the final blow, James seized the long curved hook hanging directly in front of him and swung the blunt end across the Captain's face.

Losing his balance, Claudio's gray eyes widened as his body doubled forward. Once on his knees, the merciless man looked up, grabbing his injured head. For the first time in his unforgiving life, fear spread over his polluted heart. James stepped out from within the shadows, wielding his lethal claw.

"Please—"

But he was unable to finish. A second blow knocked him onto the cabin's floor. Pushing himself up, Claudio wiped the blood off his mouth. Never had he been desecrated by what he considered to be the most despicable filth, let alone twice in a day. This only fueled the anger raging inside him. Unseen, he slyly wrapped his fingers around a blade on his waist and turned to James with blind fury.

"Bastard!!"

But his blade did not get too far.

The hook jabbed Claudio's skull through his jaw; the sharp tip jutting out from in-between his merciless, bulging eyes. The blade slipped out of his limp hand, clanking on the floor. He gargled momentarily, choking, bloody froth oozing from his mouth. Seconds later, he collapsed. Silent and still, James hesitated, warily examining the fallen brute; limp. Unquestionably dead. The ship had lost its Captain.

All James could hear now was the ocean grazing onto the vessel's hull. A sudden serenity.

Posted by the Captain's door, Claudio's guards exchanged looks; relieved the butchery was now over.

As the crew slept, the Jolly Roger continued its journey into the night.

The world below deck had already assumed and accepted James's death. Smee was one of them. He wept quietly as the slaves endured their pain in silence. Although James was not his own, he'd looked after him for three years, and he had become the closest thing to a son he would ever have. Losing James meant he had no one else to live for. He was on the brink of despair.

Suddenly, two pistol shots disturbed the stillness—one for each guard.

After a deafening pause, the hatch opened; the silhouette of a man framed by night, an elongated hook shone in the moonlight. The stranger dropped into the slave's oubliette, the deep *thud* of his boots reverberating on the wood. No one moved. No one reacted. Smee's teary eyes wavered in fear. Without saying a word, the shadow released Smee from his shackles. Once this was done, he turned, revealing his mutilated back under the moonshine. An incredulous gasp escaped Smee's lips.

With the same meticulous care, James proceeded to release every single one of the slaves. One by one, removing their shackles and restrictions. Confused, they exchanged glances. Doubt crept over them. Hope almost seemed like a forgotten myth, unattainable, if even real. But when they saw the blood on James's hands, the blood staining the iron hook, they knew.

They knew what it meant.

The white devil was gone.

XXV.
AN UNUSUAL MUTINY

EFORE THE CRACK OF dawn, under the glow
of purgatorial light, the African cargo had managed
to seize blades and pistols, securing their position
above the deck. The crew onboard panicked,
arming themselves in a futile attempt to regain
control. The naval guard, on the other hand, maintained their
ground, protecting themselves with their bayonets. Yet they were
all too reluctant to shoot. Ultimately, the slaves were the priced
cargo; killing them would have jeopardized the Jolly Roger's
enterprise. What unfolded was a staring contest of unprecedented
circumstances. The African men and women were too afraid to
throw the first blow, even though they outnumbered Claudio's
men. What would happen if they overtook the ship? Who would
navigate it? If they planned on ever leaving the entrapment of those
waters, they needed the crew. At least *some* of them. Fear paralyzed
them.

The sailor who'd whipped the African woman banged on
the Captain's door relentlessly, begging for him to come out. He
shouted frantically, announcing the savages had escaped from their

restraints. He was terrified and he desperately yearned for a sense of control and order. Yet the one who opened the door wasn't Claudio.

The sailor was greeted with the barrel of a pistol. *Click!*

The bullet pierced into his head, killing him instantly.

The ringing sound from the firing weapon caught the crew by surprise. Guards, sailors, and Africans alike all found themselves giving their devoted attention to the Captain's open door.

Boots clanked across the quarterdeck as James stepped out from the shadows into the crepuscular light. The seafarer's eyes widened at the gruesome sight; leaving a trail of black blood behind him, James dragged Claudio's corpse over the dead sailor and across the deck. With long strides, he pulled the Captain's remains by the hook attached to his perforated skull.

Hundreds of bewildered eyes followed James's every move. His gnarled face. The mutilation on his back. But no one dared to move.

Upon arriving to the mast, he tied a rope around the handle of the claw. Pulling onto the other end of the rope, he hoisted Claudio's body up by the head, like a prized fish on display. His face was mauled, carved up like a pig. Only once he was tied up to the mast—blood going *drip drip drip*—did James turn to face the crew; criminals, navy guards and Africans. He tightened his grip on his pistol in an attempt to calm his nerves; the only object truly stopping them from tossing him overboard—or so James thought. Before him, he saw despair; wandering souls yearning for guidance.

"The Jolly Roger has a new Captain," he bellowed. "If any of you find this problematic, you come to me." An African woman, familiar with the language, translated into Swahili. The other men remained silent. "This ship is no longer part of any navy or merchant enterprise. This vessel is no longer a tool for human trade. And it's no longer your prison. I free all of you!" James pivoted, locking eyes with every single one of them. "Once we reach port you may go as you wish, no one will stop you. But if you stay, you will do so as brothers and sisters. We can survive this together, or we can kill each other. The choice is yours. The Jolly Roger will no longer be your death sentence." Although James wished for peace aboard, he knew this wouldn't be a smooth transition. Men oppressed for years; punished, tortured—they needed blood. Looking around, he spotted the naval officers, cornered near the bowsprit, bayonets ready to attack. "But first,—" his face hardened; he was going to give his crew what they wanted; a *gift* from their new Captain— "slay the soldiers. Slay every man that has ever held a whip. You have been prisoners, slaves all your lives. Today you are free."

The guards' faces turned chalk-white. It only took a couple of seconds before a man—a thick thief who'd been sentenced to a life at sea for trying to feed his family—performed the first attack, digging his curled cutlass sword into a fearsome guard's skull. His action was soon followed by raining gunshots, as rapiers, daggers, and axes, buried into the uniformed men without mercy. Moments later, silence resumed. The violence stopped. Africans and criminals did not harm one another once the navy's presence was erased. Both parties halted, rooted to the spot, expecting the other to make the first move. But neither did.

Admiring what was to become his new crew, James continued. "Lower the sails and resume your posts. Let the winds deliver us. The reign of terror is over."

Tension increased as the days went by. The journey back to Sierra Leon proved to be an arduous one. Unprepared for a rerouting of such magnitude, food and water supplies were running low.

"It's only a matter of time before they slit each other's throats," Smee surmised. He'd become 'first mate' aboard the Jolly Roger, and was the only man James fully trusted.

"They won't." James observed the crew from the poop deck with scrutiny.

"Don't let arrogance blind you, lad. You may be Captain, but yer not *their* captain. Not for them. They answer to no one but themselves. They are all quietly waiting."

"For?"

"For you to fail. You must find a way to guide them, to lead them. By slaying Claudio you made a decision. You must pay the price."

"Perhaps I'm not meant to guide them," James said, faltering.

"If not you, then who?"

"How am I so different? All I ever did was kill a man. Any other criminal could have done the same."

"Yes, yer right, ma' boy. Very much so. But no one else did, now did they?"

Smee could see doubt quietly sneaking up on James. "The night I found you, I knew you'd achieve greatness. Call it intuition, a vision, or simply because you looked like a strange lad covered in vines and animal skin. We've all been waiting for someone to elevate us. I s'ppose what I'm trying to say, lad, is... people come into yer life for a reason. That's what *me* father always used to say. Whether they stay, or whether they go, there's always a reason. What's your reason?"

Weeks had passed when the Jolly Roger pushed through floating sheets of ice and past lingering mountains of pure white. Colossal slabs would loosen and detach, releasing a deafening roar every time they crumbled into the royal blue waters.

Claudio's body had been left on display, hanging from the iron hook on the mast. His skin, dried like leather, decomposed in the wide open. Flies swarmed it, birds picked at his rotting carcass. Larva nested in his eyes. Yet no one dared to touch it. It was a bad omen, and a few of his former crewmen—the superstitious kind—feared they'd be punished if they didn't avenge him.

A heavy bundle was tossed overboard breaking through the water with a splash. Two men carried a second bundle—a corpse—, disposing of it with an equally empty splash. Famine was spreading. So was disease. And the men were dropping like flies. The sailors looked up, their spiteful gaze locking with James's.

A group of Claudio's former men gathered in the main hold, looking around, alert, shrouded by shadows.

"It's been weeks. We are going in circles!" the first one whispered, his voice rough like sandpaper. "He doesn't know where he's taking us. He's a child!"

"Supplies are low. If we are lucky they'll last another week," added another.

"If the savages don't devour it all first."

"We are all gonna die," a third sullen voice spoke up.

"You speak with such certainty," said the raspy voice.

"We are cursed, aye! Cursed!"

"Shut yer yap! Months at sea have made you bloody mad!"

"It's god's word," the sullen voice added. "A man was slayed, and not just any man... without proper burial. His sacred body was displayed! It has begun to smell. It's the smell of the devil. We are cursed, I tell you! And we are being punished. We'll never get home. We'll starve to death before we do, mark my words."

"Aye..." agreed the second one.

"So we sit it out and die? That's yer idea?"

"Unless..." said the sullen voice. "Unless, we bring justice to his death."

"How?" asked the second voice.

"By slaying the one who stained his hands with the innocent's blood."

James's bloodshot eyes studied a handful of maps and scrolls, all spread over the mahogany desk. Bags big as plums hugged his eyes. He hadn't slept in days.

"The men are talking," Smee said, his voice cracking. "The rumor is... is that you're cursed. For slaying the previous Captain. For defying god's right hand and for displaying his body as an ornament on the ship."

"What do the *other* men think?" James asked, drumming his fingers on the desk; eyes on the scrolls.

"It's hard to read them. They are barely surviving. But don't underestimate them, lad. They may be following you blindly, but only because they have no other choice. You can smell the fear."

"And what do they fear, Smee?" his voice dry as ice.

"That we are in fact lost. Wandering around in circles."

A small growl escaped James's throat. "What do you believe, Smee?"

"I—," he hesitated. "I am not sure anymore. You barely sleep'n. You spend all and every night staring up at *thee* empty skies. *Where* are we going?"

The words sunk in James's mind with burdensome weight.

"Back."

"Back, where? Sierra Leon? Back to England?"

"No," James said, landing his azure gaze on the poor Irishman's eyes. "An attempt to go back to Sierra Leon would result in our demise. We don't have enough goods to supply such a journey."

"Then where, young lad??"

"What if I told you of a place—a place of untamed wilderness and vast resources? Water. Food. Land. All of it... ripe for the taking."

"It all sounds wonderful, but how do we reach this place?" asked Smee, flustered.

"Not by sailing."

Smee paused. "Then how?"

"We fly."

James's deep blue eyes widened with excitement. Smee, on the other hand, did not share his Captain's feelings. Concern brewed in his mind. He feared the sleepless nights, the strain, and the pressure had finally driven James decisively mad.

XXVI.
FLYING SAILS

LOOM LINGERED ABOVE THE Jolly Roger. The weather was funereal, with bruised inky skies. Dead winds had left the vessel practically motionless. Leaning against the railing, James observed the gray cluster. He was clenching an object inside his fist; the bone flute Tiger Lily had given him a long time ago. *Time*, he thought, such an ungrateful thing. He inspected it. A newly placed noose made out of string hung off it idly. It looked smaller than it did before. As if somehow with the passing of time, it had shrunk, shriveled into a worthless trinket. But at that moment, it represented the only glimmer of hope he had left. If the flute didn't work, James and everyone aboard the Jolly Roger would inevitably perish.

He blew into it, his breath wavering at first, scared to go beyond the *what if*—afraid it would become a failed reality. But as he allowed himself to be carried away by his last effort to live, the sound grew louder. His frustrations and fears all transcended into the piercing dissonant blow. Claudio's crewmen observed him from the quarterdeck, keeping their distance. They shook their heads. The idea of a second mutiny was gradually becoming less of a passing thought, and more of a possibility. Since James's takeover, living conditions had plummeted in the Jolly Roger. Perhaps not so much for the Africans on board, but certainly for the sailors, who not only had to share the remaining food supplies—which were barely enough for them—but the living space as well. No one dared to go back into the shackled room under the hatch. That place was forever tainted.

A faint breeze played with James's raven hair, but quickly dissipated, taunting the vessel's idle situation. The Captain's eyes remained fixed on the dreary clouds. They endured undisturbed. Defeated, he allowed his gaze to drop, losing itself on the wooden boards. Placing the flute's noose over his head, he returned to his cabin.

The moon bounced off the blueness of his iris. His stare remained fixed on the cabin's ceiling, lost, unable to sleep. He retrieved the golden watch his father had given him and faced it, as if expecting it to provide him with an answer. It had a strange power, anchoring him in his drifting state and shutting out the world around him.

Tic-toc.

Tic-toc.

This way, you'll always know the exact time. The educated with proper jobs always know the exact time, all the time, every time. The only job those boys will have in their future, will be mopping decks on pirate ships...

If he only knew, James thought. With great resignation, he exhaled, allowing his eyelids to unfold. But his attempt for peace was short-lived. A barrel hit the deck causing his eyes to snap back open. The sound vibrated throughout. It was followed by a second sound. It was the men. They were... *shrieking?*

James only had to open his door to witness the ensuing chaos.

"Where is it?" cried one.

"Aye, it was here!!" cried another.

"It's the curse!" shrieked a third.

The men ran around in the dark, frantic, their wide eyes locked on the sky.

James looked up, hoping to find the source of their fear. But all he could see was the moonlight shining through the sails. Had the men lost their wits? Would the Jolly Roger suffer an abrupt end brought on by the hysteria of long days at sea?

Until one shouted louder than the others: "THERE!!"

James's gaze followed the man's pointed finger.

That's when he saw it.

Saw *her*.

A streak of glittering starlight shot across the somber skies; in-between the masts, through the shrouds, and over and under the crow's nest. After a few swirls around the entire vessel, crystalline dust cascaded unto the ship, rapidly covering it in its entirety.

The seafarers' fear intensified, as they hid under barrels and chests, seeking shelter from the *golden snow*. *The rain of death*. Some even jumped below the deck. The level of angst spread like poison. In a matter of seconds, the entire deck was overcrowded with both crewmen and Africans, all pointing at the skies and wailing in terror. This was it, they all thought. This was the end. Judgment Day had arrived.

James's sullen eyes gaped with awe; an old, familiar smile crept up on the corners of his mouth. A sense of hope ignited in his chest, surging through his bones. *Tinker Bell!*

When a moderate tremor made the men's shrieking stop.

Something was moving the vessel.

A roar shuddered the ship entirely.

The ship... began to levitate, rising above the tenebrous waters, ascending from the ocean's rippling surface.

"Sorcery!!! It's the curse!!" several voices screeched.

As the Jolly Roger hovered above the water, a handful of spooked sailors jumped overboard, choosing the vast ocean over the cursed vessel. The rest held on for dear life, fearful they might be swept off into the same fate.

Seafarers and Africans simultaneously surveyed the fleet, their eyes hunting for their Captain. Their frantic search came to an end when they saw James's lonely silhouette standing on the poop deck, looking up at the sky, his arms rising with exaltation. A golden shroud of coruscation descended over him. Then his feet gently separated from the wooden boards. Levitating with the vessel, he addressed the shooting star terrorizing the crew.

"Take us home, Tink. Take us home."

And the men understood. They understood this was somehow James's doing. Whether it was sorcery or some type of illusion, they folded under the boy's magic. And with it, came fear. Respect. And for the first time in months, hope returned to Smee's frail heart; *"we fly"*—James's words thrashing in his mind.

Violent gushes of wind cut across the deck as the Jolly Roger broke through a swirling membrane of clouds. Three to five men were swept from one end to the other, their hands reaching out for anything to hold onto.

Once they broke through the tempestuous layer, the star-encrusted firmament revealed itself, enveloping them with serenity. Criminals and Africans alike came out of hiding, letting go of ropes, masts, and railings. An unexpected feeling of safety overtook them.

The Jolly Roger smoothly sailed through the night sky into the cluster of glimmering stars, en route to one star in particular... the second one to the right.

XXVII.

MEET ME IN THE SKY

HE MAIN SUN SETTLED on the Neverland horizon. Sunset was approaching. Peter skyrocketed through the sky, grazing the treetops below. His arm wrapped around an oval yellow fruit, similar to a watermelon with spots and intricate patterns. His other hand carried half a dozen rabbits over his shoulder. All of this, he did with extreme grace.

Time had gone by unmapped in Neverland. Peter repeated the same route everyday. He knew exactly when to swoop down, he knew exactly how fast to go. But on that particular day, an unexpected event threw his routine off course. A sight he had never seen before. And during his stay in Neverland, he had seen a whole lot.

Parting through the tinted clouds, a flying ship gently descended onto the sparkling ocean.

Peter paled as pure snow as the bulbous fruit slipped out of his hand and hit the ground, splitting into a hundred pieces upon impact.

The mesmerized crew aboard the Jolly Roger wailed with excitement, splashing into the crystal-clear waters and running towards the warm sands of Neverland's beaches. Some collapsed onto their aching backs, resting, taking the moment in. Others climbed up the trees, picking on the ripe fruit, too hungry to recline. The ones that remained on board cut Claudio's body off the mast, tossing his putrefying remains into the ocean. Their slate was to be wiped clean. They were now truly free.

Smee observed this breathtaking paradise before his eyes. He wiped his spectacles clean, forcing himself to really *see*. His eyes moistened with an unexpected surge of happiness. They had all lost nearly every shred of hope and now... they were in heaven. Smee turned to find James, but he was nowhere in sight. Taking advantage of the crew's fascination with the island, he had disembarked and snuck out into the dense jungle.

The island radiated with a magical glow. A glow one couldn't see. A glow James remembered quite well. It was in every flower, in every tree, in every spec of dust that covered the enchanted Eden. His body ached as if a part of him had been missing for years—a void eating him up inside. For once, he felt at home and complete.

After retrieving his father's watch, he looked at the time. He smiled. As expected, the arrows had stopped moving, yet the device ticked away.

He climbed up the uneven slope by the mermaids' lagoon with extreme caution, making sure he remained undetected by either the boys or the finned creatures.

The inside of the cave remained unchanged, just like he remembered it; a display of exotic flowers and forgotten trinkets. His boots ground on the pebbles with every step.

When suddenly, the air was squeezed out of his lungs, knocking him off his feet and pinning him to the ground. A sharp blade kissed his neck. This all felt too familiar, James thought.

Snapping out of it, he released himself from Tiger Lily's grip. *She might not remember me.* Bigger and stronger, he was able to match her tenacity.

She took a few cat-like leaps back, knife in hand, ready to strike.

Extending both arms, James tried to make her stop. But nothing seemed to register in her eyes. That's when he got an idea.

He used sign language to juggle her memory. Her demeanor changed instantly, softening. A trickle of memories flickered inside her mind. Her guard lowered as her face contorted with confusion. Suddenly, her eyes grew wide with shock and understanding. Cupping her mouth, she approached him, sniffing him cautiously, the knife glued to her hand. She pushed his hair back, revealing the entirety of the blueness in his gaze. Her jet black eyes looked into his, past the pain, past the sternness. He had changed. She hadn't.

Her defenses crumbling, she hugged James tightly, burying her face in his chest. This took James by surprise. Never would he have imagined such a display of emotion and affection coming from her— emotions breaking through the firmness of her exterior. He allowed his arms to gently rest on her, hugging her back. They remained locked in an embrace for what seemed an eternity.

Impervious to her surroundings, Tiger Lily did not move. Yet James noticed the sudden change of light coming in from the aperture on the cave's ceiling, casting long shadows across the rocky ground. Something was blocking the skylight above him. In the blink of an eye the shadow was gone, allowing the light back in. They were being watched. *He* was being watched.

Peter.

The roar of a firing cannon echoed in the distance. James aggressively pushed through the heavy foliage, running back to the shore. The sounds of an altercation obvious; growing more violent. A second canon fired. A third. Unsheathing his sword, he pushed past the last wall of greenery. Once he'd firmly stepped on the sand, his every muscle froze.

The cannon ball tore right through a wall of trees into the island. The Jolly Roger was under attack. By children. But these were no ordinary children.

156

Curly leapt onto a burly sailor axing his way into his skull, bashing away repeatedly, giggling with joy. The twins each had a set of ropes with small rocks attached at the ends. With terrifying precision, they swung them around a sailor's neck and feet. Nibs yielded a massive club, and wore a turtle's shell on his back. Although he hadn't decreased in size, he had increased in thickness. He swiveled the mighty weapon with ease, thrashing away anyone who crossed his way, without an iota of hesitation. Slightly wielded a dart shooter, hitting every target with acute precision; it brought the men to their knees, gasping for air. *Poisoned darts?* Tootles slayed the crew mercilessly. He switched from a bow and arrow to a curved blade, slicing through bone like butter.

The carnage developing before James's eyes caught him by surprise. His men fought back, but the ambush had found them unprepared. They scampered through the sand and into the ocean, attempting to board the vessel and retrieve their weapons. Having lived in a land without adults for what had been years, the boys had been desensitized. They had zero empathy for these men. They saw them as strangers; as equally foreign as the beasts they hunted. Slaying intruders had become a child's game, an activity they did for fun, with no understanding of death or consequences. Led by Peter, they had become animals. Dirty. Untamed hair. Unhinged violence. Wild Children.

James knew what he'd find once he looked up. As anticipated, men hung off the ship's shrouds, fighting off a flying boy. Wreaking havoc on the vessel from above; Peter swirled around the main mast, picking up both sailors and Africans like vermin, slashing their throats and disposing them into the ocean. From a satchel hanging off his side, he pulled out a ball made out of dried leaves and branches. He set it on fire mid-flight and dropped it onto the sails. Flames spread onto the fabric and wooden barrels. Men onboard abandoned their weapons in an attempt to subdue the blaze. This only made Peter's hunting easier.

Suddenly reanimated, James rushed towards the turmoil. Finding Nibs to be the closest one, he pulled him back by the shoulder.

"Nibs, it's me! James!"

Nothing registered in the rotund boy's eyes. Instead, Nibs swung his club over his head and at James, who took a leap back, evading the blow.

He doesn't remember...

"Intruders!! Trespassers!! Pirates!!!" Peter howled from above.

With a mighty battle cry, Nibs directed his attacks towards an unarmed African man. With two fast moves, James knocked him off balance, causing him to eat sand.

"PETER!!!" James roared.

Descending from between the clouds, Peter approached James, keeping his distance, hovering around him.

"You don't belong here, old friend," he muttered with a snarky smile.

"Then settle this with me, and leave these innocent men alone, coward!"

Peter's eyes sharpened; his pride insulted. "Coward, you say?! The rotten deserter calls me a *coward*!!" he barked at the boys around him. "The weakling who wanted his mummy dares to call me a coward? Let's see who's the coward. *En garde!!*"

Unsheathing his razor-sharp sword, Peter stood poised in mid-air, ready for the fight.

Seething, James pushed his feet off the sand, levitating, leveling with the boy. This infuriated Peter. James did not get to fly. Only he got to fly.

"Meet me in the sky," James taunted him, rocketing into the firmament, sand and dust clouds trailing behind him. Peter followed briskly.

With a swift move, he lunged at James. The latter evaded the attack, using his own weapon in defense. Metals clashed. Peter moved with incredible agility around and under James. James rotated, evading and counterattacking every blow. Their skills were superb, constantly trying to outmatch one another. With incredible force, Peter plummeted his body into James's chest, cannon balling them into the ocean. They both broke through the blue surface, instantly shooting back out into the clouds.

The sun reflected on their dancing blades—a swordfight shattering the sky.

Smee blocked the flare with his hand. The vaguely distinct silhouettes of two boys whirled in and out of the white puffs, swirling with extreme velocity; both driving their blades forward— an unwavering clash of equally strong, opposing forces.

Flustered, Peter flipped backwards, pushing himself away from the locked attack.

"Come get me, old man!" Peter yelled, before flying towards the forest.

James was about to follow, but he had a better idea; he darted in the opposite direction, towards the mermaids' lagoon. Two can play this game, he thought.

Peter frowned, taking note of James's move. Not wanting to be outsmarted, he doubled down on James's new path. Only, James was not heading to the lagoon. He zipped past it—past the cave with the flowers and the random trinkets—towards a colossal opening hidden around the lower side of the cliff. It housed hundreds of shipwrecks from different time periods, all trapped among the protruding rock like an elephant graveyard—their shredded sails whipping in the howling wind.

Inside, James zigzagged around the bat-infested stalactites. The ocean crashed onto the cliff repeatedly, creating a continuous thundering inside the cave. This was one of the many places the boys had been warned about by Tiger Lily. A cavity so dark and so deep, it housed creatures more vicious than mermaids. Greener. Scalier. Hungrier.

Peter's face boiled red as he dove in, searching for James. "Hiding, are we? You're better than that, James."

He stopped and listened attentively. But all he could hear were the waves crushing the rocks and the tenebrous rippling of the murky waters below him. Rivers so profound, they descended deep down into the heart of the island.

The refracting light from outside cast flickering shadows across the uneven ceiling, dancing erratically like haunting spirits hiding in the dark.

"Fine. You want to play? Let's pl—" but James leapt out from the darkness before he could finish.

Peter's swift parry pushed James's weapon aside, defending himself from the blow. Continuing their sky-high feud, their attacks increased in velocity as they made way deeper into the somber cavern.

"Why are you doing this??" James shouted.

"You broke your promise, James!!"

The furious attacks seemed endless. James sprinted weightlessly from rock to rock as Peter swirled around him.

"What are you talking about?!"

"You grew up!" Peter barked. "You abandoned me and you GREW UP!!"

James paused, if only for a second. He found himself speechless. Out of air. But Peter didn't stop, lunging straight at him.

Reacting, James spun over and nudged him back.

"Why can't you just grow up already?!" screamed James, raking the sweaty dark hair out of his face.

"And be a deserter like you? Never!"

"You kicked me out! Take bloody responsibility! Admit it!"

"Admit what?!"

"You betrayed me! You lied to me!"

"YOU lied to me!"

"You lied to *me* FIRST!" James shrieked, their attacks continuously flowing.

"I was trying to protect you!"

"From what??" asked James, latching onto the rocky wall, meeting Peter at eye level, blocking his every strike.

"From it happening to you! You know they would've done it!! It was only a matter of time!"

Mid-attack, James took a misstep and lost his footing, slipping on a boulder. Loose pieces of rock tumbled down, disappearing into the tenebrous waters. Except for one; one bounced off the surface—off a layer of green scales protruding from the murkiness.

Regaining his balance, James fought back. "You don't know that! How can you be so selfish??"

Shocked, Peter pushed himself back. Another jab at his pride. "I... am... NOT... SELFISH!!!"

He cut through the air like madman in James's direction.

"You're a lying, pompous brat!"

"And you're an old, pompous twat!"

The metal swords clanked and rattled, echoing throughout the cavernous ceiling.

"Is that so? You have terrible form!" James blurted out, aiming to sting. "And since we are being truly *honest* with one another—" pushed to his limit, his words aimed to kill— "at least *my* mother loved me!"

Peter froze and ceased his attacks. James saw this and instantly regretted it, wishing he could take it back. Peter's eyes widened with fear and anger. Until then, all of James's weak attempts to verbally wound him had simply been annoying. But those last words, and what they suggested... they had hit the cardinal nerve. James had prodded the gash open—the one that had never truly healed— exposing it to the stinging light of day, reminding Peter of those nightmarish memories he had again and again tried in vain to bury.

Releasing a primal growl, he charged towards James, weapon in hand. James grabbed Peter's arm and—using his violent momentum—swung him into a rocky wall.

Thwack! Peter's body bounced off it, launching him down to the ground. Unconscious, his limp body rolled toward the edge of a cliff, but James got a grip of the vines on his vest before Peter slid off the edge completely.

"Peter!"

He moaned groggily. Peter's body weight dragged James down, whose hovering ability had already begun to falter. James's attempts to push them off the ground failed. He was unable to fly while holding Peter. The magic was wearing off. As it always had.

Steadily, gravity pulled James down to his knees, gaining

dominance over him, landing him on a jagged overhang. Yet he held onto Peter, who slipped further down the edge, dragging James with him. Still, he refused to let go.

A deep growl rose from the river below them. Seeing past Peter, James spotted two green eyes breaking through the dark water, followed by a thousand deformed scales; the remainder of the creature's body concealed below the surface.

"Peter! Wake up!!" James panicked, trying not to lose his grip on Peter's vest.

The crocodile opened its monstrous jaws with slow precision, wide enough to easily engulf both boys with a single bite. It waited. Waited for gravity to do the rest.

Peter's weight dragged James even lower while the rock under them slowly crumbled. His feet were almost touching the beast's nose as James's upper body hung from the edge. Sliding.

A golden, shiny object slipped out of James's pocket and rolled down the cliff; his father's pocket watch. It drifted through the air ever so gently, descending right into the crocodile's massive, gaping jaws.

Tic-toc.

Tic-toc.

Tic-toc.

The sound now echoing from within its body; counting down the seconds before James would fully skid off the edge...

Tic-toc.

Tic-toc.

Tic-toc.

When Peter's feet entered the creature's jaws.

"PETER!!!!"

The boy's eyes fluttered gently. Consciousness trickled in—and with it the memory of James's last insult before his blackout. As his face contorted with deep pain and stinging anger, he began to quietly sob.

"My mother... did..." It was barely a whisper.

"Peter??"

"...LOVE ME!!!"

In a fit of uncontrolled rage, Peter propelled himself upwards—away from the reptile—, snatching James by the hand and dragging him up. Caught off guard, James accidentally dropped his weapon.

Looking into Peter's eyes, he saw a flicker of unconstrained fury. It moved James, making him regret everything once again; for this torn boy had lost the most precious thing in his life, and he was willing to bring down the entire world in order to safeguard his shattered heart.

"Peter—!"

"She did love me." His voice, distant; coarse; cold.

That was the last thing James remembered.

He felt a burning sensation as Peter's blade cut through his skin; tearing through muscle, carving through bone. A piercing shriek escaped him as his body, released from Peter's grip, fell freely, a slave to gravity. He landed on the bedrock with a dry *thud*.

Relaxing his grip, Peter let go of a fleshy object.

A hand.

James's right hand.

The body part spiraled down, plummeting straight into the crocodile's gaping jaws. The reptile's mandibles closed before submerging back into the dark waters, the ticking fading with it.

Contorting and shrieking in agonizing pain, James held onto the bloody stump with his remaining hand.

Distant drumming echoed among the stalactites. It vibrated through the rocks. Peter looked around; he found himself... afraid? He dug his fingers deep into his tangled hair as he released a distressful scream.

Tiger Lily sat by the mouth of the cave, framed by the red sky—far from Peter, far from James. But she could feel the violence; she could feel the pain. As part of an ancient and long forgotten tradition, she incessantly beat the animal skin of her drums, repeating a chant with great intensity. She was summoning something. Unleashing the darkness in the island's heart.

Tinted by the setting sun's dying rays deep inside the cave, Peter held his head firmly, screaming in anguish. A violent, overwhelming headache caused him to spin on the spot. Multiple bats awoke by the sound of Tiger Lily's drumming, flapping and screeching in alarm—their shadows dancing on the cave's inner surface. They appeared and reappeared, hiding behind stalactites, stretching long and dark, spinning Peter endlessly in the whirlpool of wings. His screaming intensified, as the pain spread throughout his body. He held onto his arms, as if someone was trying to rip off his skin.

Tiger Lily's chants increased in volume; her voice deeper; her drums louder—escalating. Without stopping her incantation, she removed a coiled snake from inside a bag. The serpent hissed, venomously. With one clean slit of a thin knife, Tiger Lily sliced it in half from head to tail. Her voice was as mighty as thunder, rattling the walls of the cave with supernatural strength.

Upon reaching the chant's climax, Peter's scathing cry deafened all sounds. All at once, the spiraling shadows surrounding him disappeared. Everything went quiet. The bats were gone.

Drained of all color, Peter looked sickish, pale. He sunk down onto a rock, resting his throbbing head, straining to keep his eyes open. Struggling to focus through his delirium, he thought he saw his own shadow detach from his body and revel on the rocky ceiling. It flew with child-like bounce, springing off the uneven walls. A few seconds later, it had disappeared, devoured by the island.

"Good-bye, friend... good-bye," exhaled Peter, before his defeated eyes slid shut.

XXVIII.

HOOK

HE SUNS HAD FULLY set. Neverland was covered in dense penumbra. In the subterranean cavern, light spliced through the darkness. Flickering feebly, a gas lamp struggled to fight off the devouring obscurity.

The flimsy boat creaked as Smee rose on both feet, his small eyes searching through his foggy spectacles. A thin sailor rowed quietly, dreading the thick waters which held onto his oar. An icy draft howled past their craft. The sailor shivered. He wanted to get out of there. But Smee would not go back. Not without James.

The two men went deeper and deeper. The air grew heavier, thicker, muskier. The sailor wheezed, finding it hard to breathe.

When, "There!"

The word came like music to the sailor's ears.

Smee pointed to a single foot, hanging off a rock above them.

James.

Somber silence oppressed the crew aboard the Jolly Roger. After Peter's departure, the men had stood their ground against the lost boys. Feeling outnumbered and without guidance, the boys had retreated as fast as they had appeared. The crew had suddenly found itself unified with a common enemy.

"They're back!" cried the seafarer overlooking the island from the crow's nest.

Wasting no time, the men lowered a rope ladder. Placing a foot on the first rung of the ladder, Smee and the thin sailor hoisted James's languid body up, each step a struggle. Unable to push any further, Smee had the crew members pull James up over the railing. Their jaws hung agape once they saw the bloody stump at the end of James's right arm. Not a single word was uttered as both sailors and Africans gathered around the limp body. In an attempt to direct him towards the Captain's cabin, James's unconscious body was elevated and passed around from sailor to sailor; from former slave to former slave, lifted above their heads like a fallen deity.

At first it started as a mere whisper. Only the African men repeated the word. One by one. Two became four. Four became ten. The word rippled through the Jolly Roger, unifying their voices into a single chant that roared into the night.

"Ndowani... Ndowani... Ndowani..."

"What are they saying?" Smee asked, bewildered.

"It's Swahili..." the thin sailor replied.

The chant grew in intensity as James floated atop the human wave.

"It means," the sailor continued, "...Hook."

Smee gasped, overwhelmed by the unexpected admiration. James had become their savior. Freeing them from Claudio's shackles was only part of it. There was nothing for them back in Sierra Leon. Just like there was nothing for the crewmen in London except for chains and imprisonment. Instead, James had delivered them to a land of endless resources. He had given them their true freedom. He had earned their trust. He had earned their loyalty.

As the chant grew into a continuous crescendo thundering deep into the jungle, James's body was lowered upon reaching a clearing by his cabin. Using iron tongs, an African ironsmith

extracted an object from a hot furnace. It glowed red with fiery heat, as if it had been plucked out of hell itself.

"NDOWANI! NDOWANI!!! NDOWANI!!!!!"

The man submerged the burning object into a bucket of water. *Fizzzzzzzzzzzz!!!*

Once the steaming stopped, he removed it, raising it in admiration, allowing the moonlight to refract off its glistening surface. An iron hook. Claudio's murder weapon. The symbol of their freedom. It had been welded onto a metal wrist-stump with careful precision.

"NDOWANI! NDOWANI!!! NDOWANI!!!!!"

The hook was brought to James. An African woman lifted his lifeless arm—his handless arm—, inserting the bloody stump into the bottom end of the reflective object before securing it with a leather sleeve. Sizzling, burning flesh itched their ears like music. James's entire body shuddered, reanimated by the extreme pain. He released an ear-splitting scream that bled into the jungle; birds broke through the treetops and into the skies, flying erratically in fear.

From a cliff, Tiger Lily observed the ship fly off, detaching from the water surface. Breaking through the clouds, the vessel disappeared into the night.

Her eyes wavered.

She wondered how different he'd be the next time she saw him?

If ever.

Yet Tiger Lily hadn't expected him to invade her dreams. His spirit had remained with her. James might have been away from Neverland, but she was able to sense his transformation. His rebirth. She was able to *feel* it.

For endless nights she tossed and turned, her face beading with sweat whenever she would awaken. She saw shadows; numerous vicious shadows—mayhem and savagery—slaughtering entire populations. She could smell the blood. She could taste the hate. Hear their macabre laughter. One image forever branded into her mind; the silhouette of an elongated hook, piercing through flesh and tearing through lives as though they were meaningless. The terror of these visions caused her body to tremble, often waking her up to the sound of her own shrieking voice.

This cycle continued night after night.

Until one night.

She woke up startled, gasping for air. Breathing deeply, she was able to soothe her nerves. The night was quiet. Not a wailing mermaid could be heard. Tiger Lily knew they often retreated deep into the island's core during the winter solstice spell, far into the subterranean caverns. Whether it was to hibernate or to feed, Tiger Lily wasn't sure. Still, she could feel their lacking presence by the empty wind carried at night.

Silence.

Too silent.

Suddenly, Tiger Lily was being choked by a bag around her head; her arms were secured tightly behind her back. She could hear muffled footsteps around her. Before she could scream, she was snagged. In a matter of seconds, silence deafened the island once again.

XXIX.

FORGOTTEN

ARKNESS. THE BAG OVER her head was removed; dread was alleviated by the faint moonlight. As her eyes adjusted to the dim room, she recognized the place: the inside of a ship. She'd explored similar rooms in the wrecks crowding the cliff near the mermaids' lagoon.

The ocean rustled outside.

Her hands and legs were restricted. Firmly. Tied to a chair, she had nowhere to go.

A bearded man with an eye patch stood guard across from her. He grinned slyly, running his purple tongue across the bleeding gums framing his rotting teeth.

She grimaced.

Suddenly, an aroma in the air perked up her nose, startling her. She sniffed. The smell—when her face distorted in horror. She had to sniff no longer. The sticky odor of blood.

"I apologize for the formality, my dear," a raspy voice split through the air like a knife.

The voice didn't belong to the toothless pirate. From within the shaded corner of the cabin stepped out a towering figure, shrouded in darkness. As he approached, the moonlight kissed his steep cheekbones, revealing his sunken icy blue eyes.

How long had it been since she'd laid eyes on him? Ten years? More.

Fear crept into the girl. Although she recognized him, he was not the same. This time around when she searched into his eyes, she only found emptiness—and it terrified her. The curious, young boy she knew, *that* boy was gone.

"You must understand," Captain Jas. Hook—as he was referred to by his men—continued, "I had little to no choice. I am persona non grata in this vicinity, as you're quite aware. You might say I did not want to stir the waters."

Her face tensed up. Although she didn't understand him, his tongue-in-cheek eloquence made her uneasy.

Reaching out, he caressed her chin playfully. "Miss me?"

Proud as she was, she tilted her head backwards, withdrawing herself from his touch, showing her contempt.

The toothless pirate approached, unsheathing a curved dagger. "Should we help her talk, *me* Cap'n? I could pry those rosy lips open," he said, while maneuvering the weapon inches away from Tiger Lily's face. "I can give'er a new one—a new mouth, that is." He chuckled; dry, sandpapery—like a wheezing dog.

Tiger Lily felt as if she'd been smacked in the face when the bearded pirate's stench hit her; his breath smelled of ammonia; his body of sour milk. Tiger Lily recoiled in disgust.

"Not today, Cecco," Hook warned the pirate.

But Cecco was too absorbed with the glimmer of his blade to recognize his Captain's tone.

"Oh, c'me on, Cap'n! I can giv'er a nice, big ol' smile!" insisted Cecco, extending his purple tongue out and guiding it to the girl's cheek.

The moment his revolting tongue grazed Tiger Lily's skin, Hook pinned him to the wall, digging his iron claw into the quavering pirate's mouth.

"I said—" Hook began, stabbing him with his icy gaze— "not

today, Cecco..."

"Mmmeapooloogeezemmmcap'n," the pirate mumbled over the iron claw.

Jas. frowned, playfully. "I beg your pardon, Cecco. I can't seem to understand. There must be something obstructing your tongue."

"MMMEEAPOOLOGIIZEEE!!!!!" the pirate shrieked.

"Oh, dear," Hook shook his head, "it seems your tongue is the problem, my lad."

Cecco's eyes widened the size of cantaloupes. "MMNOO!! MNOO!!!!!"

"I'm reluctant to say, but I believe it needs to be removed."

"MMMMMNOOOOOOOO!!!!!!!"

"Cecco, Cecco, Cecco. Now, please, do listen carefully, as this will happen as follows," said Hook, digging the tip of his claw into the engorged tongue. "You will be keeping your slobbering tongue this evening as you are to go find Smee—listen quite carefully, lad, for you must repeat this word for word—find Smee, and tell him: 'your Captain wants you to dispose the girl on the rock in the mermaids' lagoon'. Did you get that, lad? You must make sure to enunciate when speaking or else I'll make sure to remove your expendable tongue. Understood?"

Cecco nodded. A sudden stain appeared on his trousers, growing in size as his own piss trickled down his leg.

"Splendid. Go."

Cecco ran out the door and whimpered throughout the deck.

Closing the door, Hook observed the smear of blood tainting his iron claw. Then, he turned back to Tiger Lily. "The things I do for you, my dear."

She looked away, unimpressed.

"Snide temper. Fit for a princess," he said with a scoff. "It seems our mutual *friend* has brought himself a posse. Am I in the wrong? Two boys and... a girl?" Hook swished the word around his mouth, tasting it, allowing it to simmer on his palate. "My, my, isn't that—well, how shall I put it?— rather unexpected? I need your help, my wild flower. For old times' sake... I need you to smoke the rats out of hiding."

Tiger Lily looked away, avoiding his haunting gaze.

"Your soulful eyes waver, my dear. Mmm. Time, time, time. What a curious little thing time is. So unfortunate. So unforgiving. Be as it may, the time has finally arrived. For *Jas. Hook* is done running. *Jas. Hook* is done hiding. *Jas. Hook* has finally returned. And he will make this cursed land his home. He will make this his island."

Yet there was more to his return than Hook dared to admit. For the time had also come to face the boy who'd mutilated him. To face the boy who stole his home. To face the boy he'd once considered his friend. Having traversed every ocean on Earth, he eventually understood he couldn't keep away from Neverland forever. Running was futile. There was no place left for him to go. The flying boy clouded his every thought; his every dream. Years of spite and resentment had managed to spread through his every vein, allowing it to age, growing bitter and corrosive. Taking vengeance was the only thing motivating him, keeping him alive; fueling his obscure vitality.

Oars splashed quietly across the fog.

A gas lamp bled through the gloom, guiding the small boat through the mermaids' lagoon. As indicated by their Captain, the creatures were gone. Smee led the way as a massive pirate wearing a wide-brimmed hat—Snarkey was his name—rowed cautiously. Tiger Lily sat motionless in the middle. Her gaze was locked on the sky, eyes wrought with disdain.

"This is the rock, now," said Smee pointing at the large boulder jutting from the thick waters. "Leaver her on it and let her drown. Those are the Cap'n's orders."

Smee shuddered. He wanted to leave. Stepping onto the slippery rock, Snarkey lifted Tiger Lily with ease, sitting her on the lonely boulder. She showed no resistance.

Unseen by the two men, a silhouette appeared amidst the dew, observing them from above; Peter. The trees surrounding the lagoon rustled. He was not alone.

"Let's get out of here," Smee said, panicking at the sounds of darkness.

"Ahoy, there!" a voice cried out in the twilight. It was deep. And raspy. It sounded quite like...

"It's the Cap'n!" Starkey said, sluggishly. "He must be swimming our way." He stared into the billowing mist expecting him.

Unsure, Smee frowned. This was rather *unusual* to say the least. But he played along.

"We're heading back to the ship, now!" he yelled in the direction of the voice, cupping his mouth. "We put the girl on the rock."

"Set her free!" the voice bellowed.

Starkey glanced at Smee, whose tiny eyes suspiciously examined the veil of haze.

"Free, you say?" he asked.

"Or you'll feel the sting of my hook!" the voice continued.

"This does not sound quiet right, now..." Smee muttered to himself.

"Better do what the Cap'n orders," said Starkey.

"Better do so..."

Wrapping his hand around his blade, Smee stared into the wall of gray as Starkey cut Tiger Lily free of her binds. She disappeared almost instantly, slithering between Starkey's legs and into the water.

Hovering a few feet above them, Peter observed the confused pirates; a wide victorious grin plastered across his face. Continuing with his fun, his lips parted, about to resume the mockery, when a deeper, darker voice thundered across the lagoon. And this time it wasn't Peter's.

"Ahoy!!!"

Peter's muscles tensed upon hearing it.

Hiding behind a tree on the shore by the main land, was a lovely young girl. Her wide, honey-glazed eyes observed the scene unwinding before her from afar. Stealthily, she grabbed onto her sleeping gown as she made way through the foliage. Her name was Wendy Darling.

Water splashed in the distance. Both Smee and Starkey turned towards the voice. Someone was swimming in their direction. Starkey raised the gas lamp above his head, trying to get a better view. The shadow approached, swimming through the dark waters.

Curious, Wendy peeked, wondering who the mysterious voice was. Since her arrival, her stay in Neverland had been an ongoing set of surprising events. She didn't really know what to expect from a place like this. When she laid her innocent eyes on it. Illuminated by the gas lamp, the infamous hook latched itself onto the side of the boat, light refracting off the iron. What followed the angular metal was a large body; tall in size, curled raven hair dripping—soaked entirely.

A faint gasp escaped her lips. Cupping her mouth to stop herself from screaming, she hovered upwards, blending with the mist, and watched the scene from above in horror. Hook's reputation extended far beyond the ocean, haunting children's stories and invading their peaceful dreams. He once riddled Wendy's sleep for an entire week, turning dreams into nightmares. Peter had managed to listen in on these tales when he visited Wendy's home, as Mrs. Darling often left the bedroom window open during story time. Peter's antipathy grew with every word that upheaved Hook's adoration through words of fear. He wanted children to be sharing stories about him. Not the pirate. Since the first night he'd heard one of those dark tales, he'd continuously fantasized about bringing the Captain down. It became his biggest obsession.

Hook's gaze of steel scanned the area with minimal movement. "What is it Cap'n?" Starkey asked.

"The boys, they have found a *mother*."

A splash in the lagoon caused Smee to snatch the gas lamp from Starkey's hand. On the water's surface: a large nest made out of twigs and brittle branches floated peacefully in their direction. A red bird sat on it, caring for her eggs.

"T'was just the bird," said Starkey as if to reassure himself.

Hook looked into the dense fog. "What a lesson. The nest must have fallen into the water," he said morosely. "But did the mother abandon her eggs?"

Smee turned to face his Captain, illuminating him with the lamp. He was unusually down. Something was brewing inside him—a memory.

"No," he continued. "She didn't. She didn't." His voice cracked, as if for a moment recalling innocent days.

Smee's eyes widened, finding himself facing the image of the boy he found at the dock that fateful evening in London. But Jas. smoothly pushed the gas lamp away from his face with his hook, letting himself be consumed by the shadowy night. As quick as it had resurfaced, the innocent boy was gone.

The floating nest, however, gave Smee an idea. "My Cap'n, could we not kidnap the boy's mother?"

"Kidnap... it is—" Hook paused. Overtaken by a realization, his eyes snapped open in alert. "Where's the girl?" he growled.

Not until that moment had he noted that Tiger Lily was missing. He'd been too caught up in his own thoughts to notice, wandering the corridors of his mind.

"You ordered us to let her go, Cap'n!"

"What?" he barked back, his temper rapidly rising.

"We heard your voice," Smee explained. "From over there in the water, before you swam..." His words trailed off, as he noticed his Captain's breathing intensify; eyes locked on the ground, rumbling like a boiler about to explode.

Smoldering underneath his stony expression, his words came out extremely controlled, in the way of a hiss. "I gave no such order."

Smee and Starkey exchanged looks. The massive pirate with the wide-brimmed hat was shaking. No amount of terror could do Hook's notoriety justice. His men were loyal and were ready to die for him, no questions asked. In particular those who'd stuck with him from the beginning; since the day Hook was born. The ones who didn't, they met an unfortunate end. Mutiny was not an option he would entertain. As more men joined his crew, the stories of his wickedness spread east and west, leaving no dock unvisited. Pirates from all seven seas feared encountering his sails. And if they were ever so unfortunate to do so, they would meet their end under his perverse claw.

"I knew there was something odd about the voice," Smee added.

"Spirits?" Starkey uttered, as his eyes wandered in the fog.

"No."

"No, my Cap'n?" Smee asked.

"The boy. He is here," Hook growled.

When a youthful *howl* ripped through the murky lagoon like a cry of war.

"Get him!"

Dozens of feet scampered through the water in the darkness as the lost boys appeared from within the mist, leaping onto Smee and Starkey, blades unsheathed, spears sharpened.

The boys knew quite well to stay away from Hook. For Peter had warned every boy who served under him, Hook was his.

Jas. noticed an unfamiliar face amidst the ambush; a boy wearing long white pajamas. His attacks were clumsy, but the frenzy incited his violent energy. He was one of the 'new comers' that had arrived to Neverland with their newfound mother, the Captain surmised. And indeed he was—mighty John Darling, Wendy's younger brother; the middle one. Starkey shoved him back into the water with ease. The twins clawed onto Smee, hanging from each side, biting onto his thick arms. Tootles and Curly delivered blow after blow, beating Starkey to his knees. His wide-brimmed hat toppled off his head.

The boys avoided any counter attacks by jumping in and out of the water. Every charge was a surprise. John Darling reappeared. Yet this time Starkey was ready for him, grabbing him by the neck and strangling him—lifting him high above the ground. The boy thrashed and struggled, slowly turning purple. Panicking, Wendy flew out onto the rock, slamming her tiny fists onto Starkey's massiveness. As easy as swatting a fly, Starkey shoved the girl to the side, causing her to slip and hit her head on the rock. Unconscious and unnoticed in the commotion, she remained there, bathed in the shadows.

Disregarding the scene developing in front of him, Hook's rigid eyes were locked in the gray mist above him, scanning its entirety, squinting hard, attempting to find the flying boy in the twilight. His eyes caught sight of a whirring shadow across the firmament heading towards the top of the jagged rock. Determined, he stepped out of the wooden boat and marched past the boys who avoided him like the plague. Unsupervised, the small boat drifted into the haze as Nibs climbed into it discreetly, disappearing from sight.

Hook climbed onto the steep rock effortlessly but stopped upon reaching a certain point. He couldn't proceed any further on foot. Crouching down onto his hand, hook, and knees, he crawled cautiously forward, up the slimy slab. Once he reached the top, he found himself eye to eye with Peter, who had been waiting on the opposite side. Their faces inches apart. Years of built up rivalry burned in both their eyes. There they were. Back on the rock where he had once saved the boy's life. And now, he was there to take it away.

Hook stood up, making himself taller. "Pan..." The word slipped out of his throat leaving a foul taste in his mouth.

Mischievous in nature, Peter hovered, making himself taller than the Captain; tall enough to look down on his pale complexion. A devilish smile appeared on his face as he swiftly swiped the dagger Hook kept in his belt and prepared to attack. But he paused. Noticing his opponent was on lower ground, Peter outstretched his hand, cockily, and offered to help him up that one last step. "Give me your hand."

Hook's eyes locked on the boy. *Good form*. This maddened him. He did not move.

"Good meeting you, Mr. Haughty Pirate," said Peter without removing his inviting hand.

Meeting? Hook thought, brows knitting.

Peter seemed too uninterested in the ensuing battle on lower ground to even acknowledge it with a glance. This was the only place he wanted to be. He'd pictured it a hundred times. His victory over the Captain. The stories children would share about him. His imagination ran wild.

Hook stared at the boy with the scrutiny of a caged tiger eyeing his captor. His hand began to move—his arm slowly reaching; his fingers wrapping around Peter's boyish hand. As he pulled himself up, he dragged Peter down with calculated precision and buried his iron hook into his chest.

"The name is HOOK!"

It was a violent and rapid attack. The second time the claw pierced Peter's skin, it remained buried inside. Peter's troubled eyes met the Captain's; he thought he'd have the upper hand, but now, he was helpless. Confused. Hurt by this unjustified act of terror. His childish innocence had somehow remained intact. Even after so much bloodshed, his pained eyes moistened.

Jas. removed the hook and raised it above his head, prepared for the final blow—the one that would end it all. The nightmares, the sleepless nights, the ticking invading his brain. The moment he

had been waiting for, yearning for. But he stopped. He couldn't. A thought held him back. Every muscle in the Captain's body strained so tightly, he thought they would snap. Had Peter... forgotten about him?

The hurt boy landed gently on his knees, crouching; laying on his side, he covered his wound.

Taken aback by his own cruelty toward a child, Hook retreated. Crumbling. His menacing arm lowered. He found himself disarmed. Was it possible? he wondered, his icy stare melting at the sight of the fallen boy. Something inside of him had thawed. Had Peter... forgotten? Taking a step forward, he crouched down on one knee. He was going to help him. He was going to get him out of there, take him to safety. But one step was as far as he could go.

Tic-toc.

Tic-toc.

He stopped cold. Alarmed, he stood with apprehension, surveying his environment.

It was here. He remembered the reptilian monster with immaculate precision. Its green eyes hiding below the splashy surface. Its gaping jaws. It'd had a taste, and now it was back for the rest.

Hook took another step forward, towards Peter, still laying on the rock. But once again he found himself glued to the spot. His weary gaze returned to the murky waters. Ripples cut through the lagoon. Beads of sweat crowned his forehead. His face was mangled with anguish and indecision.

Tic-toc.

Tic-toc.

Tic-toc.

The echoing chime intensified. The terror was unbearable. Before he lost his nerve, Hook turned to climb down the uneven rock. As the heels of his boots reached the slippery shore, he noticed both his men and the boys were gone. Splashing—swimming—echoed in the distance. Spooked by the menacing creature?

Terrified, he looked back and forth as the ticking approached.

It was coming from the left side of the lagoon. He was just about to begin climbing back up the rock, but stopped. His boots; water had wrapped around them, ankle-deep. The tide was rising. Climbing the rock would just delay the inevitable. One choice remained. He had to swim—and fast—before the creature got any closer.

Taking one last look at the ledge of the uneven rock where he'd left the wounded boy, Hook dove into the lagoon and swam at full speed, not once looking back.

XXX.
TO DIE

ETER! WENDY! PETER!" THE boys called out toward the lagoon in unison. They had managed to snag the shabby pirates' boat—that Smee and Snarkey had arrived on—and got themselves to shore. However, they did not get a response, just the sound of water rippling over pebbled sand.

Peter laid idle, on the rock inside the lagoon. Eventually, he stirred. Pain. He let out a soft groan. The stench of dry blood stung his nose. Easing his eyes open, he turned to look down, peering over the edge of the rock where he laid. He saw Wendy sprawled on the shore, out cold, water level up to her waist from the rising tide. He knew that wasn't good—he knew that wasn't good at all.

Hook stormed into his cabin, soaked, shaking, slamming the door behind him. Burying his face in his only hand, he rested his elbows on the mahogany desk.

Starkey barged in, intruding. "Cap'n! You're back! There was something in the water, Cap'n, we called out yer name, we had to flee," the pirate explained, gratuitous fear in his voice. "Did you kill'*eem*? Did you kill *thee* boy?"

Hook closed his heavy eyes, a throbbing ache inside. "No..." he muttered, barely audible.

"What was that, Cap'n?"

"NO!!!" With a firm stab, he buried his hook into the desk, creating a long and eviscerating incision. Fearing for his life, Starkey squirmed out of the cabin.

A combination of fury, frustration, and deep-rooted sadness overpowered Hook's senses. He couldn't have, he thought. Had Peter really forgotten?

"Help... help..." Peter called weakly.

But there was no one there to help him or Wendy.

With extreme effort, he slid down the boulder, reached out for Wendy's arm, and pulled her atop the rock, next to him. She released a soft moan as he took her in his arms. Peter's skin was icy cold, having lost significant quantities of blood; a pale and purplish discoloration. Drifting in and out of reality, he battled to keep his weighted eyelids open and his vision focused.

"Wendy, can you hear me?" His voice quavered and cracked. "We are on a rock, Wendy. But the rock is growing smaller and smaller and smaller... soon it will be so small the water will be over it and we'll be swallowed by the ocean." Wendy's brow flinched, but her eyes remained shut. "We must go and find the boys," Peter continued, bordering on delirium. "Do you think you could swim or fly as far as the shore without my help, Wendy?"

Silence.

"I can't help you Wendy. I'm sorry," Peter wept. "We need help. James—" he paused, forcing the word out of his mouth— "*Hook*, that wicked, wicked man... he hurt me. He really hurt me. I'm too weak to fly... and I don't know how to swim. He never taught me. The sky seems so far right now... and the water is so close. It's rising. Don't look, Wendy." He cried, gasping for air between sobs. "Don't look." Peter covered Wendy's sleeping eyes with his hand as he shut his own.

Having covered most of the rock, the water created a circle around them, touching the tips of their feet.

Curling up into a fetal position, Peter shivered. He was scared. He was scared of the deafening silence. He missed the mermaids' melancholic melody.

When a faint smile crept on his lips. "To die... will be an awfully big adventure..."

But the smile disappeared once he realized he didn't know what that meant. *To die...* They were just empty words, empty lies from his empty mind, bringing him no comfort. It made him feel alone.

The rising water hugged both their arms and legs.

When a *squawking* interrupted Peter's drifting. He stirred.

Squawk!!

It grew louder, stubbornly wanting to be heard.

SQUAWK!!!!

Mildly irritated, Peter opened his eyes. He turned, finding the source floating on the water: a large red bird on a large nest. It squawked even louder, flapping its wings against the slimy rock.

Peter observed it with glassy eyes. Relentless, the bird continued flapping its wings. When, as if giving up, it flew off, leaving its unattended nest behind. Peter frowned. This doesn't seem right, he thought. Why would she leave such a perfectly fine, and rather large, nest behind? When something clicked in Peter's head. The nest was just big enough for two people.

Using every bit of energy he had left, Peter carefully placed Wendy and himself onto the nest. But it wasn't empty. Two large eggs had been left behind; there wasn't enough room to spare. Peter grimaced. He found himself torn. He couldn't leave the eggs on the rock. They would eventually sink.

His eyes wandered around the shore looking for an answer. When an object caught his attention; a black object with a wide brim.

To his surprise, the eggs floated smoothly inside Starkey's hat. The red bird soon descended, placing itself on the eggs, like before.

The hat held their weight perfectly.

Hanging off the large nest, Wendy and Peter floated across the lagoon, eventually reaching the shore.

XXXI.
THE TICKING

AMES FLEW THROUGH THE clouds, freely interweaving with them. His body was smaller in size, more agile, his face sunny with juvenescence; he was younger, back when he still had both hands. Spotting a pirate ship hovering midair, he approached it, curious.

The vessel appeared to be abandoned. It was completely unkempt, surely having seen better days.

SLASH!!

The familiar sound caught James by surprise. The Jolly Roger's former Captain, Claudio, whipped an unseen figure savagely—his beady eyes burning with pleasure.

SLASH!!

Approaching the victim tied to the mast, James gasped, horrorstruck. It was him, not a day past thirteen. The Eton uniform torn and stained on the back. His younger self screamed in agony.

SLASH!!

"I'm the lord's hand on this ship. The hand that yields the whip." Claudio's teeth grinded. "My word is law."

Unable to witness the violence against himself, James hid

behind his hands. It was the sound of someone's laughter that caught his attention. A familiar laugh. Looking up, he found Claudio no longer holding the whip. The former Captain had disappeared. Yet someone was still cracking the *cat-o'-nine*. Wielding the wicked tool was James's father.

"Come down off your cloud! Keep your feet firm on the ground!"

SLASH!!

"The educated with proper jobs always know the exact time, all the time, every time. Tic-toc, tic-toc!"

Tic-toc.

When the faint ticking of a real clock made James turn. It came from inside the Captain's cabin. Crawling out from within the shadows, the monstrous crocodile stepped onto the deck, approaching with steady pace.

Tic-toc.

Tic-toc.

"Come down off your cloud!" insisted his father, breaking into cackling laughter. "Feet firm on the ground!"

SLASH!!

James pushed himself up in an attempt to fly off, but it was useless. His limbs were too heavy. He found himself glued to the deck. Utterly grounded. He grabbed onto his legs, but they would not budge. He wanted to run, but he couldn't. There was no escape.

The creature got closer and closer.

"What I say is law!" his father continued.

Letting go of his legs, James looked up, but just like Claudio before, his father had disappeared. However, the whipping hadn't ceased. This time it was none other than Captain Hook, swinging the whip above his head, releasing a thundering laugh.

"I'm the one that yields the whip!" he roared. "Come down off your cloud, boy. Feet firm on the ground!" The cracking increased in violence in the hands of the Captain.

Tic-toc.

Tic-toc.

Tic-toc.

Tic-toc.

The beast picked up speed, stomping across the deck. James's younger self shrieked in pain, witnessing the abuse bestowed by his older self. James tugged at his hair, petrified. He didn't know what to do.

Turning back to the mast, he realized the boy was no longer wearing the Eton uniform. Instead, vines and leaves covered his body. Desperately grabbing hold of the ropes, Peter cried out in pain as Hook brutally whipped him.

"You promised, James! You promised you'd never grow up! You promised you'd never forget!" the young boy cried.

Distracted by Peter's screams, James did not see the crocodile coming. The beast's mighty jaws locked onto his right arm—the ticking growing louder, deeper, making the core of his bones tremble.

TIC-TOC!

TIC-TOC!!!

Hook awoke, violently gasping for air. Beads of sweat adorned his face. He looked around, disoriented and disturbed. He was in his cabin. A weak sigh escaped his lips. A nightmare.

Another nightmare.

XXXII.
THE TRUTH ABOUT MOTHERS

RUMS BOOMED, LIKE A heartbeat in the island's core, as the main sun disappeared in the horizon. A crowd of natives surrounded the altar near the caldera, where the boys almost lost their lives that first day in Neverland. Now lives were being celebrated. At least one of them was.

The same native leader who once almost slit Peter's neck now placed a necklace made out of shells, vines, and gems over the boy's head. Peter smiled proudly. One might find it hard to believe the tale of mind-numbing grief and discomfort he had suffered through just the previous night, had it not been for the jarring scar on his chest—now, a mark of valiance. Yet here he was, smiling, glowing, almost as if the events had never occurred.

Caught up in absorbing the adoration he received from everyone for saving Tiger Lily, Peter failed to notice the girl had broken away from the ceremony, escaping into the forest. All things considered, Peter hadn't truly saved Tiger Lily. Yes, he had tricked the pirates into releasing her, but that was a simple game in Peter's eyes. The boy wasn't particularly fond of her. Had he actually *wanted* to save her—like a true hero—he would have faced the pirates himself, but toying with them seemed the most entertaining choice at the time. Still, he had no problem in being rewarded for his efforts.

Peter howled into the skies. The natives joined him in celebration. A truce had been formed between Peter and these men. It was the first time he had opened up to anyone who did not look like him—who was not a boy or girl. Friends in Neverland were scarce. And with Hook in the picture, he rapidly learned to value their support.

Armed natives kept guard from above, hidden in the treetops, protecting the boys' turf. Below ground, past the large roots protruding from the rich soil, the lost boys—and John Darling, and his brother, Michael Darling; the youngest among them all—had been tucked into a round, rudimentary bed, big enough to fit them all side by side. They wrapped themselves with animal skins, squealing with excitement as Wendy sat at the edge of the bed ready to tell them one of her famous bedtime stories. All except Peter. He remained on his hammock, away from them; proudly wearing a frown, eyes firmly locked on the ceiling. Tinker slept quietly in her nook in the wall.

"Hush!" Wendy finally said, quieting the boys down. "Now... I want you to think of those unhappy parents when all their children flew away."

Moans and groans were the only response she got.

"Think of all the empty beds!" Wendy insisted.

"This story is too sad," Nibs said, crossing his arms.

"Does it have a happy ending?" Slightly asked.

"It's making me overly upset."

"Well," Wendy continued. "If you really knew how great a mother's love is, you would have no fear."

Peter cringed dramatically.

"What's a mother?" the twins blurted out in unison.

"A girl who tells you stories, bloody idiots!"

The boys were familiar with the word as a concept, but not as a reality. For all they knew, they had never met a mother before Wendy, having forgotten all about their own.

"Wendy is our mother!" Tootles educated them.

"No, now..." she began.

"No?" Slightly interrupted, nervous.

"Well, I am, but that's not what I meant," Wendy replied. "A mother is a person... who will never stop loving you... who will never forget you. You see our heroes knew that their mother would always leave their bedroom window open, awaiting for the time the children would return."

Unable to take it anymore, Peter let out a *hmph!*

The boys fell silent.

"Peter, is everything alright?" Wendy asked, sensing his disapproving remark.

"Eh..." he replied with a shrug.

"Well, now Peter. You can't interrupt a story like that and then expect me to be content without an answer."

"Wendy," Peter began, "you are wrong about mothers."

The boys let out a collective gasp.

"Is that so?"

"What does Peter mean, Wendy?" Tootles asked.

"Mother is wrong??" Slightly asked having a minor panic attack.

"Peter, tell us what you bloody mean!"

"You see," Peter confided, "a long... long... *long* time ago, I used to think like you. I thought my mother would always keep the window open. Would never forget me. Unfortunately, that wasn't so."

Wendy's story had taken a sharp, unexpected turn.

"What was it then?" asked Tootles.

"A barred window."

The boys clenched onto their bed covers in horror and disbelief. Wendy lowered her head in disappointment.

"That's what I flew back to. A barred window and a baby's crib inside. My replacement."

Unlike the boys, Peter had clung onto his mother's memory firmly, as one filled with unpleasantness and bitterness. Having been spared the trauma of abandonment, the boys didn't share his experience.

"Weren't you born out of an egg?"

"Shut your yap, Nibs!" Peter barked.

And so he did.

Luckily for Peter, their memories were as frail as eggshells. And most shells had long been shattered while keeping up with Peter's multiple realities and stories.

"Are all mothers like that?" Tootles asked.

"Yes."

"Are you sure??" Slightly insisted.

"That is the truth about mothers."

An oppressive pause overwhelmed the chamber. Michael hugged his teddy bear. Then tugged Wendy's arm.

"Wendy," he said, verging on tears. "I want to go home."

"Yes, please Wendy, let's go home," John added.

She nodded, locking her defiant gaze on Peter. "At once."

The other boys had a fit upon hearing such dreadful news. "No! Don't go! Please stay! Let's keep her prisoner!" were some of the things that were said.

"Silence!" Peter commanded. They immediately did. "Wendy, the natives will lead you out of the island, past its dangers, and into safety. Then Tinker will guide you through the rest of the journey."

"But then," Nibs said, "we'll be motherless..."

"We don't need a mother."

Wendy looked at the boys; their eyes getting lost on their laps, heartbroken. Biting her lower lip, an idea came to mind. She considered.

"No boy should ever be without a mother. I'm sure... if you'd like to, that is, my father and mother would surely adopt you. All of you." This, she said directed at Peter. "If you decided to come with."

Jumping with joy, the boys cheered and howled. They begged and begged at Peter's feet. "Peter can we go???"

"Do as you want," was his bitter response.

Yet they were too excited to notice.

Truth be told, Peter would've never asked them to stay. He refused to work for their adoration and was too proud to beg for anyone's company. Once the boys were gone, he could fly back to London and recruit other boys with little to no effort, forgetting all about his previous 'brothers' just as easily. He couldn't bear to lose. So he chose to forget.

Had the boys known what was imminently about to unfold above ground, their rejoicing would have faded immediately. A myriad of black boots crept through the jungle toward the tree house in uttermost silence. Someone stepped on a branch; *Crack!* A native perked up, alert, clutching his knife. When a wild boar appeared from behind the shrubbery. At ease, the native lowered his guard.

"Don't forget your things, Peter," Wendy said.

"I'm not going."

"Yes, yes you are."

"No. And then what? Grow up?"

"What's so wrong about growing up, Peter? What are you so afraid of?"

"It's a trap!"

"That's not true, Peter. It's only a trap if you forget how to fly."

Dismissing Wendy's remark, Peter turned to the boys, addressing them dramatically. "I hope I was wrong about all your mothers. But be what it may. Good-bye, Wendy! Boys..." Giving a firm nod, Peter bid them farewell.

Unable to find the right words, Wendy forced a faint smile. "Have it your way. But first, you must take your medicine, Peter." She brandished a small green bottle, and prepared it for him.

He pushed it aside. "Not now. Later."

Hurt, Wendy lowered the bottle, placing it on the stool next to the bed. "Promise me, Peter?"

"I promise. A 'Peter Promise'." Facing away from her, he tapped onto the wall above Tinker's nook. "Lead the way, Tink."

As soon as the fairy rose from her nest, the boys teetered in terror at the sudden stampede tremoring above them, shaking their home through dirt and rock; shrieks and metal slashing through flesh—the orchestra of a brutal battle overhead filtered into the underground chamber.

Frightened, John and Michael wrapped their arms around Wendy. The boys seized their weapons in full preparation, awaiting Peter's instructions. He, on the other hand, kept his gaze locked on the rooted ceiling just beneath where the commotion had erupted. Turning to the boys, he pushed his forefinger against his lips. *Shh...*

The chaotic clash of weapons lasted a bit over a minute. Then all was silent. Peter grimaced, waiting for something. A sign.

Silence.

Growing concerned, Peter wrapped his fingers around his blade. That's when the boys heard it: the beating of a single drum. *A sign... for victory!* Peter thought. Relieved, he howled and rejoiced at the native's triumph. His infectious delight rapidly mirrored on the boys and Wendy, who once again felt within safety's embrace.

"You're all safe to go!" And with a smile, Peter walked away, heading back to his hammock at the far end of their quarters.

Wendy observed him go, heartbroken. She understood Peter would never love her. Not the way she loved him. For if he ever did, if he were ever forced to love, to grow up, everything that made him 'Peter' would crumble, and Peter himself would no longer be. He was the axis of his entire world—of the entire island. To leave that behind, to let someone else in, would shatter his existence.

Nibs was the first to climb up the opening under the tree. He hummed happily as he crawled up the dirt tunnel. Suddenly his humming stopped, but nobody took special note of this. Wendy wrapped herself in an ivory cloak, keeping her wandering eyes in Peter's direction, hoping he would have a change of heart.

Tootles was the next to go. Followed by the twins. Then Slightly. Curly. Then John. Once they had all reached the surface, nothing was heard from them. Michael was the last one up the tunnel, having some difficulty climbing onto it. He finally managed with Wendy's help, leaving the two alone.

"Will you remember me?" she asked, fidgeting, self-conscious.

"Of course, I will," he said from his hammock. "Good-bye, Ms. Darling."

"Don't say good-bye, Peter. Good-bye sounds like forever. And forever means forgetting."

Hurt, Wendy climbed up the tunnel, leaving Peter and the tree house behind.

XXXIII.
GOOD-BYE

ERIE, WINDLESS SILENCE ENVELOPED Neverland that night. Not a single sound could be heard on the island; not even a chirp. After crawling up the tunnel, Wendy reached the surface and shoved the makeshift lid—made out of tree bark—out of the way. Releasing a deep sigh, she pushed herself up into a clearing surrounding the tree—wiping the dirt off her cloak and sleeping gown. There was something unusual about the color and texture of the dirt. It was... red. And moist. She took a closer look at the crimson pigment staining both her hands. Blood? Upon lifting her head, she was met with the end of a long, shiny blade not but an inch away from her perky nose. The expression on her face tensed up.

Across from her, the boys and her brothers had all been tied and gagged. Completely restrained.

The wall of pirates facing her parted, making room for their imposing Captain. Staring up in awe, her fearful eyes met the towering man. His shadow cast over her as the moon outlined the brim of his hat.

"Smoke the bees..." his raspy voice said. He lifted her chin up with his gloved finger, then walked past her towards the exposed tunnel. "...get the honey."

With a wave of his hand, the pirates quietly scuffled away, taking the boys and Wendy with them. She was careful to mind her step, mindful of the dismembered native corpses surrounding her.

Once alone, Hook bowed down on one knee and removed his hat in respect for the dead warriors who'd protected the tree dwellers in vain.

"Blood. Blood. Blood. The unnecessary spill."

A light breeze played with his raven hair; an unusual serenity taking over his features. As his piercing eyes caught sight of the tunnel, his icy demeanor seemed to melt. He could feel the silence coming from within. A strange silence. A void.

Removing his coat, he let it fall to the ground. He did not move any further. His gaze remained locked on the swirling darkness that laid before him.

When finally, dabbing at his dampened forehead with a handkerchief, he took a deep breath and allowed himself be devoured by the tunnel.

Unbeknownst to him, Tinker Bell had witnessed everything from the treetops, unseen by any of the men.

Inside the burrow, Hook was forced to crawl on all fours on a downward slope. The walls around him narrowed, until his shoulders were grazing the dirt off of the tunnel's sides—scratching onto the protruding roots.

Upon reaching the end of it, his squinting eyes slowly adjusted to the dim light. The chamber was small. He recalled it being quite larger. Thin roots draped from the ceiling. A melancholic cloud hung over him as he scanned the inside, remembering it very well. Random objects here and there, all feigning order poorly. By the looks of it, the boys had attempted to redecorate in order to create a home fit for a mother. Of course Peter had told Wendy they had built it just for her, in hopes of making her feel special.

James's own hammock remained untouched—covered by a

layer of thick dust and cobwebs. Next to it, Peter's hammock, also empty. Hook's wandering eyes finally arrived at their destination: the round bed at the back of the room. A small boy slumbered on it; Peter, illuminated by a faint light. After Wendy's departure, he'd crawled into bed, wrapping himself in his brothers' scents and memories.

Paralyzed and shrouded in darkness, Hook observed him from across the chamber. Peter's relaxed and rhythmic breathing disarmed him, stirring him profoundly. Hook hadn't expected to encounter Peter asleep, unwary.

Not allowing himself to be shaken, Hook's will for revenge took over; seeping through his veins, hardening him. Crouching with caution, he took one silent step towards the bed.

Then another.

And another.

Three long strides. That's all it took. Standing by the foot of the bed, he raised his iron hook. This was his moment. His victory. Yet above his head is where the claw remained, suspended. Jas. was sweating profusely, nervous for some unforeseen reason.

"Mother," the boy muttered in his sleep. "No, no... please let me back in. I'll be good." His whimpering voice was heartbreaking. He stirred and went quiet again.

Hook's arm relaxed, lowering gently. He couldn't do it. Something inside him had gone soft at the sight of Peter in this state. Defeated by his own capacity for affection, he took one step back. When he noticed something. His eyes lit on the medicine bottle Wendy had left for Peter. Curious, he grabbed it and read the label, jaggedly inked: PETER'S MEDICINE.

Investigating further, he uncapped the bottle, and bringing it up to his nose, he sniffed—the wheels inside his clouded head turning.

Tinker Bell flew into the chamber undetected, hiding upon seeing the Captain.

He retrieved a small vial from inside his pocket. A quiver invaded his one hand. *Poison.* He had learned to always carry it with him. You never knew when you would have to silently off an enemy... Or yourself..., Hook thought.

The vial's dropper hovered, suspended above the open mouth of the medicine bottle. At least this way it will be painless, he reasoned. Yet again, he hesitated. He was but a tiny squeeze away from fulfilling his revenge, but he was frozen in place. His body, his mind; both stopped him from destroying that boy.

Crash! Tinker Bell had been silent up to this point, concealing her presence behind a clay pot on a shelf; a pot which now laid in pieces on the ground. Spooked by the sudden disruption, Hook's fingers tensed up and squeezed the dropper ever so gently, producing a miniscule, yet extremely lethal, drop. On edge, Hook pocketed his vial as Peter stirred from the unexpected racket.

Gently returning the medicine bottle to where he had found it, he turned back to the tunnel. When he reached its mouth, he stopped. He could hear Peter sleeping soundly. Something inside him wanted to turn around, to look one last time. But he kept moving forward. He crawled back up the tunnel and into the night.

Retrieving his hat and cloak, he stepped into the jungle with a profound sense of dejection and unbearable sorrow. Had he been paying more attention to the details of his surroundings, he would have seen his old toy sword—the one he'd brought to Neverland with Peter—stuck on a bed of moss. But his mind was engrossed, soaring through the clouded skies of his memory.

As he made way across the island, back towards his vessel, dawn faintly broke across the horizon, announcing his last day as Captain Jas. Hook.

XXXIV.
REVENGE

INKER DARTED OUT OF her hiding place, flapping her wings frantically against Peter's face. He yawned, waking up groggily, stretching his arms above his head. "Calm down, Tink! What is it?" The dainty being zipped about the room, ringing desperately—fairy dust tracing her erratic, circular patterns. Peter grimaced, eyes still heavy from sleep, unable to understand what the fuss was about. His eyes locked on the medicine bottle. A strange emotion crept up on Peter; sorrow mixed with a tinge of loneliness. He missed Wendy. However, Tinker's ringing hadn't ceased.

"Hold on," he said, brushing Tinker Bell off. "I need to take my medicine first."

As he reached out for the bottle, she flung herself in front of it, smacking Peter's hand and wagging her tiny fingers in his face.

"Hey, now! What's gotten into you??"

She buzzed around hysterically, making exorbitant gestures, signaling him to stop.

"I know you don't like Wendy, but rest assured, she's gone now. It's just you and me, Tink. But I promised her I'd take my medicine... so that's that!"

Snatching the bottle off the stool where Wendy had left it, Peter unscrewed the top and rapidly brought the bottle up to his mouth.

Before a drop could touch his lips, Tinker slammed her body into the container, knocking it out of Peter's hand. Bouncing off the dirt wall with the bottle, Tinker hit the floor hard. The open flask swirled in the air before landing, some of its contents pouring over Tinker's tiny body. The rest fizzled on a basket of dragon-fruits—corroding them instantly—until there was nothing left but mulch.

Frenzied, Peter ran to her and picked up the bottle. He sniffed its contents; his face distorted in disgust. Scooping the fairy with both hands, he noticed her skin was burning; smoke emanating from her wings as she twitched violently, unable to withstand the pain.

"Oh, Tink! Oh, Tink!!"

Peter placed her on the bed with incredible care. What would Wendy do? he thought. Spotting a jar of water, he trickled some of its contents over the agonized fairy, washing off most of the poison and minimizing the burning sensation on her skin. The smoke ceased, causing her entire body to slacken. Consumed by the shock and overwhelming pain, Tinker Bell fell unconscious; her skin faintly glowing, pulsating.

"Tink, who could've done—" But his words instantly trailed off, as the wound on his chest seized his attention with a shooting, sharp pain; aftershocks of that heinous altercation. Wendy would never try to poison him. It made no sense. Suddenly, his face strained with anger. He knew of only one man in Neverland capable of such conniving methods.

"Hook."

Before allowing himself to be consumed by an appetite for revenge, Peter flew the fragile fairy into the cave by the mermaids' lagoon. Placing her inside one of the large flowers, he hoped the vital magic of the island would help her heal. Only when he saw she was safe, did he shoot into the sky, leaving ripples of air behind.

Heavy fog slipped onto the Jolly Roger's deck, like foam on the seashore. Dawn had begun to seep through the mist, inking shades of mauve across the firmament. A faint drizzle enveloped the ship and those aboard it.

The boys were gagged and firmly tied to the mast. As was Wendy. A plank had been placed against the railing, ready for use. The pirates aboard waited eagerly, in silence.

Hook emerged from the shadows of his cabin; thin droplets bounced off the brim of his hat. He approached the mast with slow determination, his boots hitting the deck like an old clock marking time. His body was there, but his mind wandered; lost in the turbid clouds. A sharp *crowing* made his tired heart skip a beat, mesmerized, forcing him back to life. He glanced up with anticipation—hoping for an unexpected guest—only to be disappointed at the sight of a black raven perched on the mast.

Towering over Wendy, Hook removed her gag. "Any last words... from a *mother* to her *children?*"

Hook's sorrowful expression seized her big eyes by surprise. In them, Wendy found something she didn't quite expect. Unlike Tiger Lily, her demeanor stood far from pride. She actually felt sorry for the woeful Captain.

"So much... sadness in your eyes," she finally said, overcoming fear.

This stunned Hook. The girl pitied him. His crew was far from ear's reach, so he was free to say as he pleased.

"Did your mother forget about you like Peter's?" she pressed on.

The Captain's metallic scrutiny shattered, exposed, melting in the drizzle.

"Yet you're different from Peter." She studied him carefully. "I'm sure she loved you dearly." This caused Hook to look up. "Our mother..." Wendy continued, "she's surely worried sick. Please don't take us away from her."

"Perhaps you shouldn't have run away," he said, grunting. "Perhaps you shouldn't have abandoned her."

"We didn't. We yearned for an adventure. It's true. But we had always planned on returning. We would never leave our parents. Peter told us about his mother..." she added, looking down. This caught Hook by surprise– "...and now, we are scared. What if he's right? What if she forgets us too? Then we won't have a mother anymore. We all want to go home. Even the lost boys."

Even the boys?

"And deep down, I know even Peter does," she added, crestfallen.

Her words sunk deep into Hook's murky heart. The girl had hope, he thought. He had forgotten what it felt like–hoping; it had become distant, a distorted mirage in the thin ocean air.

"That boy is lost, forever."

"Not all who wander are lost, Captain," the girl added, adamantly. "At least not forever..."

Wendy's honest words stung Hook's raw nerve, exposing the vulnerability buried under his coarse armor. The girl had a wisdom beyond her years that reminded him of his young self; a boy who was often found buried under heaps of scholarly texts until the early hours of morning.

He studied her face. Her fear was palpable. But she wasn't scared of him. She was not scared of dying. She was scared of losing something more valuable; more treasured–her mother's love. She was scared of becoming Peter. Hook couldn't do it. He couldn't do to them what Peter did to him.

Weakened, Hook turned and stared out at the vast Neverland Ocean. What had he become? He'd cloaked himself with the same darkness that had hurt him: fear. With an anguished heart, he looked down. "Let them go."

Wendy's face lit up; the possibility of returning home finally seemed a reality.

The crew on the other hand, expressed their confusion. "But Cap'n," one questioned.

"I said... let... them... go." Hook's words were dry and firm.

Reluctant, two pirates approached the mast. Wielding a knife, one cut through the first set of ropes binding the boys onto the ship.

Hook's eyes were lost in the clouds, cutting through the gentle rain, looking aimlessly; perhaps looking for *him*.

Making progress fast, the pirate was about to cut through the third and last rope, when the familiar sound of death impaled Hook's senses.

"Wait," Hook ordered, lifting a finger.

The pirate pocketed his knife cautiously.

It was faint at first, but it slowly grew louder, too obvious to ignore.

Tic-toc...

Tic-toc...

Tic-toc...

Hook's lip trembled. The ticking grew louder. Closer.

"It's here..." his voice quavered. "It's HERE."

Frantic, Hook spun on the spot, backing away from the mast, towards the cabin. His gaze bounced off the sides of the vessel, searching for the source, staying as far as possible from the water.

The crew looked around in confusion, their ears perked, unable to locate the sound's point of origin. The ticking seemed to be coming from all around them.

"Where is it?!" Hook roared.

As tension took over the Jolly Roger, pirates unsheathed their swords, pacing around the deck, alert, attempting to locate the sound, intending to kill the beast. They all knew it would glorify them in their Captain's eyes; he would cover them in riches, they thought, if they could rid him of the beast's torment.

Michael, being the closest one to the plank, allowed his curiosity to take over as he peered over the side of the ship. To his surprise, he found no intimidating creature wandering the blue waters. Instead, he found Peter, latched onto the ship's railing, *ticking*, unseen.

Peter pressed his forefinger onto his lips: *Shh...*

Michael confirmed with a nod and nudged John, who stood next to him. A small squeal escaped John, which got the attention of the boys and Wendy. Yet they rapidly looked away, so as to avoid alerting the pirates.

The crew were too distracted by the crocodile frenzy to detect Peter, who swiftly picked up two of the men and tossed them overboard.

Upon hearing the splash, Smee peered over the railing, finding nothing but rippling, bubbling water below. Strange, he thought. However, he noted something else.

"Wait... Cap'n!" he yelled out, holding his hands up, quieting the men down. He paused briefly, listening carefully. "It stopped. It's gone. It's gone, now. Listen!"

Hook did as instructed. Smee was right. The ticking had stopped. It had been replaced by faint giggling; smirking boys tied to the mast. Boiling red, Hook locked his frigid eyes on them, and pushed his way through the pirates. The boys silenced with fear. Whatever vulnerable side Wendy had been able to tap, it was long gone.

"It's time for little boys to walk the plank, don't you agree?" Hook said with a twisted grin.

Craving the amusement, his men stomped on the deck and hollered, prepping the plank without further instruction.

Refusing to give in, Curly barked at Hook like a rabid dog. The Captain delivered a solid slap across the boy's face and immediately wished he hadn't. Not once had he injured one of the lost boys; nor had he thought he ever would. The unexpected strike hurt Hook more than it did Curly. But he managed to conceal the pain extraordinarily well.

The other boys grew clammy and pale as cod. Their wandering eyes had lost sight of Peter. John was the only one who spotted him flying into the Captain's cabin through the window.

A pirate with a goatee and an earring released Michael from the mast and pushed him towards the plank. The young boy's hands and feet remained tied as he hopped, trying to keep his balance. Looking back, he met Wendy's eyes, hoping to find some comfort in them. But she was as fearful as he was.

"Please, don't do this," she begged Hook.

But he re-gagged her, shutting her up—shutting the child

inside him up.

The pirate nudged Michael onto the unstable piece of wood protruding from the ship. The small boy refused to take one step further. In response, the pirate drew his sword and used the sharp point to poke his back. Michael skipped forward in terror. He shrieked, calling out Wendy's name.

When a raucous *crowing* interrupted Michael's plank walk.

The men grew silent as Hook's frown created a deep crease that cut through his forehead.

CRAWH!!

It happened again. However, the second time it was easier to detect. It was coming from inside his cabin.

A small smile appeared on the Captain's lips. *A game...*

"Jukes," Hook called forth a muscular pirate with a shaved head.

"Yes, Captain?"

"Be a lad and fetch my *cat-o'-nine*, would you now?" Hook motioned the pirate towards his cabin.

"Yes... Captain..." he said, swallowing a lump of something dry.

Taking one meticulous step after the other, he wrapped his large fingers around his blade and made way across the deck. The Captain's cabin suddenly seemed to be further than usual. Sweat trickled down his neck.

Upon reaching it, Jukes turned the knob gently and pushed the door open with a trembling hand. It creaked, revealing the dark room behind it. A sliver of morning gloom filtered through Hook's thick curtains. Jukes wasn't quite able to see; silhouettes and abstract shapes, but nothing that felt solid or real. The old wood squeaked under his boots.

Squeak...

Squeak...

Squeak...

CRAWH!!

The slicing of a sword followed by a guttural rumble reverberated in the dark cabin. What followed was pure uninterrupted silence.

The men stepped back in fear. Hook could hear them whispering. *The curse... The devil... Spirits...* His original crew still held onto Claudio's curse, even after all those years.

One even dared to accuse the Captain while pointing his finger, stating it was he who was cursed. This was a wide man with a broad back, the face of a bulldog, and arms covered with intricate tattoos.

A nervous twitch affected Hook's left eyelid. He did not enjoy being questioned. Although patience was a virtue he often flaunted proudly, the daring pirate had chosen an infelicitous moment to test Hook's endurance. And for the Captain, timing was everything.

Like magma churning underneath the deepest pits of a quiet volcano, under the right amount of pressure, he was bound to erupt.

He approached the pirate, inching his face into the coarse bearded scum. "Matters of opinion will always be respected on my ship," Hook said, addressing his crew. "After all, you are all free men." Turning back to the pirate, he laid his icy eyes on him. "If you believe your Captain has cursed this vessel, then please, by all means slay him. However, my treacherous leeching worm, it pains me to inform you, slaying your Captain is not the pressing issue. The pressing issue, you see, concerns your draw. And whether it is quicker than your questioning thought."

At once, the thick pirate wrapped his fingers around his sword—feeling threatened, ready to draw.

"However," Hook continued, placing a gentle hand on the man's scarred shoulder, pushing his imposing body against the cur's burly chest, "it's all a matter of opinion. In fact, general opinion states long blades are not fit for short-range combat. My draw, however..."

The man glanced down: Hook's iron claw was biting into his crotch. The man froze, facing the Captain's gleaming blue eyes.

"Do you have any idea how many veins adjoin in such a particular region? My estimate is you will bleed to death in less than an hour, given the sudden quantity of sanguine fluid you'll be losing—and in a rather festive manner, some would say. But that's just my humble opinion," he taunted. "Then again, what do I know? I guess we'll just have to wait and see."

The wide man did not have time to think before he was viciously rendered immobile; wrapping his hands around his thigh, red blood sprayed from between his fingers like a geyser.

"Look at that! The Jolly Roger has its own fountain!" Hook said festively.

A few seconds later, the man stopped moving entirely; shriveled face, mouth agape—it was a ghoulish sight.

"Hmm..." Hook puffed, disappointed. "That was short-lived." Turning back to his crew: "Anyone else?"

Silence. The crew exchanged glances. The boys were petrified. "Marvelous. Let's proceed."

Nonchalantly, he stepped over the red puddle and sent Starkey in next.

The bulky pirate took a deep breath and marched towards the Captain's cabin. When he reached the door, he stopped. The dark void terrified him. With tremors shooting up and down his back, he stepped inside, devoured by the darkness.

Not even two seconds later, he appeared through the doorframe out of breath. "Bill Jukes is dead!"

The men gasped. But before any further details could be explained, Starkey was dragged back into the cabin by an unseen force. Deep slashes silenced his violent shrieks in the shadows.

Alarmed, the pirates held onto their weapons, terrified of the paranormal. But Hook's scrutinizing eyes remained locked on the dark cabin.

"SILENCE!" he growled. "Let them... go in," he said pointing at the boys.

Picking Michael by the neck, the pirate with the goatee dropped him back on deck—much to Michael's relief. Another pirate released the boys, guiding their restrained bodies towards the cabin, leaving Wendy behind. The boys were pushed into the darkness. After a brief moment of silence, shrieks and screams echoed inside the cabin. The men were now fully convinced they were dealing with a supernatural force. Hook, on the other hand, could smell the stench of a rat.

Unseen amidst the commotion, Peter flew out of the cabin's window and landed onboard. Sneaking behind Wendy, he released her, and cut her binding ropes. Undetected, he removed Wendy's cloak and wrapped himself with it, raising the hood—hiding his own identity. She took cover behind a barrel while Peter took her spot by the mast. All this was done in a matter of seconds and with precise movements.

"It's the girl!!" a shriveled pirate shrieked among the boisterous crowd. "She's the one cursing our ship! Her female presence is unlocking spirits!!"

All eyes landed on Wendy—or where Wendy used to be—, as they got lost in a unifying *Aye! Aye!*

"Throw her overboard!!" boasted another pirate.

The men cheered and howled as they approached the cloaked figure by the mast, their sense of self-worth and control somehow strengthening.

An elongated pirate with a curled stache and a vest packed with knives placed his hand on the cloaked head, while drawing out his favorite toy: An Egyptian *Khopesh*. A curved blade commonly used to behead captured enemies after a battle. It was the most feared sword in the ancient world.

"No one can save you now, missy..." he whistled through his missing teeth.

"Actually, there's one who can," a mousy voice coming from beneath the cloak responded.

Surprised, the pirate removed the cloak revealing Peter. The boy shot up into the sky, dragging the pirate with him, slicing his neck, and disposing him into the ocean.

Hook's grin widened into a full smile. *He's alive.*

Seeing past the deceit, the pirates roared with anger, their eyes frantically searching for the flying boy as they waved their weapons, attacking the air.

At that precise moment, the lost boys barged out of the

Captain's cabin, armed from head to toe, slashing and stabbing their way through the pirates—stampeding across the bloody deck. The men collectively screamed in pain. Some scrambled and tripped when attempting to snatch the agile boys. The surprise element of the attack, however, wore off rapidly. The pirates soon regained dominance over them; after all, they were only boys. One grabbed Slightly by the neck and swung his blade in the air, ready to slice him in half. But an arrow buried into the pirate's back, releasing the boy from his grip.

The arrow hadn't come from within the ship. It had traveled through the sky and across the ocean. A second one reached its target. Then a third. A startled pirate turned, finding himself facing a downpour of arrows ripping through the sky. One. Two. Three. Four arrows pierced his body before he collapsed on the deck.

Two dozen natives covered a cliff nearby, constantly reloading their bows. Pirates were dropping like flies. It was a massacre.

The pirate crew launched thundering cannon balls in the natives' direction. A handful of them were injured, while others scampered and rapidly took new positions.

The lost boys' truce with the natives had paid off. Hook hadn't expected this, let alone their sudden ambush and willingness to battle. His smile disappeared as he cut through the bloodbath, ducking past arrows and flying knives, heading with steadfast determination towards his only objective: *Pan*. With every increasing step, Peter slayed yet another pirate with savage grace.

A mutilated sailor collapsed by the Captain's boots. Peter glided towards him smoothly.

Life seemed to suddenly come to a halt.

All sounds muted as Peter and Hook faced each other in fixated silence. The brutal confrontation around them receded, leaving them in an environment devoid of space and time.

Hook's jaw tensed. A playful smirk took over Peter's face.

"So, *Pan*... here we are."

"Indeed, *Hook*... here we are."

"Proud and insolent boy."

"Dark and sinister man."

No words were further spoken. They dove into each other with weapons in hand. Peter's speed and form were superb, but his shorter limbs stopped him from fully performing a solid lunge. Hook's maneuvers were slower, but his attacks were stronger, knocking Peter back with every jab. Wielding his intricate Scottish broadsword with his left hand, every attack met an equally effective counterstrike.

Attempting to score a deadly blow, Hook swung his iron claw, aiming for Peter's scarred chest. Seizing the opportunity, the boy evaded the attack and stabbed the Captain on the back. A small prick.

Bewildered, Hook's sword slipped out of his hand, hitting the deck with a dull *clank*. He instinctively cupped the wound. Crimson blood trickling between his fingers.

Displaying an unexpected act of good form, Peter took a step back, waiting for Hook to retrieve his weapon. But the Captain didn't. The fire burning inside him had irrevocably evaporated, replaced by sudden morose exhaustion.

What was the point, he wondered, if he couldn't get himself to kill the boy?

"What is—" the words escaped his mouth— "this *Pan*? *Who* is this... Pan?" he asked, testing him.

"A boy, forever!" Peter bellowed. "Born out of an egg. I'm part bird, you know? That's how I can fly. Everybody knows that!" His every word a spectacle. Dishing out stories to an invisible audience. The spotlight on no one but himself. "A life in the clouds, never on the ground." A colorful attempt to mask the painful truth.

"Never on the ground..." Hook repeated. "Does this... *Pan* remember fairies at Kensington Gardens, another lifetime ago?"

Peter's cocky smirk did not waver. But a sudden blankness took over the gleam in his eyes; as if his face had transformed into a mask right before Hook's eyes—a mask devoid of any expression or thought. A spark of forgotten hope rekindled in Hook's benumbed features. Had he remembered? he wondered. Had he *truly* remembered? Hook had no way to be certain if all that remained of Peter's memory was an unrestrained antipathy for him. True to the island's nature, Peter could've forgotten all about young James Hope, and only safeguarded memories of the older man who once hurt him and left him behind. A nemesis for the sake of confrontation. An abstraction devoid of any true meaning. Or does he believe his own lies? Hook pondered.

Finally, the boy's lips parted. "I know not of such fairy gardens you speak of, Hook!"

Startled, Jas. took a step back, as if a fist had been jabbed into his chest; a pang spreading throughout his body. When an extremely faint whisper escaped his lips. "You promised you'd never forget."

"Promises, promises!" Peter rebutted. "We all make them, we all break them. Now, retrieve your weapon!"

At that moment, the last shred of light died inside of Captain Hook. But James Hope refused to let go, clouding the Captain's mind with doubt, infusing his thoughts with questions. Was Peter pretending? Lying? He knew the boy was proud. He knew this pride would take him to blinding extremes, all in the name of keeping up appearances—a coward's tale, forever on the run. Was he too proud to admit he'd erred?

A boy who'd spent most of his life in the sky.

Avoiding the reality that had deceived him.

It was then that Hook understood. Even if Peter did remember—admitting he had made a mistake, admitting he had lied, admitting he had betrayed him—he would never acknowledge it. Such an act would destroy him. It would shatter his existence completely. Pan's rationale relied heavily upon the fragile twisted reality he had fabricated for himself. Hiding from the pain. From abandonment. The slightest push could cause it to come tumbling down like a house of cards. Except Peter would never allow that. He'd built a wall around it. Peter would never grow up. It was his way of surviving, of hiding from the pain that never healed. Perhaps too afraid that if he really loved someone, one day such person

215

might suddenly disappear without a word, and he'd be left alone. Hook found himself sympathizing with the boy. A boy who had made himself immune to pain, by rejecting love altogether, instead of loving and losing love. By shutting out love, he was impervious to pain. Not even death could hurt him.

Tragic, Hook thought.

He picked up his sword lethargically.

The possibility of having been erased from Peter's memory pained him more than the stab on his back. A pain so bitter, so deep, it had paralyzed half of his body. Somewhere inside Pan, that innocent boy he'd met in the streets of London remained. Yet he had been buried far below an impenetrable, defensive armor; so deep, he was far beyond Hook's grasp to retrieve. Seeking revenge out on someone who'd forgotten their crime and their victim was futile. His revenge towards Peter—simply put—no longer existed. It was an illusion. And it wasn't worth fighting for any longer.

"I hope you're happy, my friend," Hook uttered. He finally had to let him go.

Peter's feet rose off the deck. "I won't let you bring me down, old man," he said, sensing something was wrong.

He swayed his sword with dance-like agility. But Hook's vitality was gone. His moves were timely, but unaggressive; purely defensive. He wasn't going to fight. He had given up, and Peter could tell.

Frustrated, Peter swooshed as fast as the wind, from side to side, pricking Hook on his lower back, then again on his shoulder, trying to stimulate his foe. But with every injury, Hook's vitality decreased. It was no longer worth the effort, he thought. He maneuvered his blade, but his eyes were lost somewhere else, locked in a mental vacuum.

"Fight, old man!!" Peter shrieked, bitterly.

He'd imagined this encounter hundreds of times; a battle of epic proportions; over and over playing in his head. But Hook had no intention to partake in such a dream. He was done with feeding the forever-thirsting lips of vengeance. With the upper hand, Peter realized victory was becoming too easy. And Peter didn't want easy.

He wanted a fight that would send him to the brink of death and back, allowing him to win at the very last second with an act of heroism and grace. But his fantasy was now dissolving; melting like candle wax; exposing the reality behind his—at first impression—vacuous act of violence. Revenge was no longer fueling the Captain's will; exhausted, he simply wanted to let go.

Stinging tears welled up in Peter's eyes. He stabbed Hook's sides repeatedly, attempting to snap the Captain out of his stupor; insulting him, belittling him, humiliating him; anything to stir the violence that had once bloomed inside of him—to awaken the bloodthirsty pirate who'd haunted children's stories and bled into their nightmares. But his provocations met no avail, and Peter himself was reaching exhaustion. With each nick, Hook's coarse shell chipped like brittle glass, exposing the unhealed wounds he'd collected over the years; a burden that had become too heavy to bear—too heavy to bear alone. Giving in, Hook left himself at Peter's mercy. If Peter had it in him to kill the Captain, then Hook had no reason to live for. But if Peter were to hesitate—if something were to hold him back—

Pushed by Peter's attacks, Hook stepped onto the plank, cornering himself, mentally prepared for the imminent end. *So this is it*, he thought when facing the breath of death. *The boy will do what I couldn't dare to do. What an eternal dance it has been.*

Performing a majestic aerial spin, Peter spearheaded down, blade on point, building speed for a final strike.

Embracing his fate, Hook let his sword be swallowed by the ocean, opening his arms wide with acceptance. "Show me what you've got—*Pan*," he murmured, closing his eyes.

When something unexpected happened. A mere few feet before impact, something changed in Peter's mind. Something he himself, had not foreseen. Closing his bloodshot eyes, he drew his sword back and slowed down. Pushing his legs forward, the bottom of his feet met the Captain's chest, kicking him off the plank with a minor—and even *playful*—nudge.

Time had, for once, fully stopped; like his father's old watch—

ticking, but not moving. Only for a fragment of a second. That's how Hook felt as his feet lost friction with the wooden plank, and he free fell into the ocean. Flying.

He couldn't do it. He couldn't do it.

As Hook descended, a bittersweet smile crept on his face. "Bad form..."

Perhaps the boy had not forgotten that night, after all.

That one night of pirate games at the tavern, when he'd playfully knocked him off the table.

That one night that changed both their lives.

The night they both, together, defied gravity.

Flying.

What followed was beyond Hook's imagination. Even Peter was surprised; a distorted grimace appeared on his face—one Hook did not fail to notice. The Captain's entry into the crocodile's jaws was unexpected, but he couldn't help finding it somewhat ironic. How had he not heard it? Had his father's watch finally stopped ticking? Gulped whole, Hook went down the beast's massive throat.

Overwhelmed by an unexpected upsurge of emotions, Peter shot up into the sky and blended with the clouds. From above, he could hear faint childish cheering; the boys. Yet for some unexplainable reason, he found it impossible to share their joy. Only once he was certain he was far from audible reach, did he slow down. Taking a deep breath, Peter observed the landscape below him; the vastness of the island disappearing in and out of the muddled fog. A sudden throb of solitude inflamed his chest. He grimaced. The game was over. "Good-bye, old friend. Good—" when he paused— "No. 'Good-bye' sounds like forever. And forever means—" but he choked up. And burying his face between his hands, he quietly wept.

But the celebration below continued; festive songs and dances aboard the Jolly Roger; a vessel soaked in the blood of a hundred men.

Smee peered over the railing. He had been spared. Tootles had shown mercy to the old Irishman. Through his spectacles, Smee stared into the somber ocean where his Captain—and not too long before, his son—had met his fate. A sorrowful cry escaped his lips as the monstrous green creature disappeared into darker depths.

XXXV.
HOME

T WAS PAST MORNING. A torrential downpour blanketed Neverland. The gargantuan reptile crawled lethargically out of the mermaids' lagoon, onto the rocky shore. It slumped down in exhaustion, dry-heaving, allowing itself to be pummeled by heavy raindrops. Exhaling deeply, its eyes half closed. It looked sick.

The sides of its scaly body bulged, as it emitted a painful squeal. Something inside wanted to come out–dying to come out.

A perforation pierced through the beast's side, splitting through its thick flesh from the inside. Foul steam and viscous bodily fluids were released onto the pebbled shore. The sharp object gored through the muculent guts, stretching the incision briskly from a small puncture to a tear, alongside the crocodile's abdomen.

A hook.

Using every last ounce of energy left, James Hook clawed his way out of the creature's belly; slime, gastric juices, and blood, covered his entire body. Halfway out, he found himself stuck. Forcing his hook through the creature's ribcage, he allowed his

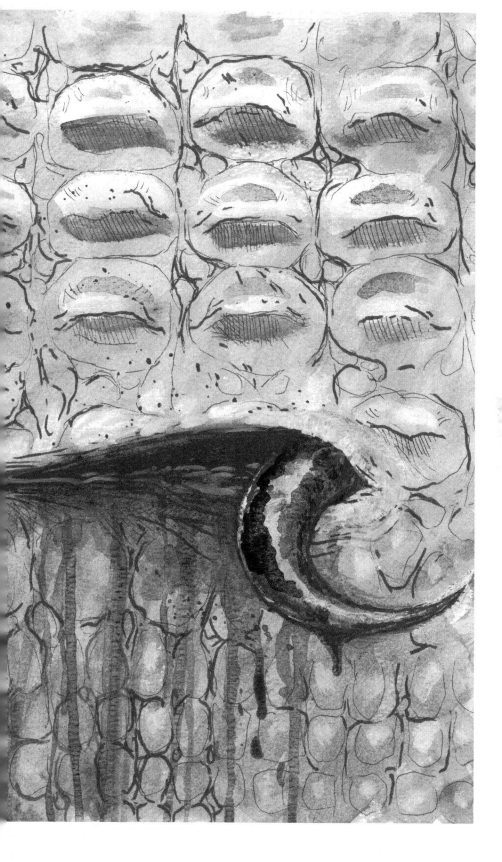

waist through. While doing so, the iron claw got caught between two unbreakable ribs. He pulled, trying to rip through, but only inflicted pain on his own arm.

Gridlocked, he rested his back on the shore, catching his breath. When a firm pull jerked on his hooked arm. The carcass was moving. Something was pulling the beast back into the lagoon.

Mermaids.

The monsoon had lured them out.

Panicking, James yanked on the hook violently. But it wouldn't budge. He propped his feet against the creature, tugging with all his might. *Snap!* His eyes rolled back as excruciating pain shot through his entire body; he'd dislocated his shoulder.

The mermaids pulled harder, submerging half of the massive crocodile's body under the swampy water. Finding no other immediate solution, James untied the leather sheathe securing the hook onto his forearm, grabbed a jagged rock sharp enough to cut through flesh, and jabbed it into his wrist, attempting to sever himself from the iron claw.

Neverland heard its most pained shrieks that dark day.

He stabbed his arm repeatedly, as uncontrollable sobs escaped his lips.

Finally, the iron claw slipped off.

Violently gasping for air, James crawled back onto the shore, distancing himself from the carcass and the mermaids. When something caught his eye; something glimmering inside the reptile, stuck in its meaty gut. James snatched it before it fully disappeared into the lagoon and wiped it clean in the soothing rain. Once the object was slime-free, he recognized it instantly: his father's golden watch. Indeed, the ticking had stopped.

Overwhelmed by the pain in his body, James collapsed. His eyes got lost in the rain-bloated clouds. He was now frozen in time. A *frozen river*. His thoughts wandered, leaving him.

When suddenly, he recalled the bone instrument tied around his neck. The small flute Tiger Lily once gave him in what seemed like an eternity ago.

Reluctant at first, he studied the tiny piece. It almost seemed foreign in his corroded hand. Doubting it would work, he placed it under his lips and blew, weakly. The flat and discordant screech echoed throughout the lagoon. It would have pained anyone's ears had they been listening. But no one was.

Unwilling to give up, he blew harder, the screech becoming louder—more dissonant. A raw cry for help.

Enveloped by the monsoon, the cave's interior ricocheted with a deafening orchestration of melodic raindrops. However, one other sound was able to filter through, splicing through nature's organic symphony; the screeching flute, faintly calling for help at the bottom of the mountain.

The call was not answered.

But the screeching did not stop. It persisted.

When a faint glow arose from inside one of the blooming flowers on the rocky wall. The glow grew brighter, yet it remained weak.

Hidden in the cave's shadows, a silhouette emerged, approaching the glowing flower among the trinkets. Tiger Lily knew whom that cry for help belonged to. Pressing her face into the flower, she recited an incantation. The flower's glow increased a touch. Yet that was all it took.

Tinker Bell emerged from inside the cave, weakly swerving through the air. She maneuvered across the torrential rain, pulsating like a dying firefly. James's cry for help hadn't stopped, screeching continuously into the storm.

His dim eyes caught sight of the frail fairy. Drained, he finally lowered the instrument with a tinge of relief; he wasn't alone.

Tinker swerved drowsily, struggling against the heavy drops that pushed her down. Landing on James's chest, she burrowed under his corroded coat, seeking shelter. James cupped his hand over her, protecting her. They somehow understood each other. A connection beyond any barrier of language. Both weak. Both abandoned. Left to die. He noticed her burnt flesh, her scarred wings.

"I am the one to blame, Tink. I am the one to blame. What I did was unforgivable. Children at play... who lost their way home. Naive and heartless."

Fatigued, James closed his eyes, allowing his breathing to slow down. A few seconds later, he was fast asleep.

After what felt like several hours, the clouds had partially cleared and the rain had fully stopped.

Lying on the shore, James remained unmoved, wandering the worlds of dreams. While he slept, Tiger Lily healed his mangled, bleeding stump. She knew the boy she once met was long gone. But she also recognized the butcher once known as Hook had perished. What was left was a ghost; a wandering shadow. And Neverland already had too many of those. Unlike Peter, she knew James had to return home. He simply didn't belong in Neverland, where time did not exist. Never aging was a curse, and she knew that first-hand. Since the moment she laid eyes on the boys the night they arrived, she had made it her mission to avoid having them meet her exact fate. They had to leave the island. With Peter, she had failed. He had made himself unreachable. She wasn't going to make the same mistake with James.

Pushing from under his coat, Tinker Bell stretched her arms and legs, fluttering her wings in the air. By no means was she fully healed, but she had regained enough of her strength to fly properly. Under Tiger Lily's instructions, she hovered over James and danced in circles, producing a meager cloud of golden dust. It was the scarcest amount Tinker Bell had ever produced, but it was just enough. After a few laps, she had managed to cover him entirely. Unaware, his body gently began to levitate.

Shielding his eyes from the blinding sun, James squinted. Damp grass tickled his neck. Disoriented, he rubbed his temples—as if rising from a hundred year slumber—pushing himself up from the ground with little strength. Bewildered, he took in his surroundings, unable to brush off his state of confusion. *Where am I?* The place around him looked, even smelled, terribly familiar, yet it held itself with a surreal quality that made it seem like a distant memory. Was he dreaming?

When, staring at a bush of lilies, he looked no further. Everything came back to him at once. He was back in Kensington Gardens. Overpowered by his emotions, he disregarded the rags he was wearing and walked up to the massive front gate, which slowly creaked open. For the first time in what felt like thousands of years, James stepped out into the cobbled streets of London.

Tears welled up in his eyes when he reached the place he once called home. The wall he had climbed down. The window he had left wide open. The garbage can that had once been overturned.

A young girl—younger than him when he left for Neverland; even younger than Peter—with striking blue eyes, stepped out of the residence wearing a uniform. Standing by the door, seeing her off, was a woman of about fifty. She waved good-bye with delicate grace.

Not once did James ever imagine that he would lay eyes on his mother again. She looked nothing like the consumed woman who had embedded herself in James's memory. With age, she had acquired a warm glow on her plum face.

An emotional tidal wave swept him off his feet. He felt...

...as if he were flying.

As the days went by, James acquired an old torn cloak to cover his rags. It wasn't winter yet, so for now, the cloak fulfilled its purpose. Having set camp across his old home, he rested his back against the wall, guarding the residence every single day—eyes fixed on the door.

The school ritual repeated itself with as much monotony. He enjoyed it. Monotony did not bother him. Except this time, something different happened. The girl waved her mother good-bye as usual, but then stopped at the sight of him. And did not move.

Perplexed by her daughter's reaction, Mrs. Hope ran back into the house, returning shortly after. Bearing a loaf of bread, she crossed the street and offered it to James with a warm smile. A hungry beggar, she thought.

Whether it was premeditated or a simple unconscious reaction, it was difficult to discern; James thanked her using sign language. Taken aback, she frowned. Then forced an uncomfortable smirk, followed by a genuine, yet mildly nervous, smile. She was both touched and vexed by the fact that this man knew she was deaf. Discomfort took over her as she quickly returned home. Once inside, she peered through the curtains one last time before disappearing inside the house.

Come nighttime, James remained, unmoved, like a willow tree that had extended its roots deep into the rich soil below. His head hung between his knees, fighting off sleep, as the rest of the city embarked into dreamland.

But it was at night that his watch truly began.

A singular bedroom window, once belonging to James Hope, glowed amongst the sleeping houses stretching across Bloomsbury. Concealed by the shadows of night, the silhouette of a young boy materialized out of the darkness. He approached James's old window, stealthily pressing his face up against the glass. Peter lost himself in the scene unfolding before him: a mother wrapping her young daughter under the covers—kissing her goodnight. It was an exquisite moment. Sublime. He'd had hundreds of adventures, more than any boy or girl could ever imagine. But that moment he witnessed through the glass, was the one delight from which he found himself irrevocably barred.

He waited for the mother to turn out the light and leave the room. The gentle creak of a window being pushed open was enough for James's perfectly tuned ears to perk up.

Peter crouched onto the windowsill looking in. When a pebble bounced off his head. Hard.

Konk!

"Ow!!" he whimpered, cupping the injured spot.

Frowning, he turned around, searching for the culprit. Squinting in the darkness, Peter was only able to locate a single man, covered in rags, sitting on the sidewalk against the wall.

Raising his only hand, James playfully shook his finger from side to side, reprimanding the boy. "*Tsk, tsk, tsk.* Bad form, Mr. Pan. Bad... bad form."

Baffled, Peter's eyes grew as wide as the full moon. He darted off into the night, startled. This made James smile.

After several decades, Hope had finally found its way back home. For not all who wander are lost, James thought. And as a wise girl had once told him, not all who are lost are lost forever. There he remained, grounded, until he drew his last breath. Until the world stopped turning. For he had made a promise—a 'James Promise'—, that he would never forget. As long as Pan existed, his counterpart would remain. Forever waiting. Never abandoning him. Waiting for the day he'd stop running. Waiting for the day he'd return.

Live fully, love fully, fly freely.

F*KTORY

[sneak peak]

CHAPTER I

MY GAZE WAS FIXED on the barrel of the gun.

The hollowness inside of it.

The rim of its mouth.

Chrome silver, smudged with dirty fingerprints.

Although the thought had once crossed my mind, I hadn't really expected to ever be held at gunpoint by my own flesh and blood. *Good ol' Frank.* My dad. The fat fuck. There'd been the few times when, upon arriving home and walking into his unexpected bubble of drunkardness, I'd ticked him off to beat-red-faced, bottle-smashing extremes, for no apparent reason; or just because I had tripped over a bottle or a beer can. Anything could propel the fat turd into explosions of Vesuvian magnitudes. By year fourteen I'd come to expect a lot from being on the receiving end of such combustions: bruises, black eyes, swollen lips. But I'd never expected *that.* Not once had he waved that *thing* at me. Not once a gun. This is how I knew he was serious.

"Put him down," the words slurred out of his crooked mouth.

By *him,* Frank was referring to my baby brother Phil. One-year-old; his entire life ahead of him, currently limp, ragdoll status, in my thin arms. His gaping blue eyes rolled white, half open, as faint seizures sporadically took over his tiny body. Phil is not prone to seizures. Phil doesn't have seizures. He's as healthy as can be. This was not normal. This was Frank's fault. But he wouldn't let me go. He wouldn't let me dial 911—run into the ER. Oh, no. He had me locked at gunpoint. Sweat glistened down his unshaven fatty chin.

Phil convulsed one more time; drool dripping down his thin lips.

That's it—I thought—I'm saving my brother.

"Fuck you, Frank."

I took one step towards the front door and then I heard the weapon click—Frank pulling back the slide on the automatic; the chamber loaded. By the time my right foot had made it in front of the left one, the blast had already echoed inside the cramped room, and the bullet had grazed my calf like a serrated shard on fire.

Fire.

I immediately thought of the stars.

Stars.

Formed by huge clouds of dust and gas bumping into one another, getting bigger, their gravity getting stronger. Once hot enough, nuclear fusion occurs. And then a star is formed.

People are shaped in a similar way—just like stars—, excessive amounts of dust and hot gas. And like stars, everyone's life has a turning point prior to their big bang. The shit-show before the creation. Y'know, one of those moments that can fuck you up.

Cleopatra's was when her father named her joint regent at fourteen. Fucked up.

Spiderman's when Uncle Ben died. Fucked up.

Charles Manson's when his mother sold him for a pitcher of beer. Fucked. Up.

Not to mention 'Helter Skelter'.

That, right there—bullet kissing my skin, me painfully attempting to maintain my balance while holding onto Phil—is my life. An intricate cornucopia of fucked up. Every second. Every minute. Every hour.

But I'm getting ahead of myself. There was a time before the bullet; a time before Phil in my arms, before Frank's attempt of infanticide. A time before the drug; a time before *Lumen*.

Twenty-four hours.

One-thousand-four-hundred-and-forty minutes.

Eighty-six-thousand-and-four-hundred seconds.
Rewind.
Go.

Everyone trusts a little girl. Fine, *almost* everyone. Fourteen, a tad
short for my age, innocent smile—what's there not to trust? Dressed
with a badge-incrusted sash and a tote bag overflowing with Samoas
and Tagalongs, I could've easily been confused with any other sun-
kissed and primed Girl Scout. Except I wasn't. Far from it. The only
thing I had in common with a GirlScout™ was that we were both
in the sales business—both pushed to sell by our loving parents; my
lard-tub father in my case. Of course the goods were different. They
sold sugar; I sold drugs. Both feeding off addiction. I learned this
when I was eight at a school fair competition or something. We each
had a lemonade stand; the one with the most sales would win a bag
of candy—*sugar*, they start them young. At first I wasn't doing very
well; I quickly realized my stand wasn't as *nice* as the other kids'. I
had no money. I quickly learned I had to adapt, forage and outsmart
them. The second day at the fair, I had a little something *extra* to
destroy the competition. I've been surrounded by pills my entire life.
Back when Frank was a small time player (before the heroin, before
the cocaine, before the ketamine), he moved buckets of barbiturates,
low-key prescription drugs (the usual suspects: Xanax, Klonopin,
Oxy, Valium, Vicodin) and—which was greatly popular back then—
ecstasy. I had ecstasy. At eight-years-old I had no idea what the pill
did, I just knew folks left and right kept coming back for it. So I
snagged a few pills and crushed them into the lemonade. Genius, I
know. All I needed was that first buyer. After that, the tables were
turned and I had a line down the block. Luckily for me, there wasn't
enough in the lemonade to raise any flags—just the right amount to
get those happy-go-lucky parents going, to get them hooked, and to
plant a seed that would make them come back for more. That day,
an entrepreneur was born.
    Fast-forward.

T-minus twenty-four hours to the bullet grazing my leg.

The countdown had begun.

At first I didn't believe the guy. He sat under a droning fluorescent light, tearing through his second box of Girl Scout cookies. It took me less than five seconds to study his entirety: at least twice my age, tall, wiry, sweat seeping through his undershirt and bleeding through the one-size-too-large tweed jacket. He sat across from me, nervous. I'm sure I was his first sale. That's why he got the little girl. *She's probably an easy target*, he thought. That's usually how it goes. Present myself as vulnerable; turn myself into bait. I'm usually good at reading people. They say you should always look for the best in them—I don't. I go straight for the meat. I look for the worst. It's easier that way.

Regardless of how seedy the transaction had been developing so far—back hallways of a club, small, dim-lit, make-shift office which resembled a cleaning supply room or a broom closet; usual drug deal setups, which in a perfect world would've meant 'legit' and 'trustworthy'—I refused to believe anything the man in the tweed jacket was saying. I didn't believe the drug did what he said it did. The product hadn't officially reached the streets yet. It was mere hearsay, information I found through word of mouth, the drug that everyone had heard of and no one had witnessed. A drug engineered in high-tech labs, top facilities hidden underground. It didn't even have a name. I'd heard every single rumor, but I still didn't believe. The sweaty man in the jacket said he would show me. Leaving the blanket of flickering lights crowning us, he approached a young man; at first I could only see the back of his messy head. Sinking in a beanbag, his glazed eyes stared at the TV screen in front of him; Sunday morning cartoons with no audio—his gaze drifting, both looking and not looking at the same time. Was he aware of his surroundings?

The wiry man in the tweed jacket removed a small white vial from his pocket and removed the cap: a portable injectable, I realized, once the small needle was exposed.

"Each vial has about eight doses, give or take," he said. Then, with a shaking hand, he injected the comatose young man on the neck. Nothing much happened at first. Glued to the beanbag, he blinked a couple of times and exhaled deeply. Then, without raising his arm, the tips of his fingers moved. I could feel myself frowning. *Was this a joke?* The sweaty man turned to me, holding out his hands, begging me to wait. So I waited. Except I didn't have to wait much longer. Following the rhythm of the young man's fingertips, a tennis ball lifted off the ground and hovered slowly midair, spinning on the spot. My jaw dropped. The sleazy man in the tweed jacket had been telling the truth. The drug had given beanbag guy telekinetic abilities. And just with a tiny shot. I approached the tennis ball and moved my hand around it, verifying this wasn't some kind of trick. No strings. I wanted to grab it, but it dropped before I could. I turned. The beanbag guy was looking at me, but I wasn't able to read through his bloodshot eyes. Perhaps he was screaming for help. Perhaps my presence hadn't even registered. Only then was I able to get a good look at him; torn sleeveless shirt exposing his long skinny arms—the left one covered with intricate and vibrant hexagonal tattoos and red dots frequented by drug-infused needles; what else were they shooting up his arms? An IV fed a transparent liquid from a bag into a vein.

"What's that?" I asked the sweaty man.

"Morphine. Helps enhance the effect while using less to achieve the same result. A little secret for test subjects. That way we keep the test doses low, y'know? I've only used a mere quarter of a dose on him, you see? So I don't waste more of the juice."

"What would happen if you gave him more?"

He shrugged. "Crazy stuff, I s'ppose. It's still in the beta testing phase. But no matter," he added, "this lil' bugger is cruising through space." As if to confirm his statement, he slapped the young man's cheek a couple of times. It's true; he showed no signs of a reaction—none whatsoever. His eyes were sunken in, resting over bags as big as plums. A faded strand of green and purple hair draped over his face; glued to his forehead with sweat. A Mohawk made way to the back of his otherwise bare scalp. The light of the

TV bounced off his olive skin. He was young. Younger than what I had initially thought—maybe a few years older than me. What could have brought him here: slouched on a beanbag, injected day and night like a lab rat? Was he pulled from somewhere? Snatched? From a different country perhaps? Well-dressed looking man telling you he has a job for you in America ('the land of dreams! Of opportunity!'); paying for your ticket, putting you up—next thing you know you wake up shackled to a bathtub without a kidney—or in this case, attached to a morphine drip; you know how it goes.

Drool dribbled down his inert lips. I cleaned it off with a tissue almost instinctively. His purplish eyes turned to mine, making me take a step back. *He's aware.*

"See? It works." The tweed jacket man said, oblivious of the young one's glare.

It worked all right.

And he wanted a ridiculous amount of money for it. That's the part where he thought he could take advantage of me; outsmart the little girl. Except by that point in the game, he had already bitten the bait; he'd gorged an entire box of Samoas. Sugar-addict; *figures*. To each his own.

I told him I wanted a dozen vials. Of course I didn't have the money, but he didn't know that. His face lit up almost instantly; yes, I was his first sale—no doubt about it. And for a dozen vials, that's a lot of green buck. I had to keep the transaction going. Just a few seconds longer. He hoisted up a large suitcase—looked more like a chrome toolbox—, dropped it on the table, and inputted a serial code onto the single screen. Sweat beads crawled down his forehead and trickled down his cheeks before dropping like engorged raindrops off his chin and onto the desk. He wiped the dampness off his face with the back of his hand. Then his stomach roared; a deep, visceral churning sound. You could tell it hurt by the look on his face; his eyes widened as he released a faint gasp. Meeting my deadpan gaze, as if about to ask for help, he squirmed out of the room without saying a word.

His echoing footsteps grew quieter and quieter until it was back to complete silence. I zeroed in on the clock on the wall: Hello-Kitty face, with her arms as the dials. A bit past midnight. The instructions on the laxative box were very clear: *'for full effect, wait fifteen minutes'*. That was for a single dose. The box had five. *'For immediate effects, apply generously'*. I was feeling generous. Locking my gaze onto the empty cookie box, my mind wandered into the steaming pits of gastrointestinal havoc. *Five doses for a single box.* And he'd eaten the entire box in one sitting. I was relieved I wasn't able to hear the fireworks.

Spinning the chrome suitcase on the table, I faced it with anticipation. The latch was open. Perfect timing. Pushing the lid up, the suitcase's contents were revealed. Endless rows of white vials adorned the inside. *This is what a normal boy or girl feels on Christmas.* After carefully removing the vials, one-by-one, I packed them with ease inside the empty cookie box. I know, shameful. But I am not a thief. I may bump up the prices every once in a while—stuffing capsules with fillers—, but I don't steal. Yet in that moment, my actions were completely out of character. I was desperate. Even though his back was turned to me, I knew the beanbag boy could tell what I was doing; don't ask me how. But he did nothing to stop me. Part of me felt sorry for the guy; felt somewhat responsible—as if it were my duty to get him the hell out of that place. But then I thought; if he wanted to leave, he would've done it already.

And then I was out the door. The guy dressed in tweed was sure to receive a serious beating—if not worse—for this. Part of me wanted to feel bad for him, but I didn't allow myself to go there. There was no point. Survival of the fittest.

T-minus twenty-two hours.

As I hid the vials behind a vent under my bed—the only secret spot in the clusterfuck shit-hole I have the joy of calling *home*—I spotted the rusty tin can not too far into the vent, just where I had left it. Flipping through the contents—wads of wrinkly cash—I quickly realized it wasn't enough to GTFO (*Get.The.Fuck.Out.*). I needed more. I was hoping my new precious acquisition would do the trick. I'd start selling tomorrow night, venturing toward the outskirts of Manhattan, veering as far away as possible from those (surely by now incredibly pissed) drug dealers. Must stay away from their turf. And then—with money in my pocket—I could leave. Leave this nightmare behind.

Dawn's rays spilled through the tiny window grazing my ceiling. You could swear this was designed to be someone's closet. Getting claustrophobic, I walked out. Once in the living room, I peered over Phil's crate. He slept soundly. In peace. This made me grimace. Peace sprouted out of ignorance. If he could only realize the rotten pit he lived in: a beaten down hotel room with no real furniture, just an uneven kitchen table crowded with cocaine bags separated into kilos, and a fridge that never stopped humming; a fridge overstuffed with beer bottles and beer cans—and the occasional hiding spot for Frank's drugs (I never understood why, but he'd stressed repeatedly that it was the safest place to store valued goods). Alas, home. Frank kept the TV inside his room—a chamber locked at all times, out of limits territory. Good. Who'd want to go in there anyway? The putrid smell of piled dirty laundry, simmering perpetually with the smell of nicotine and booze. The pig rarely showered, and he simply did not believe in doing laundry. I once caught sight of a rat squirming out of a pair of socks stiff as a board. I retched at the memory of it. At that moment, the beast slept. I could hear him snoring through the scratched up door. The paint had chipped in all the wrong places. The same could be said about the room itself: cracking molding, moldy surfaces, and a wall-to-wall carpet which was last cleaned: never. An inhospitable environment that was never graced with housekeeping. The juxtaposition between the exquisite cherry chestnut finishes, the intricate iron-laced floor-to-ceiling mirrors, and the crepuscular layer of dust and spider webs blanketing everything, was both jarring and beautiful; like a forgotten relic, stored in the back of an antique shop; or a desolate post apocalyptic city, where all its inhabitants had up and left for no reason, leaving it all behind. To be fair, the hotel had never opened for business. It was scheduled to have an extravagant inauguration sometime after the Titanic sank.

I'm not sure if they were at all related, but shortly after the iceberg ordeal, the hotel's enterprise sunk with it. Since then, there have been promises of remodeling, flipping and even demolishing, but every plan had fallen through. Good for us, I figured. Not sure how or when Frank found this spot, but it's been our home ever since I can remember. Even back when mom was alive. A home devoid of life; empty rooms and silent hallways.

I pushed Phil's ebony hair back and kissed his forehead. He smelled like baby powder. The smell soothed my nerves. Not sure why I'm taken aback by the baby smell—I've been taking care of him since I was thirteen. Usually the smell rubs off on me, and I end up smelling like a toddler for days.

I was exhausted, but there was no time for shuteye. Another all-nighter. I would try to get some sleep on the subway, but that's as good as nothing. It is what it is, I thought. I kissed Phil once again, left a warm bottle of milk by his side, swiped a bag of pills off the counter, and I was out the door.

T-minus eighteen hours.

Like any other fourteen-year-old, at 9:00 AM you could find me in school, but that didn't mean I was in class. I *attended* class, but I was never *in* class. The Principal—Mr. Hardwick—and I, we had our little arrangement. *Tit for tat. Quid-pro-quo.* Big bag o' oxy pills for the usual price; I threw in something extra; he looked the other way while I sold by the bathrooms and under the bleachers. All in the name of good business.

That morning, however, was not the norm.

"What's this?" he said, holding the pill-packed zip-lock bag in his palm with as much contempt as if he were holding a cracked egg; confusion and disgust.

I was a bit light on the extra. He could tell. "The usual."

He squinted his eyes, peering from under his rectangular glasses, in such a way that made his balding self look at least ten years older. He pursed his thin lips and dropped the bag into a drawer, before slamming it shut.

Hardwick was born with a thumb up his ass, but whenever it came to business, our transactions disregarded age and size. Yet the pause that followed was unusual. I remained standing by the foot of his desk as he directed his gaze back down over a stack of documents, pretending to read.

I cleared my throat.

"Oh," he said. "You're still here."

Oh...

"Are you looking for counseling?" he continued.

"I'm looking for what's mine, Hardwick."

Then he did that thing with his lips again. From inside his drawer, he pulled out the bag and dropped it on his desk. I repeat: this was not the norm.

We both stared at the bag for several seconds. I couldn't help thinking how ridiculous the two American flags standing on either side behind him—framing him—made him look. Because one wasn't enough.

"It's a little light, Evelyn." That's what he called me, *Evelyn*; my name. I hated it.

"Bullshit."

He didn't move.

I didn't have time for games. I reached out, aiming to snatch it back, but he slammed his hand on it before I could. "Get out."

"Pay me."

"You think you can bullshit me? You can't bullshit me. You can't bullshit a bullshitter. Come back when you have the rest, I'll pay you then."

I could feel my blood boiling. I needed that money. *Really* needed it. "Screw that, pay me now!"

He slammed his hand onto the desk before springing up on his feet. "Listen to me, you little filth. I'm doing you a favor. You're nothing. I pick up the phone, and you know who's on the other line? Social services. Or even better, I'll have my friend, the commissioner, pay us a visit with his drug dogs and bust squad. I have that power. What do you have? Nothing. Not even an attempt at a decent education. So unless you want to spend your teens in juvie, get the fuck out of my office."

My jaw clenched as my fists squeezed tight—my nails burying under my skin. It hurt. But he was right; there was nothing I could do about it. Karma crossed my mind but I quickly brushed it away. This wasn't karma, this was the oldest law of the jungle: the biggest, the largest, the strongest; those are the ones who survive. Not always the case (Exhibit A: Dinosaurs), but more often than not. Resigned, I turned and made way to the door.

Before I slipped out, he added: "And God bless."

God-*fucking*-bless, all right.

T-minus ten hours.

I spent the rest of the afternoon at Riky's. He spun in endless pirouettes around me, as I laid, fixed on the floor, glued to the ground, defeated. Also, it was a pretty good place to think. The classical music blasting from Riky's crackling speakers—a piece from Mendelsohn's *A Midsummer's Night Dream*, his favorite—provided with a soothing tranquility, embalming me in a warm, welcoming liquid. It allowed my mind to wander, to cross bridges, to find patterns, to seek solutions. Riky's elasticity added an unusual grace to his movements. The fluidity of the routine made it seem as if his limbs had neither beginning nor end, just a continuous flow of unending movement. Perhaps it was due to the angle I witnessed it from—the floor. How he moved in such a cramped space (his room could've been a closet, just like mine, except he had barricaded it with dirty clothes and sneakers), was a mystery to me. His dark curls bounced to every beat, curling back into shape after every spin. Whenever we weren't selling, and whenever Riky wasn't dancing, we spent most of our drab after school afternoons sprawled on his floor, either stuffing our minds with reality garbage television expecting to numb our brains, or—as we carelessly flunked through our own English class—reading whatever new book Riky had picked out of a freshman NYU Literary Interpretation class; we read out loud, him one page, me the next. Kafka's 'The Metamorphosis' and

Camus's *'The Stranger'* were among our recent favorite discoveries. We read Charlotte Brontë's *'Jane Eyre'* last month. Yeah. Wish I could get those hours of my life back.

Outside his parents argued. That's all they ever did: scream, swear, and smash dishes against the walls. I'm sure the neighbors hated it. But in those parts of Harlem, there was no trustworthy landlord to complain to. Dishes exploded against the other side of the wall, outside Riky's room, marking the beat in their own dissonant way. However, Riky remained composed; it was always this way when he danced, when they argued; his usual expression replaced by something more intense—more removed, as if an entire world were locked away inside him.

"Do they ever stop?" I mumbled.

"They do whenever the Earth stops spinning."

Once the piece reached its crescendo, he dropped next to me, pressing his cheek against the floor. He fixed his deep brown eyes into mine. "What are you going to do E? What are you going to do?" That's what he called me: *E*. That's what almost everyone called me. Except Hardwick. Except Frank.

"Secret savings?" I replied, playing with the idea in my head.

"Will that be enough?"

I knew it wasn't. There was only one answer to my predicament. And he knew it just as well. I could see it reflecting off the glimmer in his eyes. I had to sell. Sell. Sell. Sell. Until my feet hurt. I hadn't told him about the new drug yet; not really sure what I was waiting for.

With a lighter, he burned a mound of tiny crystals on the bowl of a small glass pipe. He inhaled. And exhaled. I hated it when he did that. The irony of a drug dealer who hates drugs, I know.

"There's only one answer, E," he added.

"I know... *sell.*"

He winced. "No, you idiot. You have to leave."

"Leave?"

"Get out of here. Leave this city, before it's too late. Manhattan is too small for you. Find a bigger pond. Get away from Frank, from all of this. You're playing with fire. No good can come out of it."

"Yeah? And where would I go?" I asked, resting my head on my elbow.

"Miami," he said, as if he'd been planning the getaway for months.

"*Miami?* Really? And do what?"

"Find a job, something. You'll figure it out. You're smart."

"What about Phil?"

"What about him?"

"I can't leave him with Frank. I practically raised him. He'd be dead in less than a week."

Riky took a moment to think about this. Then: "And he's safe with you? A fourteen-year-old drug dealer?"

I punched his shoulder.

"Only I can protect him. Once I have enough, we can leave."

"Take me with you?" he asked, puppy eyes on full display.

"And you thought I was leaving without you? Please, you're stuck with me."

"Promise?"

"I would never dream of leaving you behind—not with *them,* anyway."

We both lied on our backs, staring at the ceiling as more dishes scrapped the paper-thin walls.

"We are pretty fucked up, aren't we?" I asked.

"Could be worse."

Indeed it could.

And it was.

T-minus twenty minutes.

It was way past nightfall when I made it back to our abandoned hotel on Beekman Street, crawled under the unsupervised fence, crossed the art-deco lobby, and climbed up the dark, dirty stairs. Usually by that time, Frank was passed out drunk. Which, as I saw it, was heaven. It gave me enough time to spend a few moments with Phil—feeding him, snuggling him, cradling him to sleep—before diving into the Big Apple's afterhours scene. I had to sell. I had to sell tonight. As I was toying around with a price range for the mysterious drug, I heard an indistinct wail. At first I thought it was a cat. A dying cat out in the street. But it was coming from down the hallway; growing louder with every step. It wasn't a cat. It was human. It was Phil. My slow paced walk turned into a fast dash in a heartbeat. My chest was pounding; rapid breath burning inside my throat.

I don't even remember pushing the front door open. I don't remember walking into the bathroom. Because when I got there, everything seemed to crumble around me. I froze; the air getting pushed in and out of my mouth, dry and bitter, like sandpaper. What was he doing? What was Frank doing to him? When I caught sight of the rusty tin can—*my* rusty tin can, *my* savings—sitting atop the sink. He'd found it. The ogre had found it. Which could only mean...

The vials.

As he took a step back, still unaware of my presence, drowned by Phil's pained cries, I saw the object sticking out of Phil's small arm: a needle. A needle attached to a white vial. The shock was so overpowering that I couldn't force any words out of my mouth. My voice was stuck in the back of my throat. I was paralyzed. My mind kept screaming, but my body refused to obey. Suddenly, my muscles jolted.

"WHAT THE FUCK ARE YOU DOING???!!"

Frank turned, laying his contemptuous eyes on me, brows furrowing with confusion. Pushing past him, I snagged Phil up, and in a failed attempt to subdue his cries, kissed his forehead, rubbed his back, inspected his arm.

"Oh, well look who it is. Little Ms. I-come-home-whenever-I-please."

Ignoring him, I pressed Phil against my chest, nuzzling him.

"So what's this stuff anyway?" he asked as he stared deep into the white vial.

I picked up on the slur in his voice; noticed his heavy eyes and his puffy red cheeks. He was piss-drunk. He put the vial down and grabbed the tin can. His eyes narrowed, and then he directed them at me.

"Saving up for father's day?" he asked with a grin.

It was a trap. I had to get his attention away from the rusty tin can, to something else that could hold his currently dazed mind.

"You want to know about the vial," I finally said.

But he didn't lower the tin can.

"Is this my money?" he asked, his voice an octave lower.

"No."

"Then what is it?"

"It's nothing."

He must have detected the desperation in my voice, because he pulled out a cheap lighter from his pocket and sparked a flame. "Nothing, huh?" With his free hand, he opened the lid and raised a crumbled bill. I gulped hard. The bill got closer to the flame. He was playing with me, he wouldn't dare, not even him; he loves money too much. My eyes were fixed on the dancing flame as it joined the green bill, creating a thin trail of smoke.

I remained composed, dying inside. I could not give in, that's what he wanted: a reaction. Taking a deep breath, I buried my face on Phil's neck, whose cries had decreased significantly. When Frank dropped the burning bill into the tin can setting off a cloud of black and grey. My eyes widened. All my efforts falling apart; dissolving into ash right before my eyes. The contents of that tin can represented the only glimmer of hope I had to move on from this towering troll. I couldn't let him take that away from me. I refused. With two quick moves, I snatched the can out of his hand, dropped it into the sink, and allowed a weak stream of water to cover it entirely. The fire had stopped and the bills were soaked, creating a blackish liquid when mixed in with the ash.

Before I could react, Frank yanked me by the arm, pushing his burly face inches away from my own. His breath smelled of sweat and rancid beer.

"I own you. Understood?"

I nodded, genuinely terrified, eyes locked on the dirty bathroom tiles.

"I can't hear you."

"Yes, Frank," I whimpered.

"Yes... *daddy*. Say it."

My nose twitched. An involuntary reaction. I couldn't stomach the words. My voice was caught again.

"Say it."

"Yes—" I paused, breathed. "—*Daddy*."

"Good girl." After patting me on the head as one would to a stray mutt, he salvaged a few of the wet dollar bills in the sink. Then he left the bathroom, making way into his cave. That's when I noticed Phil was no longer moving. His arm; limp. His eyes were half closed, showing only a strip of creamy white.

"Phil?" I shook him. "Something's wrong with him." My voice cracked. I charged across the room to grab the only phone in the hotel, when Frank beat me to it and snatched it.

"I need to call 911!" My voice had significantly grown louder, more frantic.

"I'm expecting a call."

"He needs a doctor!"

"He's fine."

That's when the seizures began: weak at first, but rapidly increasing in vigor and frequency. There was no time to lose. I bolted to the door, when Frank intercepted me with his heftiness.

"Where are you going?"

"To the ER! There's something wrong with him!" I was beyond panicking.

"No you're not."

"FUCK!" I swerved around him and took two long leaps, inching away from the front door.

"You're staying." And that's when I knew it. The firm, yet calm tone in his voice was enough to inform me I was being held hostage by something more than his massive physicality. I could feel it. The air was denser, as if the pressure in the room had suddenly plummeted. I turned, and there it was, the barrel of the gun, staring back at me. Who would've thought? Me held at gunpoint by my own father while my toddler brother convulsed in my arms. Too many surprises in a day, and being held at gunpoint was the last thing I expected. That was until he shot me.

T-minus zero.

My calf burned as if it had just been sprinkled with acid and prickled with glass. No matter how hard I struggled, how hard I kicked; Frank ripped Phil out of my arms and threw me into the bathroom, locking me in. I banged at the door only briefly—Frank had already blasted the TV's volume and who else was going to hear me? The rats and raccoons living in room 1314? Being loud wasn't going to get me anywhere. I took a peak at my calf; it was bad, but not too serious. The bullet had only grazed my skin. However, that wasn't my biggest worry. I was terrified as to what would happen to Phil. I felt so helpless, locked in the bathroom. I surveyed the compact room. No windows, of course. Just a small rectangular vent that led to a pitch-black shaft that cut through the building for ventilation purposes. I climbed on the toilet seat to get a closer look. I could crawl out, and up the shaft, hoping to reach another vent. But that seemed closed to impossible. There had to be another way. When, while doing another quick scan of the bathroom, my gaze landed on an object on the sink: a white vial with a small needle at one end. A thought crossed my mind. Frank couldn't have used the entire vial—could he? As if grabbing onto a lifeline—Phil's life—I snatched the vial firmly and shook it by my ear. Nothing. It felt light on the palm of my hand. Still, I refused to give up. I gave the doorknob another chance, pulling on it. But just like before, it didn't budge. I hated the idea of injecting myself. *'Don't shit where you eat?'* But I had to draw the line somewhere, and this was an obvious exception. I was hoping—hoping there would be enough left to at least budge the door open. After that, I would manage. I held the tip of the needle against my forearm, just as I had seen the man in the tweed jacket do to the beanbag guy. My hand faltered, shaking. *What the hell am I doing?* No. *What the hell am I waiting for?* Refusing to let Phil die, I perforated my skin, and pushed onto the back of the vial. A sudden shudder took over my entire body. A chill; as if my veins had suddenly been pumped with a cool liquid. There was some left all right, not much, judging by the rapidity of the injection, but *some*. Dizzy, I collapsed into the bathtub, pulling onto the shower curtain with my free hand. Everything spun around me. When all at once, my thoughts reorganized themselves with steadfast fluidity. I was lucid. I was thinking clearly. My focus was spear sharp. I could feel it growing inside me. Dropping the white vial into my pocket, I knew what had to be done. With a tilt of my head, the bathroom door magically ripped off its hinges and landed flatly on the floor. Easy. As easy as knuckle cracking. I couldn't help but think: this is going to revolutionize the world—or destroy it. Drowned by the loudness inside his room, Frank hadn't heard me tear down the bathroom door. But I wanted him to. I wanted him to see what I could do. So I tore down *his* door.

Startled, he leapt off his old faux-leather recliner, frozen mid motion—he'd been trying to light up a cigar. Phil lay unconscious at the foot of his bed.

"What the fuck did you just do?!" Frank roared, moving his arms around like a ticked off Italian—flaming lighter in hand. "What the fuck did you do that for??!" he hollered, motioning towards the ripped off door.

I guess he was too drunk to acknowledge the fact that his one-hundred-and-twenty-pound daughter had just knocked his bedroom door down.

"You are in so much fucking trouble, you little bitch—" the word was never fully completed, as Frank flew across the room, smacking his back against the wall with a crack; all with a simple hand gesture. To be fair, he didn't exactly *fly*—I might have been exaggerating. But he did get *shoved* against the wall with a simple hand gesture of mine; which was way more than I could've accomplished with my tiny fists. The lighter and cigar hit the musky rug. Frank rested his hands on his knees and released a pained groan. When he looked up, his eyes widened with disbelief. Then his gaze shifted; following it, I saw it land on the gun. With one quick hand swipe, I knocked it off the dresser where it had been sitting, before he could reach it.

It hit the floor with a dry thud. He locked eyes with me, sensing my defiance. He leapt across the room, once again attempting to grab the weapon, but I made it skid across the floor just as easily—away from him. I soon realized this had become a fun game I wouldn't mind playing for a while. But I wasn't familiar with the drug's effects or duration; the last thing I wanted was for the drug to wear out, leaving me exposed and vulnerable to the boiling volcano which was now Frank. I had to be quick. I had to get it done. After leading him out of the room by chasing after the revolving gun, I *nudged* him once again, sending him *flying* (it's my story, fuck off) across the room and into the bathroom. He landed inside the bathtub, banging his head against the wall—hard. Using his momentary blackout to my advantage, I snatched the remaining—dripping wet—bills from inside the sink, and shoved them inside an old diaper bag sitting under the sink.

"You—you—" the words slipped out of his mouth with a wheezing mumble. "You're mm—mine." He smirked. I had briefly forgotten about my wounded calf, but the blood trickling down my ankle acted as a quick reminder. He shot me. Not only had he shot me, but he'd also injected Phil with an unknown substance—tarnishing his innocent self. Seeding, my mental grip wrapped around his fat neck. His eyes bulged as his legs kicked the air erratically. Frank deserved to die. He was a disgusting specimen of a human being; deceitful, selfish, uncaring. He would have killed me. He would have killed Phil—when the thought hit me like a concert-hall piano: *Phil!* Caught up in my own anger, I had forgotten about the urgency of his condition. My distraction had been as reckless as Frank's actions. I released him from my mental grip and trotted back into his bedroom, but, upon arrival, I immediately stopped. A small patch of flames danced almost too playfully on the dirty rug, next to the silver lighter. How could I have been so careless?! Not wasting another second, I swiped Phil off the bed and bolted out of the room. The fire crackled behind me. I turned to look. Nothing I could do was going to subdue it; it was already too late, and it was spreading fast— up the stained curtains the orange glow went. Thick black smoke had begun to materialize. Unaware, I began to choke. We had to get out. Before I reached the front door, I heard Frank moaning in the bathroom—it made me stop. I couldn't move. Why wasn't I moving? *Dammit.* I turned, facing him in the distance. I motioned towards him with my hand, but his body barely nudged. I tried again, but got the same results. I couldn't lift him. Was I getting weaker? I took a step forward but stopped as flames shot out of his bedroom, creating a wall of fire between us. I stood there, for half a second, Phil wrapped in my arms. *Shit,* I thought. With a nasty grimace tattooed all over my face, I motioned over to the bathtub's faucet, allowing the grimy water to flow onto him with ease. Then—with some mental effort—I plugged in the tub, allowing it to gently fill. I wasn't really sure what this would accomplish. At that moment— dying toddler in my arms, firewalls blazing around me—I, for some reason, believed it would save him; or at least protect him. Because water—and fire—you catch my drift. I wasn't thinking straight. The charcoaled smoke had made my eyes teary, burning as if they'd been heavily Maced. There was no time to think. I swung the front door open, and before I knew it, I was skipping down the stairs—three at a time—at full speed until I was past the hotel's side-door and a good three blocks down the street. Only then did I turn.

Tentacles of smoke crawled out of five windows on the twelfth floor, and two on the thirteenth. And as the sirens blared in the distance, I ran, pressing Phil tightly against my chest. I ran and I ran and I ran, and I didn't look back. Not even once.

For updates on
F*KTORY
visit **www.goofactory.tv**

ACKNOWLEDGEMENTS

WHILE THIS STORY STARTED off as a personal project aimed for no one but myself, I want to take a moment and thank the reader and the story itself, for after being dormant for several years it grew past and beyond what I had intended it to be, outgrowing me and hence becoming a story for you and you and you. This is for all of you and I want to thank you because in an indirect way, you made this happen.

I want to thank all friends, mentors and family, without whom this idea would've never come to fruition. Thank you all for enduring me during those moments of intense reclusion and hermit status, when, overwhelmed by the process, I locked myself indoors, working for hours, until I could get it all out of my head. I am extremely grateful and want to acknowledge the great impact you all had on this book.

J.M. Barrie, thank you for creating such a wonderful character, a heartfelt story, and a wonderful mythos. Without it, this novel would've never materialized. Your story touched, changed, and inspired many lives, mine included, and I'm deeply grateful for it.

Thank you to all those stories that came before this one, those that paved the way to a world of understanding, bringing to light the duplicity of life and not just the black and white of good and evil. Bad people can do good; good people can do bad; good comes out of bad and bad comes out of good. In the end, we are neither, but just a bit of everything, and hence often misunderstood.

I want to thank my parents for not only allowing me to immerse myself in books as a young boy and bask in my own silence, but for encouraging the cultivation of the imaginative world blooming inside my head and the wings that would later help me take off. I want to thank both of you, and my sister, for exposing me to a world I was lucky to be a part of, a world, which I absorbed as swiftly as a sponge.

Shani Vellvé, my editor; thank you for your time and patience. Thank you for telling me how it is, and for sharing your knowledge. With your help, this story went from convoluted to enjoyable.

Nick Perlman, thank you for bringing to life these beautiful images, and for constantly surprising me with compositions and renderings I myself hadn't previously imagined.

I want to thank my dogs, Lola and Pudger, for showering me with gratuitous love and for, with every passing day, strengthening my sanity.

And Chris, I cannot even begin to express my gratitude. Thank you for feeding the air under my wings especially during those times when gravity tried to ground me the most. Thank you for inspiring me. Thank you for believing in me. Thank you for pushing me. And thank you for being the first one to read everything I write, no matter how bad, no matter how long. Thanks to you, I was able to take flight.

Jorge Enrique Ponce is the author of R^3 and the writer/director of several films, including #OMGIMTRENDING and Interview with a Zombie. He was born in Lima, Peru and now lives in Los Angeles, where he's currently working on his new book and film.

Nick Perlman is an illustrator and filmmaker whose work has appeared in a variety of venues, from American Illustration to a number of different film festivals. When not covered in gouache and ink he earns his living as a television editor in his native city of New York.
www.nickperlman.com

Made in the USA
San Bernardino, CA
25 June 2015